Company Ink

Tinsel and Tentacles 3.0

TA Moore

Rogue Firebird Press

Readers love TA MOORE

Dirty Work (Dirty Deeds #1)

"The bad guys shift as we work out the puzzle, but the new feelings between Clay and Grade just keep getting stronger… TA Moore never lets her fans down." —Paranormal Romance Guild

Bone to Pick (Digging Up Bones #1)

"If you're looking for a book that will keep you on the edge of your seat, make your heart race, and make you laugh out loud all at the same time, then this is the book for you. —A Wonderful World of Words

Shift Work (Night Shift #1)

“Damn Ms. Moore, it’s like you got me at hello. Or was it naked in the elevator? Either way the hook was set and as I read, I was all yours.” —Paranormal Romance Guild

Every Other Weekend

“It entertained, it kept me riveted and it increased my fate in writers… Definite recommendation to anyone who likes MM romantic suspense.” —Alpha Book Club

Collared (Devil Take Me)

“TA Moore has written a gem filled with a world that kept me shuddering in fear as I couldn’t stop reading.” —Rainbow Book Reviews

Footwork

“Footwork has everything: heart-wrenching and sweet moments, suspense, banter, snark, action, fun, love and lots of steam.” —QueerRomanceInk

Swipe

"*Swipe* has just about everything one could want in a bad-boy romance. The action was explosive, the relationship dangerous, and the men very, very hot. Buckle up for this one it is a wild ride that has a very satisfying outcome." —Joyfully Jay

Company Ink by TA Moore

Tinsel and Tentacles 3.0

Don't get him wrong, Davy hadn't been thrilled to end up face-down in a shallow grave...but he'd not been surprised either. With the life he'd lived, and the work he did, it had always been a possibility. So he'd not been bothering to hold his breath–metaphorically speaking, being dead–for a chance to get his own back on his killer.

On the other hand, death was kind of boring...even for a mercenary who wore the stigmata of his sins as occasionally too-independent tentacles. So when
someone opened a door to the living world for him he wasn't going to say no. He figured he could knock out the revenge in a couple of hours and
then spend the rest of his time on this side of the Veil getting take-out, getting laid, and getting into fights. ...the order didn't matter.

Unfortunately, it turned out to be a bit more complicated than that. If Davy didn't know better, he'd have thought this whole set–up was the universe trying to get him to learn something.

All Hill had learned was that death wasn't what he'd expected. When he had opened the door to the afterlife he'd been prepared for winding sheets and bones, maybe a few chains. Not for the vengeful ghost to be a hot, dead man who'd mug him for his skin and bones. The tentacles had been a surprise too.

But then necromancy didn't come with an instruction booklet, or a restart button.

The deal had been struck, and the two of them would just have to make it work.

Published by Rogue Firebird Press

This is a work of fiction. Names, characters, places, and incidents either are the product of author imagination or are used fictitiously, and any resemblance to actual persons, living or dead, business establishments, events, or locales is entirely coincidental.

Company Ink

http://www.roguefirebird.com/

Paperback ISBN: 978-1-954159-81-5 | Digital ISBN:

978-1-954159-80-8

Printed in the United States of America

To the Five, all of us and forever, to my mum who's always thought I could do anything I put my mind to, and to the Writing Staffies who make sure I get some fresh air daily!

Also, to Brian and Penny who keep me honest and are firm about interrobangs! Good to have you back, Penn!

Contents

1. Chapter One 1
Dec 21, 11pm
2. Chapter Two 15
Dec 22, 12.20am
3. Chapter Three 33
Dec 22nd, 10am
4. Chapter Four 43
Dec 22 12.10 pm
5. Chapter Five 57
Dec 22 2.30pm
6. Chapter Six 73
Dec 22, 8pm
7. Chapter Seven 87
Dec 23, 6am
8. Chapter Eight 101
Dec 23, 9.40 am
9. Chapter Nine 111
Dec 23, 11am

10. Chapter Ten 129
Dec 23, 1pm

11. Chapter Eleven 143
Dec 23rd, 1.30pm

12. Chapter Twelve 159
Dec 23rd 3:30pm

13. Chapter Thirteen 173
Dec, 23rd 6.30pm

14. Chapter Fourteen 187
Dec 23, 7.00pm

15. Chapter Fifteen 199
Dec 23, 8pm

16. Chapter Sixteen 215
Dec 23, 11.10pm

17. Chapter Seventeen 229
Dec 24, 8.10pm

18. Chapter Eighteen 241
Dec 24, 9.10pm

19. Chapter Nineteen 255
Dec 24, 10.40pm

20. Chapter Twenty 267
Dec 24, 11.40pm

21. Epilogue 281
21 Jun, 11.30pm

About the Author 289

Fullpage image 301

Chapter One

Dec 21, 11pm

It was almost Solstice, and as the sun started to set there were bad men at the gates of every cemetery in Dudley.

Most people put their faith in good works and solid church-forged padlocks. They weren't the ones who had to worry in the first place, though. It was only the people with enemies who needed to worry about the dead.

Enemies and secrets.

Hill Rosen paused on the street opposite St. Januarius Church and watched the thugs and mercs take up their stations along the boundary lines of consecrated ground. Most of them wore guns in shoulder holsters under their parkas, pointedly visible to passersby. Some just depended on their fists and the promise of red-faced, spittle-flecked rage to keep the bereaved back from the walls.

It had been over a century since the last confirmed invocation of the dead. That was according to the Church, of course, whose current doctrine told congregations to seek redress for their wrongs through temporal authorities.

What was the verse Father Thomas had used this morning? Hill narrowed his eyes as he tried to remember the content of the solemn drone of the sermon at his family church.

Render unto Caesar the things that are Caesar's, that was it.

Unofficially, based on Hill's two-year-long deep dive into the subject, it had been fifteen years ago in Idaho. A factory fire that corporate lawyers had successfully passed the buck on, leaving the bereaved families to shoulder the medical and personal costs...including a local priest who'd either forgotten to lock the gates or handed over the keys to bitter parishioners. Either way, he wasn't a priest anymore.

What the summoned dead had thought was a fit response to that wrong was up in the air, but by New Year's, the company had reversed its decision and the families had been made whole...financially at least. A few True Haunting enthusiasts speculated that—based on the high suicide rates in the upper echelons of the company around this time of year—the dead hadn't been satisfied with money.

Hill could see why fifteen years wouldn't be long enough for anyone with a guilty conscience and money for muscle.

On the other side of the road, one of the mercs noticed Hill. The man scowled and dropped his hand pointedly to the gun holstered on his hip. A sharp jerk of his chin to one of the other men sent a wiry fair-haired man who looked uncomfortable in his jeans and sweater loping over the road.

"You lost?" the man asked as he stepped onto the sidewalk in front of Hill. A quick once-over—from messily cropped brown curls to cheap sneakers—made him visibly untense as he dismissed Hill as a threat.

Hill shook his head.

"Late," he said. He nodded toward the padlocked gates. "I wanted to stop by my dad's grave while he's close."

The man narrowed his eyes. "He die bad?" he asked.

"It was a heart attack," Hill said. That was what he'd told them at school, a lie so old it almost felt like the truth. The next bit just was. "I just miss him."

Despite the professional detachment, the merc briefly softened.

"That's a shit one," he said. "And when my dad goes, I'll wanna talk to him. But not tonight."

Hill glanced over at the well-guarded church and swallowed hard. "Not tonight," he agreed.

"Get home," the merc told him, not unkindly. "You don't want your dad to look down and worry."

Hill nodded and left. The soles of his feet scuffed along the road as he walked away. He could feel the merc's eyes on the back of his neck, but he didn't look back.

Albie Rosen had been a nice guy. Funny. He gave great piggy-back rides and was good at explaining why people did what they did. His hands had never been sweaty.

He'd also been weak. He let people walk all over him rather than stand up for himself.

Even dead, Hill couldn't imagine he'd be much good at being a vengeful spirit. He'd probably be more disappointed than angry. It would be nice to see him again, but it wouldn't fix anything.

But that was OK. The only reason he was here was so his stepdad's thugs, whoever they were, could report back that he'd given up.

Hill zipped his hoodie up as he reached the end of the block. He hunched down into it as he rounded the corner. His bus, the 229, was already at the stop, and he broke into a jog to get there before it pulled away.

Fraser had always kept a few degrees of separation between himself and any dirty work he needed done. These days he used money. That wouldn't have worked on Hill's dad, so maybe back then it had been threats. Either way, it kept Fraser's hands clean.

There was just one problem with that.

If you didn't know where the bodies had been buried, it was difficult to put a guard on them.

***

Two transfers later and the 447 bus pulled in to the curb. The driver looked dubious as she leaned over to peer through the open doors at the Player and King stop as if she'd not seen it before.

"Here?" she said. "You sure, kid? It's not the best area. Especially not at this time of night."

Hill ignored her concern, and the "kid." People always thought he was younger than twenty-four. He didn't know why, but apparently one day he'd be grateful for it. The "when" on it was unclear too. It definitely wasn't today, when he'd rather avoid any unnecessary attention.

"I'm meeting a friend," he said. "Thanks."

The driver turned her mouth down in an unhappy grimace, but didn't try and argue the point. Hill stepped down onto the pavement, and the cold pinched at his ears. He pulled his hood up, hunched his shoulders, and stuck his hands in his pockets as he walked away.

He closed his left hand around the key he had in there and squeezed until the edges of it bit into his skin. It hurt, but he was used to it. Hill had carried the same key around for the last five years. It had taken him that long to work out where the lock it went with was situated.

145 Player Street.

Hill stopped on the sidewalk and looked up at the house.

There had been tenants there until a few days ago. Somehow the house still looked run-down and unloved. Maybe it was the lack of Christmas lights on the eaves. It was the only house in the street that wasn't lit up.

The last tenants hadn't wanted to leave this close to Christmas, but it had been unavoidable. Hill needed access to the basement and didn't have the wherewithal to fake a gas leak.

He climbed the worn stone steps to the front door and tried the key in the lock.

It wasn't his first visit, so he *knew* it would fit. Something in his chest still tightened, ready for the tumblers to lock or the mechanism to jam. It just turned smoothly, and when he turned the handle, the door swung open.

He stepped in, over the handful of pizza flyers and spam mail on the rug, and closed the door behind him. It didn't feel any warmer inside than out. If anything, it might have even been colder, with wisps of Hill's breath visible as he cleared his throat.

One theory had it that unconsecrated burials created "soft spots" between the worlds. Not weak enough to allow passage except at the right times of year and with the right invitation, but enough to allow leakage. Like a chill that lingered in the height of summer.

Or a smell in the basement like the one the Pollon family had lodged multiple complaints with the property management company about...for years before Hill ever got in touch with them.

It wouldn't actually matter to Hill's plans, but it did give weight to the theory.

Hill went into the kitchen. He'd turned the fridge on the last time he was here. The sound of the electricity humming through it was surprisingly loud in the otherwise silent house. He glanced at his watch to check the time—fifteen minutes until midnight—and then opened the door to lift out the double-bagged carcass he'd stashed in there. The plastic crinkled under his fingers as the bloodied beast in the bag shifted and sagged down as he moved it. He let it hang from one hand while he picked up the pot he'd left on the stove.

He didn't actually know why he'd put it there. It could have been set anywhere. It had just seemed out of place anywhere else.

Everything else he'd left downstairs already.

He propped the pot on one hip as he opened the basement door. The smell that the Pollons had talked about wafted up to him. It was dank and vaguely green, like standing water...even though the property manager's plumbers had never been able to find any issues with damp. Hill flicked the lights on and hesitated, one foot on the top step.

All he had to do was stop.

Hill tightened his grip on the edge of the pot as he stared down the narrow stairwell into the disorientingly mundane basement. There was a dryer and washing machine shoved into one corner, a cracked basketball backboard propped against a wall, and a stack of stained, crumpled groundsheets that the Pollons hadn't wanted to take with them.

It wasn't too late to go back. Not yet. It would be soon, though.

That was one thing that the Church, folklore, and all the forums on Reddit and the dark web agreed on. Knock at Death's door, and you had to complete the rite. No one knew exactly what happened if you tried to ding, dong, dash it, but the consensus was it wouldn't stop just because you died.

So this was Hill's last chance to change his mind.

This wasn't what his dad would have wanted. Hill knew that; it was for the same reasons that Dad would have been a bad vengeful ghost. And up until three years ago he'd been happy enough. He'd never liked Greg, and Greg had never understood him, but mutual disinterest could work a lot like tolerance under the right conditions.

If he'd not found out...

Except he had, and he couldn't *unknow* it. He'd never been good at pretending or playing along. The truth was...it just *was.*

Hill took a deep breath, regretted it as the smell hit the back of his throat with an afternote of boiled cabbage, and started down the stairs. The wood creaked under his weight, and the cold bag of murdered animal bumped against his leg with each step.

Ten years ago Greg had murdered Hill's dad, and then he married the widow to keep her onside. Except there was no proof, nothing but an overheard conversation and the man's general character. Take that and everything else Greg had ever been suspected of to court and see how far the case would go.

No.

Hill reached the bottom of the stairs and started to prepare the space. He unfolded one of the ground sheets and spread it out on the floor, anchored at the corners with old cans of paint. Then he got a pocket knife out of his back pocket and sliced the bag open so he could empty the contents into the pot.

The bloodied jackrabbit slid out of the plastic in a limp tangle of limbs and ears. Hill had caught it himself, out in the woods with a snare that Greg had shown him how to make.

Back when he was still Uncle Greg and he brought his Christmas presents to Thanksgiving, and Hill hadn't understood why he made Dad nervous.

The original ritual requested a hare, but outside of Europe records showed this substitution was close enough.

He checked his watch again. Two minutes. He waited somewhat patiently for them to tick over into the next day. As it turned midnight, he got to work.

Hill had thought the butchery would be easier. The animal's skin was tougher to carve through than he'd expected, his wrists sore and palms blistered by the time he finished. He was sweating under his hoodie despite the chill that seeped out of the walls.

Hopefully the next part would be easier.

He put the remnants of the carcass, hide and bone, into the plastic bag, bundled it up, and set it to the side. Once it was out of the way, he swallowed hard and then leaned over the pot of thick blood and organs.

The smell of it had a similar base to the basement reek.

For some reason that thought sent a chill through him. It wasn't like he didn't know, or to be accurate, strongly suspect, the source of that smell. Both chemically and metaphysically. The meaty reality of it, though, was somehow still daunting.

You don't have to do this.

Hill knew that. He was still going to do it.

He spat into the pot. It landed on top of...something dark and clotted...and floated there.

"Listen to my prayer," Hill said. He had learned the words by heart, until he could have said them in his sleep if he wanted to. Somehow, tonight when it mattered, they tried to slide away from him. He had to strain to find the word that fit the *shape* his mouth wanted to make.

"Hear me. Answer me. The threats of the wicked bring suffering on me, set violence and strife on the streets of the City."

The blood in the pot stirred, greasy bubbles roiling the surface. It made the smell worse.

"They—"

Was that right? It felt like there was a gap, something that had slipped away. Fear grabbed at Hill's tongue. That would *not* be good. That would be—

Hill talked over the swell of panic that tried to choke him, the words forced out through stiff lips. Getting the invocation wrong would be a problem; not finishing would be worse. He tightened his grip on his pocketknife.

He gritted his teeth, steeled himself as best he could, and stabbed the knife through the palm of his hand. The blade carved through *his* skin easier than through the jackrabbit's hide. Hot red reaction washed over him as the pain separated itself into distinct layers: the cut, the bruise, the scrape of metal on bone.

That was the most disorienting bit, Hill thought with unexpected clarity. Nothing was meant to go around touching *bone*.

"Let death take my enemies by surprise. Bring their dead up to the living," he choked out. "Call them from decay, from the chains of sin."

He shoved his bloody hand down into the pot. There was more blood in it than made any sense, considering the size of a jackrabbit. His arm sank into it until it was above his elbow. It was so cold it scalded him as it soaked through his sleeve. He gasped in shock and then squeezed his eyes shut tight as he used that breath to force the rest of the words out.

"But as for me, I trust in you," he said. "Davy Jones."

And something, down in that cold boiled stew of blood and lung and liver, grabbed his arm.

It didn't feel like a hand. Too wet and long and...wriggly.

Hill recoiled. It was stupid, after everything he'd done and planned to get here, but he couldn't help himself. His stifled yell and lurch backward was instinct, hard-wired into his marrow.

It just didn't do much good.

Whatever was down there tightened its grip on him. Hill winced as he felt his wrist bones creak and ache. The cold dulled the pain, but not enough. He clenched his teeth and pulled. It felt like trying to pull a mastodon out of a tar pit.

One-handed.

He could feel the tendons and muscles in his shoulder strain and fray as his arm took the strain. The pain crawled up his neck, through his jaw, and into his skull. It wasn't like he had a choice, though.

Pull it out of the grave, or he went in.

Hill dragged it out. Strings of dirty, matted hair broke through the surface of the blood first. He grimaced and braced himself for the memento mori decay of a spirit more than ten years in dirt and concrete.

He expected rot, grease, and naked, stained bones.

There might have been guilt.

Davy Jones broke through the barrier between the grave and the living with a gasp, clots of blood dripping from his stubbled jaw and sandy hair. His skin had gray undertones, the spray of freckles over his nose like flecks of ink, but was intact and smooth over the sharp bones of his face.

The only injury was a thumbprint smudge of bruising at his hairline, just off-center from his nose.

His eyes were wild and black, edge to edge.

Lust was *not* a reaction Hill had expected to have to worry about. Did it count as necrophilia, he wondered distractedly, or since there was no carcass involved, was it still just necromancy?

Blood splashed Hill's face, cool and sticky thick, as something pale and boneless writhed up out of the pot. He tasted old salt and metal on his lips. Before he could spit it out, the pale...limb?...wrapped around his neck and pulled him down into a kiss.

Davy's cold tongue darted into his mouth—it tasted like fresh blood, after all this time, and dirt—and Hill's breath caught in his throat. He wasn't sure if it was from attraction or the wet noose of muscle and skin wrapped around his neck.

This wasn't...

He tried to grab at the spirit's hair, tangled and clotted with blood, but another pale whip of flesh snapped up out of the bloody mixture to grab his wrist. Slow, dark hunger twisted uneasily under Hill's skin, and his focus scattered at the departure from what he'd expected.

First-hand accounts of what happened after the rite was complete were rare. Those who survived it rarely wanted to talk about it. Those who didn't were even more retiring on the subject. The scraps that *did* exist mentioned the spirit's rage and unpredictability, not...this.

What they *had* all agreed on, though, Hill reminded himself grimly, was that not finishing the ritual was a bad thing.

He struggled to his feet and dragged the dead man—heavier the more of him there was in the world, all long bones and pale, tangled tentacles—with him.

Part of him was rattling around the inside of his brain in a panic. Whatever it wanted to say was muffled by lust and fear, but Hill figured it was probably the tentacles.

The pale, blood-smeared whips of them wrapped around Hill's thighs and toyed with the ends of his hair. It definitely seemed like someone would have mentioned them, even if they left out the way they squeezed your cock through your jeans.

Blood dripped onto the floor as Davy planted his bare feet back into the living world. He gripped Hill's jaw with one hand and deepened the kiss.

The taste of bones filled Hill's mouth and seeped down into his lungs. The chill made his marrow ache and his blood feel slow and sludgy as his heart labored to move it on.

He couldn't breathe.

Hill tried to pull away. He clawed at the spirit's bare—broad, hard-muscled, *not the time!*—shoulders and yanked at handfuls of matted blond hair. Only the parts that were bloody, slick and cold, felt solid. The rest gave like smoke or candy floss under his fingers. Neither made the spirit react, except to tighten its grip and kiss him harder.

It wasn't...

This was...

It wasn't that bad.

Hill relaxed into the dead man's cold embrace and kissed him back, fingers knotted through bloody hair. He just had to let go.

Of his breath. Of his anger. Of everything.

Hill staggered back a couple of steps. He stared in confusion at the back of someone's head, a cowlick swirl of dark hair at the nape and a mole just under his ear, until he realized it was him. His back. His hair. He assumed his mole, but he'd never actually noticed it before.

If that was him, though, then who was he?

He looked down at his hands. They looked the same, felt the same. They moved the same when he clenched them into fists, bony and knuckly. His hand wasn't bleeding anymore, but the wound was still visible. Sort of. It looked more like a bruise or a birthmark, a smudge of color against pale skin.

"Yeah, count yourself lucky," someone said, their words thick with a Texas drawl. "That hurts like fuck."

Hill looked up and watched with disoriented horror as his body turned around to face him.

It didn't look like him.

Or it did, but only if he squinted. The line of Hill's jaw was there, Hill's hairline, Hill's *ears*, but it was overlaid with *his* face.

Davy Jones's short, straight nose, sharp cheekbones, and the stern, thin mouth that Hill could still somehow taste. The smirk was nothing that Hill's mouth had ever managed either, cocky and pleased with itself.

On impulse, Hill flung himself at *his* body. He didn't have any idea what he was going to do, but if he could be ousted, so could Davy. Before he could get close, one of the tentacles that squirmed around Davy snapped out. It grabbed Hill by the throat and hauled him up off the ground.

It squeezed until Hill's eyes bulged, and he grabbed at it, fingers dug into the dense, heavy muscle that collared him.

"You knocked on my door, kid," Davy said, his voice amused. He lifted his hand and licked blood from the open wound. "What did you think was going to happen? I'd go yell 'boo' at your enemies?"

Chapter Two

Dec 22, 12.20am

HIS NEW COCK WASN'T circumcised.

That was the *second* thing Davy noticed.

He finished his first piss in nearly thirty years, surprisingly fun, to be honest, and shook his borrowed cock off before he tucked it back into the jeans. Then he turned to wash his hands, the smart sting of pain as the water hit raw meat making his eye twitch, and studied "his" reflection in the mirror.

That had been the first thing he noticed, that he'd no fucking idea who this kid was.

Dark hair hung in unstyled curls over a narrow, expressive face. Pale green eyes stared warily at the world from behind thick lashes, and his mouth...

The memory of the kiss flickered quick and vivid through Davy's brain. Warmth and softness, that moment when the kid had leaned into it. The taste of his breath—coffee and Skittles and life. An unfamiliar heat flushed through Davy, and he felt that uncircumcised cock twitch with quick, eager response.

His hands tightened unconsciously against each other, and he flinched at the sharp ache from his injured palm. He loosened his grip and flicked the tap off, giving a quick shake to shed the water.

He glanced at the mirror again, lean cheeks now flushed and eyes darker as his pupils expanded, and licked his lips. *His* lips.

Let's just say, it was a good mouth.

Just not one that he could place, or the face around it.

Although, to be fair, Davy couldn't think of anyone he *would* recognize that would want to bring him back from Beyond. Hell, he doubted anyone had even gone looking when he disappeared, just in case they found him. He'd not been a likable man, and his profession hadn't encouraged him to try and hide that.

Still didn't.

So? That begged the question: what did a pretty kid with green eyes want with him?

There was only one way to find out, he supposed.

Davy turned and reached for the door. His tentacle grappled with the handle, but the best he could do was rattle it before the jellyfish-translucent feeler slid through it. He stared at the door in bafflement for a beat and then remembered...

Hands.

He snapped the thin end of his tentacle to underline the realization, a pop of soft skin.

Of course. He'd forgotten how much he used to use them for... pretty much everything, really. He reached for the door. The metal was cold against his palm, almost painful, but he managed to fumble it open.

Out in the hall, the kid was caught mid-pace as he waited for him. He turned to glare at Davy as he stepped out onto the cheap lino.

"What took you so long?"

"You know, you *could* have just walked through the fucking door?" Davy asked as he jerked his thumb over his shoulder.

The kid stopped, mouth open, as he looked at the door, then back at Davy.

"I can?" he asked.

Davy snorted. "I fucking wish," he said. "Nothing's that easy in this life. Or the next."

The kid looked pissed off. He started to say something, stopped himself, and took a deep breath. It wasn't really necessary in his current situation, but Davy understood the impulse. The kid narrowed his eyes. The pretty green had faded to almost silver, pale and striking against dark lashes and sallow skin.

"Am I dead?" he asked.

Davy held his arms out. The span felt slightly off, and he spared a breath to be mildly annoyed to realize the kid was taller than him.

"Do you *look* dead?" he asked.

The kid looked down at his hands and flexed his fingers to watch the tendons move under thin, desaturated skin.

"Kind of," he said quietly.

Fair enough, Davy supposed. He patted himself down briskly. Hoodie first, then his jeans, and then the back pockets. He found the wallet in the back left, a well-worn flap of leather roughly stitched in one corner where it had started to come apart. It was full of cash, but no cards or ID.

At least the kid made an effort.

"Think of it as more of a...*Face/Off* situation," he said absently as he pulled the cash out to count it.

"A what?"

Davy glanced up and took in the look of utter confusion on the kid's face. OK, so that wasn't the easy cultural touchstone he'd expected. He weighed up the advantages of trying to prompt the way to mutual understanding, and then decided to just change tack.

"OK, like a house swap," he said. "I get to be alive, you get to be dead. We have fun, we both learn important lessons, and then we probably go back to the status quo."

That got him a frown and the dubious repetition of, "Probably?"

Davy shrugged. "Things happen," he said vaguely.

What things, he couldn't say. There was no handbook for the dead, just the slow drip of information from the dry dead down to the wet dead. The threat of "things" had definitely been muttered about.

Davy tossed the wallet and folded the cash over to tuck it back into his jeans. He turned and headed toward the front door.

"H-hey, wait," the kid stammered out. "What are you... Where are you *going!?*"

Davy paused on the threshold of the house and looked back over his shoulder.

"It's been thirty years since I had something to eat," Davy said. "I'm going to get a burger."

"I'm a vegan," the kid protested weakly.

"Going to suck to be you when you get this back," Davy said. He waved his hand in a sweeping "after you" gesture at the door. "You coming or what?"

It took a moment, but the kid shook off his bafflement and broke into a graceless, ungainly lope to catch up with Davy. He squeezed through the propped-open door and stumbled down the step onto the path, looking around like he'd never seen the street before.

Davy stared after him and then looked down at his body, all long arms and lanky legs. Shit. If he needed to run, he better not look like that. He stepped down onto the path and let the door slam behind him.

As his foot hit the cracked pavers, he felt a brief jolt of disorientation as his brain tried to stitch his last real flesh memory and this one together.

...boots instead of Converse, comfortable but heavier as he walked, and that low-grade but constant ache in his knee from a misstep on old stairs in a Moscow apartment block. His hair had been damp with rain, and he'd shoved a door open, palm flat against the glossy green wood, as he glanced over his shoulder to say, "You didn't have to do this."

"Do what?" the kid asked.

Davy tripped over his own feet as he staggered out of the memory. He caught himself against the fence and then straightened up, brushing his hands together.

"I didn't say anything," he lied in a rough voice.

It wouldn't have convinced anyone who'd ever known him, but the kid just looked confused and shrugged it off. He stuck close to Davy's heels, unconsciously tucked into the mantle of his tentacles, as they walked down the street.

Davy had plenty of questions he needed answers to. Time was short, and the stakes might even be high. So he was a little surprised that the first one he asked was, "So, what's your name?"

The kid looked startled too. Maybe at hearing that question from his own face.

"Hill..." the kid said, and then glanced sidelong at Davy. He added the rest reluctantly. "Hill Rosen."

Huh.

That cleared up...fucking nothing.

Davy took a bite out of the cheeseburger. The heady taste of cheese, hot meat, and warm, starchy bread filled his mouth. He closed his eyes and groaned in satisfaction as he chewed. Even the sting on his tongue from not letting it cool only added to the experience.

Thank the Reaper that restaurants still did Lost Souls opening hours on Solstice.

"Albie Rosen," Hill said. "You seriously don't remem..."

He stopped and glanced uneasily at something that Davy couldn't see. Something dead, presumably. Being incarnate had drawn the veil over the Beyond that the living enjoyed. All Davy could see of it was Hill, who was essentially haunting him, and his own tentacles...who'd been haunting him since Davy died.

On principle, he raised one of those and swatted whatever was taunting Hill away. Opposite, Hill unhunched a bit and rubbed a bony, elegant hand over his face.

"You really don't remember my dad?"

Davy licked grease off his fingers. "It's not ringing a bell," he said.

"He worked for Fraser since...forever. He's the one who buried you in that house."

"I was dead at the time," Davy pointed out. He picked up some fries and dunked them in the curry sauce before he took a bite. The pop of starchy potato flavor was better than sex. He sucked the salt off his fingers and caught the flicker of lust in Hill's pale, clever eyes as he watched. His body—Hill's body, technically—tightened in reaction...and yeah, well, maybe the fries weren't *that* good. "We didn't do introductions. Besides, it's not like he killed me. Right?"

Something bleak and angry crossed Hill's face, tightening his jaw and twisting his lips. He gave a short, hard shake of his head.

Davy took a noisy slurp of soda.

"Don't worry. It's good enough as far as the powers that be are concerned," he said. Water ran down the side of the paper cup as he set it back on the table, puddling on the scored Formica. He left a smudge of blood overlaid across the logo and frowned as he checked his hand. Blood had soaked through the rough dressing, but not enough to be a problem. It would stop soon enough. Davy blotted his hand against his leg as he went on. "Otherwise I wouldn't be here. If you want something bad to happen to dear old Dad, I'm still your man."

Hill gave a small, humorless twist of his mouth.

"Something bad already did," he said. "Someone killed *him*."

"Huh," Davy said. He scratched the side of his jaw as he thought about that. "Look, I'm not trying to be precious about this—fuck, I'd do it for the fries if it was up to me—but my remit to do shit to assholes, at least on this side, is tightly regulated. I could swing 'helped cover up my murder,' but I need to have some skin in the game."

So he'd been told anyhow, and he wasn't interested in pushing his luck about it. Consequences in Beyond tended to the...unpleasant, and you'd no choice except to survive them. Davy was a shark, but still a small one in a very big ocean.

Some of the big sharks had been there for centuries.

Affiliation with the Company could buy you some protection, but...well...that was all about appearances. Davy had expected to be punished for his sins when he woke up dead, just—he pulled the spiritual stigmata of his tentacles in and wrapped them around his feet in a tidy knot—not by the afterlife's equivalent of High School cliques.

"How about this?" Hill said. "The same person who killed him? They killed you."

Davy drew back as he took that in. That was...

He should want to hear this, but suddenly he didn't know if he did or not. It turned out he didn't get a choice.

"My stepdad," Hill said. "Fraser Jones."

Yeah. That made sense. Davy supposed it wasn't really a surprise. He'd not *known* who killed him. Most didn't. It took an hour, give or take, to write a memory from the brain to the spirit. That meant the dead only ever had their best guess about the moment of death, but Davy's guess was pretty fucking informed.

He just wasn't sure how he felt about being right. Emotions had never really been his thing. He *had* them, but other than the big two—fight or fuck—they'd always been behind a paywall.

Luckily, being a smartass came with the free tier.

"So what you're telling me," Davy said as he reached for the burger, "is that my little brother got married, and I didn't even rate an invite?"

He took a bite and chewed as he watched realization dawn on Hill's expressive face as he put the names together and realized it wasn't just chance and the fifth most common surname in the US.

It was OK.

He wasn't the first to miss the connection. He might well be the last, though. Gravestones were good for making that sort of thing clear.

"So, what," Hill said in a shocked voice. "You're my uncle?"

Huh.

Davy blinked as he thought about that and then put the burger down.

Gross.

Step-uncle.

It was, Davy decided, an important distinction. Besides, it wasn't like Davy had been on speaking terms with Fraser before the murder. Even if he'd been alive, he'd probably not have crossed paths with Hill. And as it was, he'd been dead longer than Hill had been alive.

Davy mentally weighed the justifications up and...yeah, it was fine.

That sorted, he tuned back in to what Hill was saying.

"...they said my dad killed himself," Hill said. "For a long time I believed them, but then I found the files Dad had hidden on his old e-reader. Files about you. About the things he'd done for Fraser."

Davy slouched back against the cool copper-clad wall of the elevator and stared at his own reflection in the doors. Both of them, as Hill paced back and forth over the carpet anxiously. He kept having to step over Davy's tentacles where they spooled out slack and lazy over the floor. The urge to trip him with just a twitch of one appendage swelled in Davy's chest and was quashed again.

"And you think Fraser killed him?" Davy asked.

"No," Hill said. "But it made me wonder, and either way it's Fraser's fault, isn't it? Either he killed my dad, or he's the reason my dad killed himself. And he definitely killed you."

"Fair enough."

Davy idly hooked a finger into the collar of his T-shirt to pull it away from his neck. The long line of his own neck, all tendon and pale skin, made his mouth go dry.

I swear, the memory of his mom's voice hissed the unwelcome interruption in the back of his head, *you were hung in another life.*

She'd been dead longer than him. Habit still made him knock it off.

Besides, they were nearly there.

Davy glanced at Hill, who'd stopped to stare at the slow flick of the last two floors. He didn't slouch. With a sigh, Davy pushed himself up off the wall and straightened his hoodie. It wasn't quite parade rest, but he managed a rough approximation of good posture as the elevator stopped.

The doors swung open, and the smell of fresh cookies wafted over Davy.

Next to him, Hill fell back a step. His mouth went slack as he glanced around whatever was on the Beyond side of the Veil in confusion.

"Where is..." he stammered. "What's happened to my apartment?"

...

Yeah. That was a metaphysical lesson that Davy didn't want to get into today. Mostly because of time; partially because fuck if he actually understood how it worked.

"Just stick close to me," Davy said as he draped one long, boneless arm over Hill's shoulder. "You're not going to be dead that long, and you won't remember it afterwards."

Hill started to shrug Davy's arm off, flinched away from something that came too close, and decided to stay where he was.

"So this is your place?" Davy said. He followed his nose over the wooden floor to the open-plan kitchen and a covered plate set out on a counter. There was a card propped next to it, a cardinal staring festively from a white, expensively printed background. Hill ignored it for now as he unboxed the plate. "It's nice."

Hill hung on to the end of Davy's tentacle, and the thin fingerling length twirled through his fingers as he trailed after him.

"It's Fraser's place," Hill corrected him. "I just live here. They didn't think I could cut it on my own."

Davy made a pleased sound under his breath at the platter of cookies he'd exposed. They weren't hot anymore, but they were the size of his palm and shiny with sugar crystals.

"Yeah," he said as he picked one up. "Rich kids are easy marks. Just tell them 'I like you for you' and they leave you in the same room as their wallet."

He lifted one and took a bite. His nose wrinkled as the taste exploded on his tongue.

It was...

He chewed as he tried to identify the flavor that flooded his mouth. It was chocolate. He knew it was chocolate—what the fuck else would you put in a cookie—but he couldn't get his brain to believe it. The taste of meat had been *instantly* familiar, but this just wouldn't click. He swallowed and poked his tongue between his teeth after a hard chunk of biscuit.

Today he'd learned you could be old enough to forget the taste of chocolate.

"It's carob," Hill told him as Davy took a second bite.

Davy grimaced and spat the mouthful out into his hand.

"Why the fuck?" he asked.

"Vegan, remember?" Hill said. "No dairy."

Davy wiped his mouth on the back of his sleeve. "You know what, life is wasted on you."

A humorless smile twitched Hill's mouth. "You're not the first to say that."

Davy picked up the card and flipped it open.

"Hey," Hill protested. He grabbed at the card with one hand, his fingers wisping through the thick parchment. "Where did you get that? It's for me. You can't just–"

"And yet I am," Davy said with a shrug. He hitched one tentacle up to block Hill. Maybe Hill couldn't grab the paper, but his fingers swiping through it made it hard to read. Davy glanced over the neat, angled script that said it hoped to see him—well, probably not *him,* but not like they'd know—on Christmas Eve. He fanned the invite idly in the air and raised his eyebrows. "Look at that, back from the dead for—" He checked Hill's watch. "—two hours, and already my social calendar is filling up."

Hill scowled. "You're not going."

Davy shrugged as he turned away. "Shouldn't be dead if you want a vote," he said as he headed down the hall to find the bedroom. There were still a few hours till dawn, but he was on a deadline, so he couldn't waste the wee hours. "First lesson you learn."

It wasn't, but...why spoil a nice night with that sort of detail?

Hot water battered the back of Davy's neck. The steam filled his lungs, hot and sweet with the raspberry and chamomile smell of the shower gel.

It was on the label. On his own he'd just have called it "sweet."

Close his eyes so he couldn't see the squirm of his tentacles against the glass walls of the shower, and it was almost like he'd never been dead.

"You can't go."

Well, it was as long as he ignored his tentacles *and* the original occupant.

Davy ducked his head under the steam to rinse his hair, raspberry scented foam shedding in sheets to swirl around his feet. He emerged, blew drips of water from his nose, and turned to swipe one hand over the misted glass. Hill stared at him for a beat and then looked away, his expression flustered.

Hell if Davy knew why. It was Hill's body; presumably he'd seen it naked before.

"We already covered that you don't get a say," he said. "But for the sake of argument, why not? What better place to kill Fraser than at the company Christmas party? Trust me, you won't be the only one there who wants him dead. Not unless he's changed."

Hill's eyes snapped back to Davy's for a beat as confusion overrode whatever weird hang-up he had about his own naked ass.

"What?"

"He wasn't likable when I knew him," Davy said. "Most people don't get nicer."

"That's a pessimistic view of human nature."

Davy shrugged. "It's my experience." He scratched his wet collarbone as he thought about it, then shrugged an acknowledgement. "To be fair, I'm an asshole, and like attracts like."

The glass had started to steam up again. Davy let it as he turned back to the shower. He cleaned under his nails to get rid of the rime of hare's blood and filth, then turned his hand palm up to let the hot water soak into the wound. He hissed softly under his breath at the sting of it.

"I didn't... I *don't* want..." Hill said from the other side of the glass. "Are you listening?"

"Hmm," Davy said affirmatively. He shook the water off his hand, the water pink-tinged as it circled the drain, and got out of the shower to grab a towel to scrub his hair. "You didn't want...?"

Hill stared at him, cleared his throat, and managed to flush—not easy when you didn't have a body to hand. He glanced down at Davy's cock and then dragged his attention back up to his face.

"Could you at least put a towel on?" he asked.

Davy started to ask, but what the hell. Maybe he'd have been thrown to watch someone else walk around in his meat suit. He gave his wet curls one last scrub and then slung the damp towel around his hips, one hand needed to hold it closed at his waist.

He waited.

"I didn't say I wanted Fraser *dead*," Hill said. "What good would that do?"

That was really *not* the sort of question that Davy was equipped to grapple with. He stared at Hill for a second and then rubbed the bridge of his nose.

"I don't know," he said. "It'd make my two days on earth a lot easier? Does that count for anything?"

"I want Fraser to understand what he's done wrong," Hill said. "And to make right what he can."

A glib retort about how Hill still didn't get a say was on the tip of Davy's tongue. The seal snapped his jaws together before he could get it out, the cold, inexorable grip of it so tight he could feel it in the memory of his own cold, dry bones all the way back on the other side of town.

Hill had summoned him, and apparently Hill did get a say in what he'd summoned him *for*. Good to know.

"I've got it," Davy said. "No killing. Justice it is."

The clamp on his jaw relaxed as he gave Hill his way. Fine. It would have helped if he'd gotten a rundown on the rules to start with, but Davy could take a hint. Although considering *he* was the one Fraser had murdered, you'd think he'd get a say.

That...

Wait.

Davy narrowed his eyes at Hill.

"When you say you want Fraser to understand what he's done wrong, you just mean killing your dad?" Davy asked. He poked Hill in the shoulder with a tentacle for emphasis. "Maybe throw in that it was a gray area to go ahead and marry the widow. Right?"

Hill shook his head. "I mean everything," he said. "Everyone he's hurt, every friend he's let down, every deal he broke, every business partner he's betrayed. All of it."

Davy started to say something, stopped himself, and took a deep breath. He held it until he remembered what it felt like to be dead. Then he asked, "Seriously? Do you have any idea how many...how *often* he's... What do you care who else he's fucked over? *They* obviously don't care enough about it to stick a knife through their hand."

If there was actually *any* justice, even just a fucking mote, in the world, that would have done the trick. Davy had smooth-talked a *bunch* of people into getting fucked, or fucked over, without making as good a point as that.

Instead of agreeing, though, Hill just grimaced and shoved his hands into his pockets, his shoulders hunched up to his ears. His voice was low and scratchily reluctant as he said, "Despite what he did—what he does—Fraser's been good to me. To my mom," Hill said, his voice low and slow. "He paid for my school and my therapists and a whole life with us. A good life. A life he funded with money from fucking everyone else over, including my dad. All these years, I benefited from what he did because he cared about me and Mom. Meanwhile, the people he didn't care about suffered. If all that bothers me now is my own pain, in making that whole for me, then that's just the same thing, isn't it? People that matter to me matter; the rest don't. How would that make me any better than him?"

There was a *lot* that Davy wanted to say in answer to that, but the cold muzzle of the rite had snapped shut around his jaw again.

Nobody *got* to be "better." Everyone played the game. Then they died and played some fucking more.

Apparently Death didn't want its favorite little idiot here enlightened on how the world worked.

Davy tried to squeeze a "fuck" from between his teeth, but the icy bite of the geas pushed down on his tongue like a salt-cured thumb.

"Fuuuu...ine," he conceded, pulling his lips back in a frustrated snarl. "You bled for this. You get to call the shots."

Hill wasn't quite dumb enough to look relieved. He just relaxed his shoulders and nodded before taking a deep breath.

"Right, first of all, you're not going to the party," Hill said. "I don't want my mom or anyone else—"

Davy tapped the end of a tentacle against Hill's mouth to hush him.

"No, I think I'm going," he said, and waited for the icy bite of the rite's muzzle around his teeth. When nothing happened, he worked his jaw from one side to the other to loosen up the ache and smirked at Hill. "I should say 'hi' to my new sister-in-law, if nothing else."

Hill went pale.

Paler.

Davy's tentacle caressed the sharp line of Hill's jaw and tangled through his hair.

"Don't worry," Davy told him. "Moms love me."

It was a waste of a lie—seriously, even his own hadn't much cared for him—since Hill didn't look comforted. There was only so much you could do to help people, though.

Davy dropped the towel to the floor, the expensive cotton soaking up the water that dripped off him, and sauntered naked back into Hill's bedroom. He ignored the choked sound that came out of Hill's mouth.

They only had until Christmas Day to work with. He needed to get started....

Chapter Three

Dec 22nd, 10am

THE GOOD WENT TO Heaven, the wicked to Hell, and the unquiet dead lingered in Purgatory.

That was the Church's party line. They mostly avoided dealing with Purgatory, though, except in the vaguest of terms. Even in the rabbit holes that Hill had gone down over the last year, there hadn't been a lot of detail to find.

Still, he'd formed a vague concept of what it was like.

Empty. Uneasy. Somewhere there was no rest. Misty and soft-edged.

Maybe he should have realized that the dead took up more space than the living. The...Beyond, Davy had called it...was a slightly undersaturated magic-eye version of the Dudley that Hill knew. The familiar streets and most of the buildings were there, but just with more *folded* into the geography to make them fit. An alley would open up like origami to reveal trees long since uprooted and streets that had been renamed or buried years ago. Every building extended beyond what he remembered, stacked up toward the sky with layers of mismatched architecture and clumsily proportioned windows.

It made his head hurt if he looked too hard at it, so he tried not to. The closer he stuck to Davy, the more "real" the living world seemed.

A tentacle wrapped around his waist, casually intimate in the way it hooked into the pocket of his jeans, and nudged him away from a pothole in the road he'd not noticed.

Hill touched it absently in thanks and then shook his head.

"Real" obviously needed a bit of a mental update, he supposed.

The tentacle uncurled from his waist and reached up to push a long hanging branch out of Davy's way. Davy didn't seem to notice, and Hill wondered idly if the tentacles were somehow sentient or just autonomous in the same way that blinking and breathing were.

He'd fallen a few steps behind Davy as he thought about that and almost missed it as a cafe door swung open. A lifetime of not paying enough attention to his surroundings made him hop back in time to avoid crashing into the man coming out.

Mostly avoid it.

His foot caught around the man's ankle and made him stagger; hot coffee sloshed over gray slacks and very expensive shoes.

"Sorry, I didn't..." Hill got that much out on autopilot, before his tongue caught up with his eyes and went numb and stupid.

The man made an annoyed noise as he brushed the liquid off his legs and shook it off the newspaper he had in one hand. Gray speckled feathers bristled over human eyes and the start of a human nose—enough to support a pair of reading glasses—before it melted into a pointed yellow beak the length of a forearm.

"Watch where you're going," the man snapped, a blunt black tongue wriggling around the words. Then he shook his head and tossed his coffee-stained paper down in disgust. "If you weren't still wet, I fucking swear."

He stalked away.

Hill stared after him and then shook himself quickly. He started to jog after Davy, then stopped to grab the paper. The coffee—and how, the thought briefly distracted Hill, had the man planned to *drink* it?—stained the front page and smudged the ink. Hill could still make out a few words.

The masthead read *The Dudley Pomp*, and the date was *today*. Apparently the big news of the day was something to do with a road. The picture of a multi-level interchange took up most of the space above the fold, with a stern DISRUPTION just visible above the headline.

A tentacle snaked back and latched around Hill's wrist. He didn't resist as he hurried past the other...dead? ghosts?...on the sidewalk until he caught up with Davy. A few gave him a look on the way by, somewhere between pity and hunger.

"What did that mean?" Hill asked.

"Huh?"

"That guy had..." Hill trailed off and sketched the outline of a beak in front of his face with one hand. Then he nodded over the street where the bird-faced man had stopped to look in a window. Davy looked that way and then made an annoyed face at himself. Hill ignored it as he pushed on. "Why? Is it like your..."

He trailed off again and wriggled his fingers in the air. The tentacles pounced on the movement and wove through his knuckles like they were playing.

Davy whapped at them, his fingers passing through them like they were smoke. They still retracted, pulled in close to his body and curled gently.

"No," he said flatly. "That's...look, you're not actually dead. Does it matter?"

"I will be," Hill said. "One day."

"Yeah, well, do good deeds. Hope for the best."

"I prefer to plan for the worst," Hill said.

The words were out before he remembered *why* the answer came to mind so easily. It was what Fraser always said. From Davy's sidelong look, he'd heard it a few times himself...back when he'd been alive, presumably.

"Muzzles are a sign of office," Davy said after a brief pause. He kept walking as he talked. "Birds, dogs, maggots, hares. Anything to do with the dead. It confers status and conveys position. The tentacles are...."

He stopped on the curb to wait for a truck to pass, and then glanced back at the obedient cloud of tentacles.

"Well," Davy said. "Think of them as like...more like a rap sheet."

He stepped into the road. A passing silver Bentley clipped him as it growled by, hip and knee getting the brunt. It made Hill flinch in an immediate atavistic response to the thought of how much that would hurt.

Davy didn't even notice. The car exploded around him, streamers of dust and smoke unspooled in the air, and he just kept walking. As the car passed him, it knit itself back together. There didn't seem to be a driver that Hill could see.

He tried to blow out a relieved breath and realized he hadn't anything in his lungs. It felt a bit stupid to breathe in just to sigh, but he did it anyhow. It made him feel better.

"Did you—" he started to ask. Except he knew Davy hadn't. OK. Hill wiped his hands on his jeans, the ones that his body *wasn't* wearing any longer, and stretched his legs to fall back in next to Davy again. He gave one of the tentacles a leery look as it draped casually over his shoulder, the weight of it a surprise. "What does that mean, a rap sheet?"

Davy made an exasperated sound and pulled his hand down over his jaw.

"It's...when you die, your sins come with you," he said. "What they look like when they get here depends on...fuck knows, to be honest. Some people get chains, some get a *rache*-a hound or cat or beast- that sticks to their heels, some get—"

"Tentacles?" Hill said dubiously.

Davy shrugged and idly reached up to poke his ear, as if he had an earpiece in. Of course, Hill realized uneasily, even this early there would be people on the streets. Living people. It was just that Hill couldn't *see* them.

That gave him a strange, "turning up naked to English class," dream feeling.

"You know my mom didn't name me Davy Jones, right?" Davy said.

Hill had...not. The only information he'd had about the dead man had been that name and his dad's guilt. Even the address had been something he'd had to dig through shell companies and bank transfers and old calendar entries to narrow down. So that explained *that*, he supposed.

"Why—"

"I made problems go away," Davy said. "They never came back, just like they'd been sent to Davy Jones's locker. Since I was already called 'Jones,' it stuck, and then I died and my sins...I guess they thought it fit too."

"What was your real name?" Hill asked.

Davy glanced at him. He quirked the corner of his mouth in a smirk. The lazy confidence of the expression made Hill struggle to find the lines of his own face under the handsome blond overlay of Davy.

Not gonna ask how many bodies I sent down there?" he asked.

That *would*, Hill supposed, have been a good question. Logically, it was the important one, but what Hill wanted to know with sudden, unexpected need was the name.

When he didn't edit the question, Davy shrugged.

"It was..."

He trailed off. Surprise flickered over his face, chased quickly by consternation. He reached up to rub his forehead, frown lines indented under his fingers.

"It was... umm..." Davy tried again, face pinched as he tried to shake down the answer from his brain, and then laughed instead. He shrugged it off dismissively. "It wasn't important then, and it doesn't matter now. Come on. We're here."

The afterlife as a concrete experience was new to Hill. He would be willing, however, to put money on Davy being wrong about that. It probably wasn't the time to push, though.

He stopped on the pavement and looked up.

Unlike some of the buildings, Fraser's offices didn't look much different in the afterlife. The tinted glass was nicotine brown instead of black, and the long white concrete pillars were chipped and gray. CIRATTA HOLDINGS was written in a discreet gold font on the main doors. Shadows moved against the windows, just visible enough that you could see some of them looked inhuman.

Hill took a shallow breath and rubbed the back of his neck with one hand.

"I still don't know what good you think this is going to be," he said. "If there was any useful information at Ciratta, I would have used it before summoning the dead."

Davy took the ID badge out of his pocket and clipped it to his shirt. "You're not me," he said as he straightened the badge and headed up the low flight of well-worn steps.

He changed how he walked as he climbed. The lazy, cocky confidence of Davy Jones, not currently dead and enjoying it, changed to something hesitant and careful. Hill didn't know what he was doing at first.

Then he realized it was him. He walked like that.

"I really doubt that was necessary," he muttered under his breath as he squared his shoulders and headed up the steps.

The doors had started to swing shut as he got there, and he had to jump through. A tentacle caught him by the elbow and steadied him when he stumbled. He didn't know if he should thank it or not, so settled for a quick pat. When he looked up, his stomach sank as he saw the tall sandy-blond man leaning on the reception desk.

Or didn't, he supposed. His stomach was currently a foot to the left, possessed by a dead man who was about to be caught out by one of Fraser's more...embarrassing...lackeys.

"That's Luke Reynolds." Hill leaned in toward Davy. "He knows me. He's going to know you're not—"

"Hill," Reynolds said as he pushed himself off the desk. He didn't give Davy—or Hill—a second look as he instead pointedly glanced at his wrist. "Early for you, isn't it?"

Davy blinked at him and hunched up one shoulder in a scarecrow-awkward shrug. The gesture did not look the same way that Hill remembered it felt from inside the shoulders.

"I left something upstairs," Davy said. "I want to get it before the party later."

Reynolds mugged surprise. "You?" he said. "You're actually going to turn up and socialize with us cogs in the machine, Fraser's lackeys? That's a change."

"I said I wanted to get it before the party," Davy said. "Not that I was going to the party."

The receptionist chuckled. Reynolds's expression soured.

"Suit yourself," he said. "At least we won't have to worry about you throwing a tantrum over the food, Little Lord Fauntleroy."

Hill's ears burned with the memory of *that* humiliation.

"It wasn't—" he started to defend himself, then realized it was pointless.

"Don't worry about it, sweetheart," the receptionist said as she unplugged a lead from her desk and pulled the collar of her shirt down to click the jack into the connector in her throat. When she spoke again, her voice came from the intercom inside the elevator as the doors opened. "The living aren't real; they can't hurt you. I've buzzed you up."

Oh.

OK.

Right.

"Thanks," Hill said. He pointed self-consciously at Davy. "I should probably wait for him."

The receptionist smiled at him and pushed her cat-eye glasses up her nose.

"Don't worry about him," she said. "He knows his way around. Thing is, he's a results man. If you want answers...well, the dead see a lot. The doors won't stay open forever."

Hill licked his lips as he hesitated. He'd ridden that elevator every day for the last three years. It had always been glass and polished metal. Even when his dad had worked here. The worn cherrywood panels and musty orange carpet had never been part of the design. That, somehow, made him more nervous than the box's undeniable resemblance to a coffin.

"Shit or get off the pot, love," the receptionist advised as she fished a packet of cigarettes out of the drawer. She tapped one out into her fingers and winked at Hill when he looked at her. "Terrible habit. Never get started. It'll kill ya."

She struck a match. The flame was wispy and more smoke than light. It still worked to light the cigarette. As the receptionist breathed in, the doors started to close.

The smart thing to do would be to let them.

Hill's death was—hopefully—temporary. By Christmas he'd have his body back, and Davy would be...wherever spirits that finished their business went. Agreement across the board, from Church doctrine to Reddit boards, was that being *too* informed about the dealings of the dead ended...

Badly. Or well. Either way, the important part in that was the "end."

The problem was that, while Hill might have consistently tested as *intelligent*, among other things, a smart man would have let sleeping dogs lie. Not gone to Player Street and kicked them back to life.

He bolted for the narrowing gap of the elevator doors.

Out of the corner of his eye, he saw Davy's head jerk around to see what Hill was doing.

"What is it?" Reynolds said as he turned in the same direction. "There's nothing there."

Davy's tentacles shot out to grab at Hill. One snatched at his ankle. He managed to jump over the thick cable of it and stepped on another as he staggered on landing. That gave him a flash of unnecessary guilt. He blurted a muttered "sorry," even as another tentacle grabbed his hoodie. The collar jerked up under his throat and...even when you didn't need to breathe, that still felt unpleasant. He yanked his arms free, the jacket left to dangle from the tentacle's grip, and threw himself at the gap.

The last and longest tentacle grabbed his wrist, and Hill braced himself for a rude halt. Except it didn't tighten its grip and just slid away, the dry, cool tip of it caressing Hill's palm as it let him go.

He made it to the elevator just in time to squeeze through the doors. His momentum crashed him into the back wall of the cab, his hands braced flat against the fly-speckled old mirror. When he turned around, he had just enough time to shrug an apology to Davy's glare before the doors slammed shut.

A distorted reflection stared back at him from the beaten copper that clad the doors. The warm tones of the metal tinted his skin with brown and pink instead of gray, but somehow it didn't look like his living face. Just an idea of what he'd look like dead in the flesh.

He looked down at his feet and started to put his hands in his pockets. When he only found empty air, he remembered the somber flag of his hoodie left where he'd shed it, dangled from one of Davy's tentacles.

"Shit," he muttered, briefly at a loss for what to do with his hands.

"Language," the receptionist's voice chided him from the speaker. The mechanism cranked, and the cab rattled upwards, fast enough to make him stagger. "Hold on to your bones."

Chapter Four

Dec 22 12.10 pm

HILL HAD DISAPPEARED.

And to add insult to injury, it had looked like a shitty special effect from an '80s movie. He'd been dolly-zoomed from existence. Davy could guess what had happened, but it *itched* at him to work with conjecture. Even if it was well-informed.

"What's wrong with you now?" Reynolds asked. "Do you need to go stand in a corner and look at a wall or something?"

Davy wasn't sure whether it was contempt or disgust in Reynolds's voice. It didn't really matter. Both put his back up.

He'd forgotten how *satisfying* the dull roil of his old black temper was in the flesh. Not that he was an even-tempered dead man, either, but chemicals definitely added a little zest to the experience. His tentacles, already agitated, responded to his mood by lashing out.

One wrapped around Reynolds's neck. The pale, leathery length of it looked stark against a professionally topped-up tan and a black collar. There was no blood to flush with, exactly, but the shadowy pattern that blotched the length of it darkened as it squeezed.

It did fuck all, of course.

What little influence the dead could impose on the living did *not* extend to popping their heads off like Pez dispensers. It wasn't fair, but nobody had ever said death was except the Church...and they had good reason to lie.

So Davy could throttle the man all day and—

Reynolds rapped his knuckles against Davy's forehead.

"Anyone home?" he asked. "Seriously. What's *wrong* with you?"

Davy stared flatly at the man as his brain stalled out trying to process the *what the fuck* of what had just happened. For a *fucking* start, people didn't just touch him like that. Living him had been an asshole with a temper; dead him was an asshole with a temper and tentacles. People with *any* sort of survival instinct usually got the message that he was someone to give a wide berth to.

His lack of response made Reynolds snort and shake his head.

"Might as well talk to a rock," he said as he reached over the reception desk to swipe his pass. "You're lucky you're the Old Man's kid. Only reason you got a job here."

Huh.

Davy looked down at himself. Or more accurately, at Hill's lean, elegant body. That was right. He wasn't an ex-SEAL merc with a hard-earned reputation for being not-quite-right. He was currently a nepo-baby analyst-twink with pretty eyes.

Funny how easy that was to forget.

"I'll walk you up," Reynolds said as the doors to the sleek, all-curved-lines pod of an elevator opened silently in one wall. "Make sure you don't end up anywhere you're not meant to be. Again."

He walked away. Davy stared at his back with narrowed eyes and then followed him.

So the "fuck around and find out" vibes were only skin deep. He was a bit offended by that.

He could fix it, of course. Even in Hill's body. It wouldn't take much. Pain was a distraction; it was the fear of *more* pain that focused the mind. A broken finger. Or...as he stepped into the elevator behind Reynolds...a hand to the back of the head to smack his smug-ass face into the furred reflection in the matte metal walls.

The thought made Davy's fingers twitch.

Food. Fuck. Fight.

The only three things on his to-do list for this brief return to meat and chemicals. He'd ticked food off the list already, and he really did need to get a move on with the other two.

"What floor?" Reynolds asked as he bent over to squint into the scanner. The light from it flickered briefly over his face as it checked his ID.

Davy indulged his fantasy of violence a second longer, then reluctantly abandoned it. Whatever form "redemption" took for Fraser, it would probably still be best if there was no suspicious behavior on Hill's part to tie him to it.

And despite the fact Hill's departure had left Davy to deal with questions like "what floor" on his own, he didn't want anything...Fraser...to happen to him.

So he stuck his hands in his pockets and gave Reynolds his best blankly unhelpful look.

"My floor," he said, as if he genuinely thought it was the obvious answer.

Reynolds gave him a withering look, rolled his eyes, and jabbed one of the unmarked black buttons. It was a sure bet. When people thought someone was stupid, they were only ever too happy to be proven right.

"The fact you thought I'd *ever* be into you?" Reynolds said as he crossed his arms and stared at the shut doors. "That should be part of the diagnostic for whatever you've got."

Davy gave the nape of the man's neck a sour look as he regretted his decision to practice moderation. He could probably have given Reynolds reason to keep that sneer off his face for the next five years. At least.

Instead, here he was, stuck not doing something he wanted to do. His "No.1 (Step) Uncle" mug better be under the fucking tree.

Um, yeah, no. That was still creepy.

Davy hooked his finger into the collar of his T-shirt and gave it a tug. The gesture caught Reynolds's eye, and he glanced over. Davy irritably curled the end of a tentacle and flicked the man in the eye.

Useless but...

"Fuck," Reynolds muttered as he screwed up his face. He rubbed around the bony orbit of his eye with his thumb as he blinked. "Fucking migraines."

Davy glanced from him to the web of his tentacles.

He hadn't expected that petty bit of spite to do anything other than frustrate him. The dead might be able to *see* the mortal world, but that was it. They couldn't touch it or taste it or fuck it over. Not unless they went polter...but there were *some* fucking lines even Davy wasn't going to cross.

It could be coincidence, he supposed. There was only one way to find out.

He reared up one pale, narrow tentacle and held it for a second, swaying slightly from side to side like a cobra as he aimed. Then he struck and jabbed it straight through Reynolds's eye and twisted it through the honeycomb of his sinuses.

It felt weird. Like nothing where he *knew* he should feel something. Hill's body responded to the lack of feedback by pulling up something analogous, the wet, slick warmth of blood thick and slippery as it coated Davy's hands.

Reynolds seemed to like the experience even less. His face went gray, the sickly color stained around his mouth and eyes, and he had to catch himself against the wall. He bent his head forward; it looked like he was about to puke on his shoes, and Davy's tentacle flicked up into his brain.

That Davy felt.

The jolt of it went through him like a shock and made his tentacles recoil, knotted in tight around his body.

...Hill's mouth moving, all lips and tongue and sticky, sweaty irritation. The brief thought that it wouldn't be bad *for his career as he looked at Hill's cautiously hopeful face and the sour "No" that scratched out of him. Shame—he liked women more, but if you got the chance to fuck the boss's son, you fucked the boss's son—but this one was a liability. Fraser didn't trust him, and that wasn't something that Reynolds wanted rubbing off on...*

Gone.

Davy staggered as he tried to hang on to the thoughts, but they ran out of him like water. The details first, and then anything but the vaguest idea of what they'd been. He wiped the back of his nose on his hand. It was dry, but it *felt* like it should be bloody. He could taste the salt and metal of it, the expectation that when he sniffed the hot liquid would hit the back of his sinuses.

His eyes caught his reflection over his raised hand, fractured and misted in the roughed-up metal, and stalled for a second in surprise when he saw...himself.

Davy...that *hadn't* been his name, had it?...Jones, with his hard-edged good looks and too dark to read eyes. The lack of any white was a post-death evolution, but they had always been...off-putting. Or so he'd been told.

Although the squirming mass of immaterial flesh that writhed agitatedly around him probably took the heat off the eyes a bit in the "off-putting" stakes these days.

He glanced up in the corner of the cab at the camera he was pretty sure was there and wondered if it could see that. If it did, then discretion was pointless. Fraser had grown up in the same sweltering brand of Catholicism as Davy; he knew about the ritual, and he knew how many people he'd pissed off who might use it against him.

Davy checked on Reynolds. The other man looked queasy, and as Davy watched, he wiped blood out of his nostril onto his thumb. Not even a glance at Davy's reflection. If it was an act, then it was a good one. So it was more likely some little-known effect of the Beyond that Davy saw himself in there.

Just in case, though...

He winked at his reflection, just one quick flick of an eyelid before his image faded back into Hill's hair and mouth and hands.

Best-case scenario was that Fraser didn't work out who'd pulled his unfinished business out of the ground. But if it did come out, Davy wanted his brother to know he was enjoying the parole.

Davy left Reynolds to puke in the toilets and went to find Fraser's office.

It didn't take him long. The biggest office with the least personality. Davy swung the well-cushioned black leather office chair around and threw Hill's body down into it, all lank and careless grace. He swung a sneaker-clad foot up onto the corner of the desk and reached for the top drawer.

It turned out that thirty years, give or take, did change a man. Fraser had moved his candy from under his pen tray down to PERSONALACC_26. Davy unwrapped the sucker he pulled out and stuck it in his mouth. The plastic crinkled in his hands as he balled it up and dropped it onto the floor.

Davy scraped the thick sugar-scrub waxed coating off the candy with his teeth to get to the sweet-sour pop of raspberry. That hadn't changed. Fraser would still rather *have* the candy than actually *eat* it.

Hill wasn't the only one life was wasted on.

He rolled the sucker around his mouth, hard shell clacking against his teeth, as he gave the space bar on Fraser's computer an idle tap with his finger. The screen flickered to life—a bland gray background with a half-translucent corporate logo of an octopus floating in the middle of it.

Davy stared at it. He'd forgotten that.

Sweat itched under Davy's armpit. He scratched absently as he shoved his soaked hoodie into the locker.

"We can't let what happened in Palmyra go unanswered."

Davy shifted the door so he could see his brother without having to turn around.

In the reflection, Fraser frowned at him. He looked, like always, like someone had drawn Davy from memory.

"I saw you already sent a reply," Davy said.

Fraser clenched his jaw. "This is the private sector," he said. "It's not enough to be good at what you do; you have to be seen *being good at it."*

Davy smirked at him. "I look good enough," he said.

"Not that good."

"Better than you."

"Older than me."

They glared at each other. Blood had always been enough reason to stick together, but not enough to like it. But...Fraser was good at what he did—crawling up rich people's holes—too.

And, like it or not, black ops was a young man's game. Davy wasn't old, but he'd run himself hard. After a workout, these days, the ache lingered along stress lines that he could feel weren't going to get any better.

He knew where people like him ended up when they lost their edge. In a grave.

He'd come very close to one in Palmyra.

"I know." Davy gave in to the inevitable. "But we also can't look scared. So if your slap on the wrist works, we'll call it even."

Fraser gave him a thin-lipped smirk. "And if it doesn't?"

That was a good question,

Davy closed the locker, briefly making his brother vanish, and then turned around to look at him.

"It will," he said. "I know Coate. He's not stupid."

"Stupid enough," Fraser interrupted him. He pulled his Blackberry out of his pocket and frowned at the screen. "He nearly killed us. Rosen and his wife were there too, and they're civilians. She lost the baby."

"Don't pretend you care."

"I care about keeping Rosen happy," Fraser said. "He knows where to find the money. So answer his email about the corporate logo. Make him feel like he's got a reason to stay. That he's an equal partner."

"Is he?"

"Where money's concerned? Yes," Fraser said. "Don't be a dick about it, either."

Davy didn't check his email until the next day. When he did, he'd rejected all of them. He might start to slip one day, but right at that moment, he was still good. So why not lean into his rep?

Davy Jones and CIRATTA HOLDINGS. What else could you have but an octopus? He'd gone over to their house to go through the designs, though. That had shown willingness.

A thick tentacle curled around his throat and draped over his shoulders. He couldn't *feel* it, but the memory of the dry, fidgeting heft of it still made him shift his weight back automatically.

"Yeah, I get it," he said as he popped the sucker out of his mouth. "One way or another, I picked you, not the other way around."

The tentacle tightened, long straps of muscle moving visibly under the pale skin. It could have been meant affectionately, or not, but either way it didn't have much effect. Davy left it to it as he twiddled the chewed white stick of the sucker between his fingers and stared at the computer screen.

Thirty years, give or take. That was how long ago Fraser had started his day *and* ended it with a reminder of fratricide. It seemed like the sort of thing that implied something about the person who did it.

Davy didn't know what exactly—guilt, pride?—but it had to have a psychological impact. He stuck the candy back in his mouth and tucked it into his cheek. The sickly-sweet taste seeped slowly into his teeth as he pulled the keyboard toward him.

The box on the screen, brusque and free of a user-friendly interface, demanded a password.

Davy hovered his fingers over the keys as he ran through his options.

ikilledmybrother didn't work, which was a surprise.

Neither did *hedeservedit.*

The computer told him that if he got the password wrong one more time, it would lock him out.

"That is the point," Davy said absently.

He flexed his fingers. The knuckles didn't pop. He grimaced to himself. Between this and the fight that never was in the lift, he was getting blue-balled left, right, and center today.

DavyJonesLives.

He hit enter and smirked as the computer shut down. With luck, whoever got tapped to fix his system would actually do the legwork to log the failed run of passwords. That would be awkward for Fraser, which would be a shame.

Now, for what he had come here for.

Davy braced his propped foot against the edge of the desk and pushed. He rolled jerkily back toward the floor-length windows, the wheels of the chair bogged down in the plush gray carpet. His tongue curled around the tacky paper of the candy stick as he dropped his feet to the floor and looked around the room.

If he were a go-bag, where would he be?

Under the floorboards was industry standard, but—

Davy pushed himself up out of the chair and walked over to the bookcase that took up one wall. There were only a few books in it, all industry titles and uncracked spines. Like Fraser hadn't been the weird neighborhood kid with no friends, three library cards, and an addiction to pulp sci-fi and Westerns.

As opposed to... Davy picked up a workmanlike silver frame from a polished black shelf and looked at... a heavy-set middle-aged man with high cholesterol, a classy wife, and a hot stepson.

Now that was creepy in a different way, but Fraser wasn't that sort of asshole. He'd never had anything but contempt for the perverts who'd come sniffing around when they were kids.

Davy studied the posed, postcard-perfect family portrait for a second longer. It was fairly recent from Hill's haircut—he had the vibe of someone who didn't think about that often—and age. Fraser looked content, or at least pleased with himself, and like someone who'd consider the comfort level of his having to crawl around on the floor.

So, make it eye level.

Davy set the photo back down and stepped back to take in the rest of the room. His gaze hooked on the bookshelf, and he cocked his head to the side. Maybe, but it wouldn't be Davy's first choice—if you were in the shit that deep you wanted to get in and out—and, like it or not, he and Fraser had the same instincts.

He moved it down the list of possibilities as he turned on his heel to check out the rest of the room. It didn't take long. Fraser liked *having* expensive things, but it gave him no pleasure having them *around.* Unless there was a need to posture, he preferred things to be "clean."

It was why they'd worked so well together. Davy made problems go away, and Fraser cleaned up the mess.

Funny that he'd swapped those roles with Hill's dad after he killed Davy.

Davy snorted to himself at that and rubbed the back of his neck. Probably something pretty fucking psychological there too, but not real useful right now. He walked over to the only other prominent decor in the room, a clutch of letters of commendation and Fraser's commission framed and hung prominently on the wall over the narrow couch.

Without him thinking about it, his tentacles squirmed over his shoulder and groped through the glass and paper and plaster into the wall behind. It felt—

Davy screwed his face up as his brain tried to map sensation onto a body that didn't have the actual *bits.* It wasn't unpleasant, just very weird to feel dust and dry wood on his earlobe and in his ass crack. The gossamer stickers of spiderwebs *in* his nose made his stomach turn, and it took a lot to do that.

Finally, he felt the graze of rough fabric and cold metal trail down his back. He squirmed his shoulders back in reaction and then pulled in all his tentacles but *that* one. It lingered in the wall, a pale, fleshy pointer straight through a framed medal that Fraser had never actually gotten.

Davy snorted and withdrew the last tentacle. It hung attentively over his shoulder as he reached out to move the wooden frame and set it neatly down on the couch. He tapped a finger against the smooth gray paint underneath and listened to the light, hollow thump of it.

Just in case.

He punched through the wall.

It fucking *hurt.*

Davy recoiled in surprise at the jolt of pain that brought tears to the back of his throat. He pressed his lips together on a yelp and shook his hand as if that would make it better.

What the hell? He sucked in a ragged breath and stuck his hand into his armpit as he waited for the sting to subside. His mind raced from confusion to paranoia that Fraser really did have some sort of anti-spirit measures worked into the structure of the building.

Salt or relics or some shit like that. Davy leaned forward cautiously to peer into the hole he'd made. He'd heard the dry dead talking about stuff like that before, but he'd never paid much heed to it. It hadn't seemed relevant to his problems.

Nothing looked out of place. Just a dark cavity in a wall and a battered canvas bag hung from a cheap hook.

So why the *fuck* did Davy's hand feel like he'd shoved it into a nest of angry wasps?

He gingerly took it out from under his arm to look at it and grimaced. His knuckles were split open, blood slowly oozing out over ragged chunks of skin, and already stained with the start of bruising. It looked like...

Davy mentally trailed off as he realized that it looked like the hand of someone who'd never punched something before. Probably because it hadn't. He lifted Hill's hand to his mouth to suck the blood out of the scraped skin. Between this and the hole in his other hand, currently bandaged up with gauze pads and Band-Aids, Hill's deal with the dead was going to leave a mark.

Something in Davy's chest pinched like that was his problem. It caught him off-guard. Nothing about this deal was new to him. OK, possessing someone who'd never been in a fight before was kind of novel. The rest was SOP. He had always been a targeted-strike kind of operative. If he saw the fallout, it was because something had gone to shit somewhere.

Hill would have to deal with the New Year on his own. All Davy could do to make that any easier was his job.

He grabbed the edge of the hole and broke off chunks of the wall, paint chips and plaster dust scabbed over his bloody knuckles. Once it was big enough, he reached through, grabbed the bag, and pulled it out.

It felt usefully heavy, but there wasn't time to make sure.

Davy picked up the frame he'd set aside, the medal inside askew on its mounting from being handled, and hung it neatly back on the wall. It didn't *quite* hide the edges of the hole.

Again, though, that was the point.

Davy brushed himself off, slung the bag over his shoulder, and headed back out. He grabbed a package from the Secret Santa pile on his way out. It was neatly wrapped and felt heavy enough that the fact it didn't rattle when he shook it suggested that—he checked the neat, smiling Santa tag—Steven Wills had scored a good present.

Sucked to be him.

Davy pulled the tag off and tossed it in a bin on the way past. He whistled tunelessly to himself as he went to find Reynolds. Halfway there, he paused as the thought of Hill nudged at him. There wasn't much he could do to find Hill in the Beyond, but he could give him a heads-up that he was leaving.

Somehow?

Chapter Five

Dec 22 2.30pm

"BEING DEAD," THE MAN behind the big desk said, "it ain't so bad, huh?"

Hill sat on the edge of a hard leather chair, coffee cup and cookie balanced on a small plate on his knee, and tried to work out where to look. The more or less human eyes, pale brown and lightly creased around the edges, or the blunt brindle dog-muzzle that sopped up coffee with a long red tongue.

He thought that it was probably polite to focus on the eyes, but he wasn't sure how anyone managed that.

"I guess you get used to it," Hill said. "I prefer being alive."

"Call me Seb" sat back in his chair. It creaked under him as his weight shifted. He cocked his head to the side. For a second Hill forgot

about the teeth as he instinctively glanced up, half expecting to see pricked dog ears stuck up through the well-cut auburn waves.

"Do you?" Seb said. His chops stretched back from his teeth in a wide, toothy grin as he asked, "Why?"

He sounded genuinely interested.

Hill grimaced a smile and wondered if he had somehow stumbled into a job interview against his will. It had happened before. That was how he'd gotten his job at CIRATTA, ambushed in the break room when all he'd been there for was to drop off some paperwork before Fraser left on a business trip.

His stomach felt the same, and he was drawing blanks on what he was pretty sure should be easy questions to answer.

Why did he prefer being alive?

Was "people do" a good enough answer?

Hill awkwardly took a bite of his cookie to buy himself a second. It looked like a double-stuffed Oreo, but as the cream and biscuit coated his tongue it tasted like...

With Janet? Out of everyone she'd picked fucking Janet?

The memory rolled over his tastebuds and down his throat before he could choke on it. Frustration, jealousy, and bitten-back tears for the filling. Hill coughed and set the rest of the treat back down.

"The food's better," he said.

Seb laughed. There was a crack in one of the dog's teeth, a line of rot that threaded brown and deep up toward the gumline. Hill watched it with uneasy fascination as the man shook his head and wagged a dirty-nailed finger.

It looked like blood rimed under his thumb.

Years of lessons in being normal told him that it wasn't; of course, it wasn't. Why would a man have blood under his nails in a nice office like this? He was just oversensitive.

The part of Hill that was always sharp and intolerable about things, made of sandpaper and unapologetic about it, grimaced at him inside his head.

Why would he have a dog face? The rules clearly don't apply.

"The spirit of a biscuit," Seb said and nodded to the plate on the table. "Sometimes you get a bad one. Try again."

Hill licked the taste of someone else's heartbreak off his lips and was queasy about how much he was tempted. He'd always been told to think about how the other person would feel, and he had always assumed that was literal. An internal IFTTT process. That had been raw, immediate as his own pain or anger. He could still taste the hot salt of her—he felt sure it had been a woman, although he could not say why—anger in the back of his throat.

"No." His voice was dry and scratchy. He leaned forward and gingerly slid the plate onto the edge of the desk. The untouched coffee sloshed over the side of the cup and stung his fingers. It hurt, but...it didn't spill over and spread. It stung his knuckles, and it was done. Hill would have been amazed if not for...well, everything else. "I'm good."

Seb shrugged. "Your loss," he said as he picked up an Oreo. He tossed it in the air and snapped at it like a...well, a dog. Sharp white teeth caught it in midair and sheared it in half, a swipe of that long, wet tongue getting both into his mouth. "But there's more to death than food."

The image of Davy's ass, tight and firm and still glistening from Hill's shower gel between the veil of lax, squirming tentacles, strolled through Hill's mind. It felt like he blushed. He didn't know if it was possible to do that without a heart or blood supply.

Of course, other things depended on blood flow too, and as Hill shifted awkwardly in the chair, it didn't seem to be having any trouble.

Hill crossed his legs and folded his hands over his lap as he tried to focus on Seb.

It shouldn't have been this difficult; the man had a *dog face*. But Davy had long, lean thighs with a scar carved into one like punctuation, and he walked with a cocky strut that shouldn't even have been possible in Hill's body. It was hard to keep that imagery caged up in the "Unachievable crushes"—for so many reasons—area of his brain.

On the other side of the desk Seb gave Hill a wet, wide smile. "You've seen some of what we have to offer," he said. Hill wondered with quick, cringy embarrassment if the other man somehow knew what he was thinking. Could spirits do that? If they could, and Seb was aware of Hill's mortification, he ignored it as he went on. "And there is the question of inevitability."

"Everyone dies," Hill admitted. "That doesn't mean I'll have unfinished business. I could go to heaven."

Seb chuckled. That was...unnerving, but he pressed on before Hill could ask what was so funny.

"Or...hell," Seb pointed out, still somehow smirking with his dog lips. "But if you don't, and you end up in the Beyond, the Company is a good friend to have. I'm sure that your new...associate...has had some stories to tell about us, but—"

"No," Hill said.

Seb blinked. For the first time he looked genuinely off-balance. "No?"

Hill shook his head. "He's not mentioned you."

"Huh," Seb said. He scratched along his jowls as he absorbed that, and brindle hair stuck to the white cuff of his sleeve. "I suppose he's been dead longer than most who get Invoked, but... nothing? Not even about the men with snares and knives at the end of the tunnel?"

"Wait. The *what*?"

"Oh, don't worry about them," Seb said as he waved one hand dismissively. "No point, is there. Still, didn't expect discretion from Arms, of all people."

"His name's Davy," Hill said.

It occurred to him, a little late, that maybe he shouldn't have made the correction. It didn't matter, though. Seb was already shaking his head dismissively, slobber dripping from loose chops.

"No. No, it's not," Seb sighed. "Trust me. I would know. He is a problem for another day, though. Right now we're talking about you."

"I would rather talk about the men with knives,"

"And snares," Seb corrected him cheerfully. He shuffled through the paperwork on his desk. "You can't forget them."

He glanced up, his eyes suddenly old. *Old*-old, cloudy and wet and wrinkled. "You *mustn't* forget the snares."

Hill swallowed and cringed back in the seat. He glanced at the door and weighed the option of making his excuses to leave.

"I..." he started to stumble his way toward a polite out, but Seb wiped his dirty hands over his eyes and recovered himself before he could.

"*You* came for answers," Seb said. "And you thought they'd be free, because you have a winning smile and a pure heart? No such luck. Life is generous, death is not. It is, however, straightforward."

That did *not* sound true. Hill squinted at Seb as he asked dubiously. "It is?"

"It can be," Seb said. "You invoked the spirits to punish your stepfather, and that's all in motion, no hiccups there, but that leaves you with questions about your dead dad that only he could answer."

Seb paused, one perfectly manicured brow raised expectantly as he looked at Hill. The breezy, human resources in a private firm, callousness of his delivery made *something* catch in Hill's chest. He wasn't sure if it was a sob or a laugh, and he wasn't going to let it out to find out. It caught in his throat like a dry bit of bread as he swallowed hard.

"I'd like to know—"

Seb shushed him with an upheld hand. "Not my circus, not my monkeys," he said blithely. "I'm the big-picture man. I don't need to know the details. It's enough that you want something we can give you. In return, the Company wants a catspaw in the mortal world."

They stared at each other.

"Is that a joke?" Hill asked after a long, stiffly awkward pause.

"Why would it be?"

Hill reached up and gestured vaguely around his chin and jaw area to indicate the slobbering dog muzzle that jutted out of Seb's face.

"Because of the..." He trailed off as Seb just looked confused. "Um...never mind. Why do you need one of those?"

It was not easy for a dog to purse its lips. Seb managed to pucker his around a mouthful of sharp teeth.

"Oh, don't worry your pretty head about that," he said. "You've already flouted the laws of God and Man—"

"Rules."

This was the interruption that made Seb look annoyed. He sighed, his loose dog chops flapping. "What?"

"Technically, they are rules, not laws," Hill said. "A law would have wider scope, more enforcement, and legal consequences of some kind."

Seb rolled his eyes and started to say something, but he didn't get a chance. The Invocation of the Spirits had been Hill's special interest for the last three years. This particular element hadn't been his main focus, but it still felt reassuring to fall back onto. He would much rather info-dump about ecclesiastical conspiracy theories and metaphysical loopholes than...

...well, men with snares that waited for the dead.

"It's also the laws or rules of the Church, not of God," he blurted out. "Since God, by definition, is omnipotent and therefore is aware of the Invocation and, based on the fact it's not been removed from existence, approves of it."

Seb picked a chunk of cookie out of his teeth and licked it off his fingers.

"That assumes you're capable of understanding God's will," he said. "Maybe the Invocation is a test. Or a trap."

"Maybe," Hill said. "But that's not a law, and honeypots are generally frowned upon."

Seb leaned over to the table and picked up Hill's abandoned cup of coffee. He tipped his head back and poured it into the dog's mouth, long tongue lapping it out of the air.

"Tell that to the men at the end of the tunnel when they get out their burlap sacks," he said as he set the cup down and glanced briefly at Hill to enjoy his disturbed reaction to that. "But this is sophistry, and that's a Thoth's remit. We're men of the world."

"I would not describe myself like that," Hill said.

He wasn't sweating. That was one advantage to being disembodied, apparently. The sensation of knowing he should have been was almost as distracting, though. He shifted and resisted the urge to mop his face for nonexistent drops.

Seb wiped his mouth on his sleeve, fresh stains joining old ones on the cuff. "You used to be simple."

"Me?"

"The living. The invokers. When they called the dead they wanted punishment, plenty, or both. Then you discovered solipsism and nihilism and priapism."

Hill blinked. One of those things was not like the others, but he wasn't sure if Seb was aware of that or not. While he tried to decide if it was mockery or ignorance, Seb chuntered on.

"Now they pull us up from the grave dirt, brush the worms from our brow, and shake us down for contentment or fairness or justice... Give me the days when all you had to do was scare up a turkey for a feast or scare some syphilitic old bastard to death."

"And what you got in return was a...catspaw?"

Seb held a finger up. "No. That's penitence," he said. "An act of service to discharge the spiritual judgment against us. That exchange is baked in. This is more...like double-dipping. You get a little something extra than what you asked for, and in return you act in our interests in the mortal world."

He held up one hand, cupped as if he held what he was talking about already in it.

"Answers about dear old Dad," he said. Then his other hand came up to join it. "Little bit of necromancy. Who's it going to hurt?"

The implication there was "no one," but Seb had always pointedly not promised that. Hill picked absently at a hangnail on his thumb as he tried to find the answer in the static of *things* in his head.

He already *knew* his dad hadn't killed himself, so was it a "want" or a "need" to have an answer as to why Fraser had done it? On the other hand, he didn't *want* to know what else his dad had done for Fraser, or why, but part of him dug its heels in on needing that information.

How could he demand anything of Fraser if he just handwaved away any of his dad's sins?

Did his mom know...

No.

"No."

He'd not meant to say that out loud. Seb looked startled at it. The corner of his mouth curled up to reveal the ragged row of teeth and the wet, red inner lip. Slobber pooled and dripped.

The thought of the offer being retracted cut through Hill's doubts like a hot knife. It was only Fraser's voice in his head that stopped him.

"Make them wait." The rough, clipped advice had been delivered dispassionately long enough ago that Hill couldn't remember what the negotiation had been about. A bike. Pocket money. Skipping therapy. It could have been any of them. *"You already know how badly you want it. Find out if they want it more."*

"Not yet," Hill choked out. He pressed his thumb down hard into his thigh. The pain didn't work quite as well as with meat and bone, but it still helped focus him. "I need to think about it."

Seb wiped a string of drool off his lips with his thumb.

"You don't have much time."

"I have some."

Seb took a deep breath, a flash of pink just visible as his wet black nose flared. "Usually this is a 'take it or leave it' offer," he said. "You need us more than we need you after all, but I like you."

It was not. He did not. Hill hated the fact that he needed to be grateful to Fraser for something else.

"Here." Seb produced a card from his pocket and leaned over the table to offer it. The thick, glossy black stock was pinched between his two dirty fingers. "When you decide, call me."

Hill took the card. It was blank. He turned it over twice to make sure. "Um...how?"

Despite everything there was something bizarrely, infectiously compelling about the big, toothy smile that Seb directed at Hill. He winked at him.

"Think about it," he said. Then he twitched his head around sharply. It took a second, but then the insistent, shrill tone of a fire alarm cut through the air of the room. Seb's head twisted, lip curled, and he physically grabbed his muzzle in one hand to pull it back down. Between his fingers, he said, "Well, I think that's our cue, Mr. Rosen. Give my best to Arms."

It was hard enough to think with the fire alarm scrambling Hill's brain. The abrupt dismissal left him even more flat-footed, and he gawped at Seb. A snarl pulled Seb's muzzle tight, and he slapped his hand on the desk.

"Don't let the door hit you in the ass on the way out!" he snapped. The crack of flesh on wood made Hill flinch, but didn't help him pull together the disparate threads needed to *move.* There was too much going on, and it *rattled* through him as he— Mid-panic, Seb suddenly switched to affable as he pushed the plate of cookies forward. "And do feel free to help yourself."

Hill stared at him. He wished it was that easy, but he was locked down. Locked in. His brain wouldn't stop *screaming*, and his body was stuck in sleep mode. He couldn't even breathe easily; every breath squeezed through the tight grip on his throat.

Then he realized he already had a cookie in his hand. He could feel the dry, crumbly texture against his fingers and smell the sweetness of it as he pulled it back. It didn't smell like heartbreak or grief or anything but a cookie.

For a second his jaw ached with the urge to take a bite, just to confirm the content of the confection. He managed to squelch it and grab a napkin to wrap it in as he stood up.

"I'll think about what you said, but..." Hill stumbled over his own tongue, then looked past Seb's shoulder at the window. Dudley-in-Death spread out behind the glass, ramshackle and stitched together. It was bigger than the real one...the living world's one. "My dad. Is he out there?"

Seb just tapped a finger against his wet nose.

"You know how to find out."

Hill supposed he did. His hand tightened around his contraband, and he felt it break within the flimsy wrapper. Crumbs spilled between his fingers onto the floor. Still on autopilot, he shoved the napkin in his pocket and turned to leave.

"If I were you, I'd not tell Arms about my offer," Seb said to the tense spot between Hill's shoulders. "He was bad when he died, and he ain't got no better."

Hill nodded his acknowledgement of that without looking around. It was true. Davy was self-interested and amoral, and possibly a contract killer. He hadn't claimed otherwise, though. That was more than Hill could say of most people in his life.

He let himself out.

The receptionist was on her break.

A jack from the board was plugged into her ear, and she stared with placid amusement at nothing while she ate a sandwich. The fleck of mayo on her painted red lip made Hill's hand move to his confection-stuffed pocket to check it was still there.

It was safe to assume that all food in the Beyond shared the same quality, as far as being a medium for memory went. That just unlocked a cascade of other questions in Hill's mind.

Did the memory adhere to the whole food, or could something layered like a sandwich retain different qualities with each slice?

What if someone ate something and halfway through the meal something happened, bad or good? Would the "taste" here change halfway through?

Did someone need to *eat* the food in order for it to manifest in the Beyond, or did some of it have the memory of it being made inside?

He was so engrossed in his thoughts, he tripped over something on the ground.

Before he could measure the length of himself, a loop of something warm and firm caught his elbow. He steadied himself and gave the tentacle a distracted pat...until he looked around to see what he'd tripped on and saw another tentacle pull sheepishly out of view. Another rose up in front of him and offered the hoodie he'd lost earlier back, the black fabric slung over the end of the tentacle by the hood.

"They like you," Davy said from the low-slung steel and leather chair he sprawled in. The lengths of his tentacles were tangled around his feet, some lazily draped over his thigh like a favored pet, while others picked and poked boredly at the carpet or a discarded pen. He pulled a chewed paper stick out of his mouth and tossed it to the tentacles. They tried to catch it, but it fell right through them and landed on the carpet. "They'd have let most people fall."

One foot was braced on an old, battered-looking duffel on the floor. The other was propped up on the low coffee table, dirt smudged over the December edition of the *Things to Do in Dudley* magazine from the Dudley Commerce and Visitors Bureau.

It had a list of local graveyards in it, along with a curated selection of historical untimely deaths in case anyone wanted to risk trying to raise the spirits.

For the first time, Hill wondered if the dead got fed up with that.

"Then why trip me to start with?" he asked as he took his hoodie and shrugged it back on.

Davy reached down to give the tentacle slung over his knee an affectionate slap. "That's 'cause they're assholes," he said. "They are sins, remember?"

He lifted his foot off the table and grabbed the duffel with one hand. It got slung easily over his shoulder as he stood up, with the sort of careless grace Hill was, again, vaguely irritated to realize, came from his body.

"Or *you're* an asshole," he pointed out.

Davy smirked as he started toward the main doors. "Naw," he said. "I'd have let you fall. I've no problem with the idea of you face down on the floor."

This time Hill didn't need any help to stumble. He caught himself and gave Davy's back a hard look as he tried to work out what that meant. Insulting or...suggestive.

He'd just about settled on insult when one of Davy's restless tentacles wove back. It wrapped around his thigh, warm and solidly muscular, and goosed him. He jumped, and the tentacle whipped away, grazing between his legs as it went.

Usually it was heat. The sticky, inconsiderate flush of hunger that kindled in his balls and spread up to prickle at the back of his neck and the tips of his ears like sunburn. The mix of discomfort and desire was familiar, even though a lot of it had been...solo engagements.

This felt different.

No warmth. No tightness in his chest as his breath caught. Instead, he felt a *shift* in the pit of his stomach, like the way sand slipped on the beach.

It was strange, but then so was the fact that it had been in response to a caress from a tentacle with no respect for personal space.

Hill groped through his memory for a second for the exact way Davy had put it.

We have some fun and we learn some important lessons.

Something like that. Hill guessed this could count.

He filed it away to think about later and broke into a jog to catch up with Davy before the main doors swung closed behind him. Hill supposed there was some way to get out—logically, there had to be—but he didn't want to have to ask.

To Hill's surprise, Davy stuck his arm back to brace the heavy glass door from closing. Hill muttered thanks as he ducked under it. He wondered briefly what would happen if he *did* try to just walk through it instead. The wave of nausea that hit him was vicious enough to feel like a warning.

He stopped to let it ebb again and looked at Davy.

"What happened to Reynolds?" he asked.

A smirk crooked the corner of Davy's mouth as he tilted his head back, one hand raised to shade his eyes. His hair had been shorter than Hill's. The overlay faded away into an ombre of black curls at the end of caramel brown waves.

"He put something in his mouth that disagreed with him," he said. "I don't think he's going to make the party."

Hill grimaced at the reminder.

"Lucky him," he muttered sourly.

It made Davy laugh, a low, unforced snort of amusement. Unlike the strange experience of getting turned on while dead, Hill was very familiar with the queasy, heady feeling that pushed at the walls of his chest.

Great, Hill thought sourly to himself as he padded along in Davy's shadow. He had a crush on the vengeful spirit. Hill thought being turned on by tentacles was probably the healthier of the two.

Chapter Six

Dec 22, 8pm

"Aren't you going to ask me what happened back at the office?" Hill asked from the other side of the bathroom door.

"No," Davy said.

He peeled the bandage off his hand and grimaced at the dry, sour edges of the wound. When he poked at it, it felt hot and tender. Either it wasn't a good idea to stab yourself with a knife you'd just dissected a rabbit with, or being dead fucked with your immune system.

Either way, it would be Hill's problem soon enough. For now—Davy flexed his fingers quickly to make sure everything still worked, and hurt—it would do.

"Why not?" Hill asked.

Davy shrugged for no one to see.

"Because I already know what happened," he said. "The Company made you an offer."

"Don't you want to know what I said?"

"No," Davy said. He liked Hill—it would definitely be practical to kill Fraser, but the idealism was kind of admirable...and Hill was cute—but not enough to cross the Company. It was best to stay out of Company business...even their dirty business.

He ran hot water over his hand, as hot as he could bear, as if it might help, and quickly redressed it, the fresh tape clumsily smoothed around the crease of his thumb. Then he headed back out into the main room of the apartment.

"I don't know what I should—" Hill broke off mid-sentence. He held his hand up, fingers spread, between him and Davy. "Why are you naked?"

Davy stretched and reached over his shoulder to scratch his back. "Your clothes are itchy," he complained. "Either you've got fleas or you need to change your detergent."

"All the other spirits I've seen are dressed," Hill said. "Why can't you keep your pants on?"

"They're your pants, and they're itchy," Davy said. "We've just covered that."

Hill threw up his hands in exasperation and turned his back. "At least put a pair of briefs on," he said in a strangled voice. "Please?"

"Fine," Davy said as he rolled his eyes. "It's your cock. If it gets a rash, that's on you."

He headed into the utility room to grab a pair out of the wash. It was done, folded, and stacked in a basket on top of the dryer.

"Your mom did your laundry," he noted over his shoulder, before he looked through the pile for something that wouldn't feel like poison ivy. "She used dryer sheets and everything."

He found a pair of black briefs. He stepped into them and pulled them up over his thighs until the fabric cupped his ass and balls. The fabric was soft and cool, any heat from the laundry process long since faded.

"She wants me to go to the party," Hill reminded him from the other room. "But not as *me*."

The moment of glee that Davy felt was unexpected but undeniable. He let the band of the briefs snap against his stomach and hurried back to stick his head out the door.

"It's a costume party?" he said.

Hill turned toward him, looked flustered, and averted his eyes to something over the top of Davy's head.

"I...no, it's not," he said. "I just meant that I'm supposed to look like a credit to them instead of, well, me. Why? Do you *like* costume parties?"

Davy leaned against the door frame, one bare arm braced on the wood, and his head tilted to rest on his forearm.

"I mean, shit," he said as he scratched the hinge of his jaw. "I guess?"

When he was alive, nothing short of torture would have dragged that out of him. He'd not even have admitted it to himself. Hell, dead, he wouldn't have been keen to admit it. In the Beyond, masks and mystery balls were the preserve of the Company. The whole point of *these*—the thought made Davy's tentacles rear up to mantle around him—was to stop him hiding what he was under swagger and a pretty face.

His brief return to the world of flesh and bone and incarnate cocks, however, had apparently unlocked something in him. Only to immediately let him down. So no chance there from his last time drawing breath.

"You know, this isn't the first time that Fraser's fucked me over," he grumbled. "But this is the one that hurts the most."

Hill lowered his gaze from the ceiling long enough to give Davy an exasperated look. "He killed you."

Davy shrugged. "I said what I said."

For a second Hill stared at him. "How do you do that?" he asked. "Just...forgive people, without them being punished or showing any regret for what they did. I can't. I've tried so hard, and I can't let go of it."

Davy pushed himself off the door frame. He rubbed the back of his neck and shrugged awkwardly. In general, he avoided too much introspection. It didn't lead anywhere good for a man in his line of work, on either side of the Veil.

A Company man could do pro bono hours working off their sins. The likes of Davy still needed to hustle to make ends meet. Death was more expensive than the Church ever told you.

Whatever something had unlocked in him, though, wanted to give Hill an answer. Davy had a feeling that nothing else the kid was going to get from this was going to be that satisfying. Even if he did pull it off.

"It's not that I'm *not* pissed," he said, "but someone was always gonna kill me. I was that kind of asshole, and so was everyone I knew. It wasn't like I was gonna marry some hot twink with a trust fund."

"I don't have a trust fund," Hill said primly.

Davy winked at him. "Made you think about it, though."

He went back into the laundry room to finish getting dressed. A pair of sweatpants and an old T-shirt seemed like the least hair-shirty of the selection available. He swore that rich people were different. He'd worn the same fatigues two weeks straight and had enough sand in his ass crack to fill a play pen, and he'd not wanted to strip his own skin off this much. He pulled the sweats on and wandered back out with the T-shirt dangled from one hand.

"Him marrying your mom *after* killing your dad is probably what sticks in your craw," he said. "Insult to injury."

Hill gave a tired snort and sat down on the edge of the coffee table. Sort of. It was close enough.

"It's kind of a package deal for bugging me," he said. "Killing my dad. Marrying my mom. Raising me like he'd not been the one to screw me up."

Davy pulled the T-shirt on. It was washed, but the worn cotton still smelled vaguely of *Hill* in a subtle, sweaty way.

"How long did they wait after your dad died?" he asked.

There was a pause as Hill gave him a suspicious look. "My mom had nothing to do with it," he said. "My dad's death. Fraser's business dealings. None of it."

Davy sat down on the edge of the couch and reached out to grab the duffel bag and drag it over to him.

"I didn't say she did."

"You were about to."

Davy paused with his hands on the loose metal buckles of the bag. He was definitely better with the baser emotion, but he was pretty sure the confidence that Hill said that made him feel *something*.

Pity, maybe.

"You don't know me, Hill," he said. "Don't fucking assume you do. It won't end well."

Hill gave a dry little snort. "So you're saying I *shouldn't* trust the undead mercenary who corpse-jacked my body and doesn't have any skin in the game?" he said. "Thanks. That would never have occurred to me."

It wasn't like Davy wasn't aware of the irony that Hill agreeing with him hurt his feelings. Irony just didn't make it hurt any less. His tentacles tucked in close around him, the ends curled around his ankles and tucked behind his knees. The posture felt sullen.

Davy ignored them as he pulled the bag straps loose and flipped the top of the duffel open. The inside smelled like old fabric and gun oil.

"I wasn't accusing your mom of anything," he said. That part was a lie; he had definitely been about to imply something, but the next part was something he genuinely wanted to know. "Just whether Fraser put his severance plan here together before—"

He tipped the bag upside down and gave it a shake to empty the contents onto the table. The taped-up envelopes landed with a thud, the gun with a crack that made Hill flinch. Davy slapped his hand down to stop it sliding onto the floor. Habit curled his hand around the butt, the plastic and metal a familiar shape.

"—or after he said his vows."

A hundred thousand sounded like a lot of money. It was actually a surprisingly portable amount of money.

Davy riffled the edge of the last strap of notes before he dropped it on top of the pile. The nice new scent of money had faded from the bills a while ago, but the feel of it against his thumb was still as good as he remembered.

"So, all these years," Hill said, "Fraser's just been ready to go, just leave us behind, the minute anything happened?"

Davy glanced up from the tightly stuffed A5 manila envelope he was about to open.

"So?" he said. "I thought you didn't like him."

"I don't," Hill said. "I love him, but I don't like him, and I can't forgive him."

Yeah. Sometimes Davy was glad he'd never invested in enough therapy to "feel" more shit. Hell, make that most of the time. It looked complicated, and nobody seemed to enjoy it.

"But I thought he...I don't know," Hill said as he shook his head. "I thought we mattered to him. Or at least that my mom did. People always say that the two of them are 'couple goals,' that they're perfect for each other."

Davy peeled the flap of the envelope up. It came away easily, the glue brittle from its time in the wall.

"Fraser's good at being perfect," he said with a shrug. "And this isn't personal. It's worst-case scenario insurance."

Hill reached out and flicked a ghostly finger at the pile of cash. It moved, just a little. "So in the worst-case scenario, he runs and we're left behind?"

"I...yeah, I guess," Davy said.

He poked at the cash with a tentacle, and it just passed through the paper, dipping through the table beneath. It felt the way that nails on a chalkboard sounded and made Davy squirm, but it didn't shift so much as a note.

Huh. He filed that away for later. It might be useful, or it could be a problem. Either way, Hill didn't need to know about it just yet.

"Look," Davy said. He laid a tentacle on Hill's shoulder. "Fraser probably does value being part of your family."

"Interesting way to put it."

"Cut him a break. To him, that's a lot," Davy said. He pulled an ID out of the envelope, flicked the card in his fingers, and read the front of it. Then he held it up so Hill could see. "Anyhow, it's not that Fraser doesn't care, it's that Kyle Bennett from Idaho doesn't have a family, so..."

Hill didn't look comforted. He pointedly shoved Davy's tentacle off his shoulder.

"You sound like you'd have done the same thing."

"Well, I wouldn't have married your mom," Davy said.

Something told him to leave it there. What was it the social worker used to say, "It might be true, but is it *helpful*?" The fact that taking marriage off the board as a way to monitor whatever threat the dead man's widow posed made it more likely Davy would have just...removed her from the board. That was true, but probably not helpful.

And people thought he didn't listen.

"Look, once we show Fraser the error of his ways...I'm sure he'll sort it out so it's a family affair if he has to flee the country," he said.

"Or maybe he'll stop doing things that might lead to him fleeing the country?"

Davy hesitated for a beat to see if the rite thought that particular request came under the whole "invoker gets what the invoker wants" thing. It didn't feel like it, as much as Davy could tell that sort of thing, anyhow. Apparently even dark, metaphysical contracts of unknown, and best to keep it that way, origin knew when clients were pushing their luck.

"Maybe," Davy agreed vaguely. "Sure."

He grabbed the emptied-out duffel and pulled it back over the table. Most of the contents were on the table, but a quick pat down of the pockets turned up a believably worn wallet with 250 bucks in used money and, zipped into a hidden pocket, a lime-green burner phone.

"That's a Samsung Galaxy S21," Hill said in a cool, precise voice. "It came out four years ago, and I upgraded two years ago. Just before Fraser redecorated his office. So definitely after the vows were said."

Awkward.

Davy groped for how to respond to that and came up with nothing. He'd already thrown his best at the wall to try and make Hill feel better, and there was nothing else in the tank. So...

"Fraser always was a cheap bastard," he said. "Do you still have a charger for it?"

Hill pointed to a set of drawers on the other side of the room.

Davy pushed himself up and went over to hunt through them. The sullen silence started to weigh on him as he fingered through the spaghetti junction of old leads, so he cleared his throat and kept talking.

"Anyhow, it looks like Fraser still uses Gallagher for his fake IDs." He pulled a long woven pink cable out and looped it around his fingers. Only to find out it was micro-USB. That was useful. "She always makes Fraser from Idaho. I have no fucking idea why. It was always...ah...Texas for me."

"You're from Victorville, aren't you?" Hill said.

It wasn't like it *mattered* anymore. Hell, even if Davy hadn't been dead, it was decades past being actionable information for anyone. It still gave Davy an itchy feeling between his shoulder blades. He didn't like being seen. It was bad OPSEC, and it just made him feel weird.

"Is that what Fraser told you?" he asked.

"He said he grew up in New York," Hill said. "But I did a lot of research to find out who my dad put in that shallow grave. Nothing went back as far as childhood, probably because Davy wasn't what you went by then, but there were a few mentions that tied you to the place."

There it was. Davy pulled the right wire out, checked the connection connected, and plugged it into the socket on the wall. The phone did nothing. He wiggled the lead a couple of times and held the buttons down until the screen begrudgingly lit up.

"For the record, the grave wasn't that shallow," Davy said. He looked around at Hill. Despite the fact he'd been the one to bring it up, Hill looked uncomfortable at the reminder his dad was an accomplice as well as a victim. "And at first you don't know you're dead, so you don't know that you don't need to breathe."

It was snowing.

Not much, but enough to attract Davy over to the window. It never snowed in the Beyond. Sometimes there was snow on the ground, but it was never *snowing*. Maybe it did up in the Company's towers, high above the streets, but Davy had never made it up so high. The Company had hired him a few times—good people were hard to find, good people who'd do dirty jobs even harder—but he'd never gotten beyond human resources. Third floor. The coffee was shit and always tasted of corporate depression.

Davy leaned his shoulder against the glass and watched the skiffs of white powder get tossed around outside as he let the phone ring. His tentacles tested the window until they found a spot where the Beyond didn't overlap with the living world. It was only big enough to let one squeeze through to try and grab the flakes out of the air as they fell.

The chill surprised Davy. Not that it was cold, but the way it mapped the bite of winter air against his tentacle down the backs of his legs, a stripe of iciness that clenched his thighs and made his balls tighten.

"Exactly what's the plan?" Hill asked. "You just going to tell people what Fraser did?"

The ringtone cut out as the call dropped. Davy let it. He held the phone loosely in one hand as he shifted around to watch Hill pace. His cock ached with the dull reminder that the *best* use of nervous energy was fucking.

Davy adjusted the waistband of his sweats and reminded himself of the minor obstacle that he couldn't *touch* Hill. His cock didn't care. It thought he just hadn't tried hard enough.

"Trust me, they'd not give a shit," Davy said, trying to sound like he wasn't thinking anything filthy. "Neither would Fraser. My death wouldn't be a problem for any of them."

The phone buzzed back to life in his hand. A different number than the one he'd dialed was on the screen. Davy smirked to himself as he held his thumb over the screen.

"Me being back, on the other hand?" he said. "That would be a problem for a lot of people."

He hit answer and lifted the phone to his ear. There was no way he was going to be able to make Hill's voice pass as his. He'd given it a go while he waited for the phone to charge, but Hill was not a natural mimic. To be honest, Davy wasn't actually too sure what his living voice had sounded like anyhow.

So instead he went with cool and precise.

"I have a job for you," he said. On the other end of the line, Gallagher snorted and started to say something. Davy didn't give her a chance. “It’s from Davy. He said you’d know better than to ask too many questions.”

There was a brief sound of choking and then silence, except for the faint sound of glass on glass. Davy could almost see Gallagher’s nicotine-stained fingers grinding out a cigarette in one of the big ’70s orange ashtrays she’d kept around the place. Every one a keepsake from some Belfast bar she used to drink at.

“Davy’s dead,” she said. Her voice sounded *old.* Somehow, that was more of a shock than it had been to see Fraser in all his middle-aged spread in the office. “And that ain’t a question, if you were wondering.”

“He told me you’d say that.”

“Fucker, it’s been thirty years. Only thing anyone says about Davy Jones is ‘he’s dead’ or ‘who the fuck is that.’”

“Pensacola. Twenty-two.”

There was a pause. It wasn’t much, but Davy could *feel* the hook catch in that slight hitch of her breath.

“Asshole, how old do you think I am?” she said.

“Pensacola. Twenty-two. Wawa.”

She hung up. Actually, from the brief “whoosh” and crack, she’d thrown the phone across the room.

The tentacle finally snagged a snowflake out of the air. It actually hung there for a second, a pinprick of chill against the pale end of the limb, and then started to slowly slide through as it melted. A flick sprayed the melted droplet into the air as it finally seeped all the way through.

“What was that?” Hill asked, sounding baffled. “A party game?”

The phone rang for a second time.

“Yeah, but not the fun kind,” Davy said and took the call. He didn’t bother to pretend he needed to go through the dance again. They both knew Gallagher would do what he wanted. "Davy needs three things from you. A full set of fake papers, two phone calls, and a location."

He listened to Gallagher's attempts to hedge until a yawn hijacked his stolen body. Once he'd given in to it, the exhaustion of the last few days sank deep into Davy's borrowed bones. It had been, he realized, as he ground the heel of his hand into gritty eyes, a while since Hill had gotten any sleep.

"I sympathize," he said. "Davy doesn't. He says just make it happen by Christmas Eve."

He hung up, tossed the phone aside, and stretched.

Davy also needed a nap. Now that he thought about it, it had been even longer since *he'd* gotten any sleep. Thirty years. The phrase wasn't "the restless dead" for nothing.

Chapter Seven

Dec 23, 6am

DAVY STOOD IN FRONT of the open fridge, phone pinned between his shoulder and ear as he checked the contents of the shelves. He seemed unwilling to give up the idea of a secret stash of bacon.

Finally, he plucked a grape out of a bowl and tossed it into his mouth.

"I'm just the messenger," Davy said, voice slightly muffled by grape. He burst it between his teeth and swallowed it. Hill, reminded, reached down and touched the crumbled cookie packet shoved in his pocket. He resisted the urge to sneak a bite, and Davy reached into the fridge to grab a carton of milk. He didn't read the label. "I know it's early there, but Mr. Jones is calling in his debt and..."

He paused to listen to the angry objections on the other end of the call. While he waited for them to finish, he rolled his eyes at Hill and made a "blah-blah-blah" gesture with his free hand.

"I think I see the problem," he said finally. He grabbed the top of the carton and twisted the lid off with a pop. "It's just not *my* problem, and I don't think you want to make it *Davy's* problem. Whatever deal you made with Fraser, take that up with him. It's nothing to do with Davy."

He added the milk to his coffee, a generous glug that lightened it nearly the color of his hair, and smirked at whatever was being said.

"Yeah, I thought so too," he said and hung up.

"You're enjoying yourself," Hill said. "Sleep well?"

Davy shrugged as he tossed the phone down and picked up his cup. Steam spilled out over his hands, and one of his tentacles curled around his hip to flick at it. Like a cat with a length of string.

"Like the dead," he said cheerfully. "Besides, the Beyond doesn't have phones. It's fun to yank people's chains without having to back your mouth up."

Hill thought of the receptionist at CIRATTA. He was about to ask, until he remembered the...wet...sound, like a swallow, as she plugged the wires into her body.

"And it's for a good cause," Davy reminded him. "To save my little brother's soul...after I give him an ulcer."

He snickered at his own joke and took a drink. The face came a moment later as he wrinkled his nose and smacked his lips. He jabbed his tongue out like a lizard. Hill rolled his eyes at the drama.

"It's potato milk," he said and pointed at himself. "Vegan, remember?"

Davy narrowed his eyes and then picked up the carton to check. He pulled a face.

"Who thinks 'you know what, let's milk a potato'?" he grumbled as he tossed his coffee down the sink. "When they die, I wanna be there. Their stigmata is going to be weird as hell."

Hill shrugged. "I prefer oat," he said. "But they didn't have any so close to Christmas."

"That makes sense," Davy said as he rolled his eyes. "There's always a run on oat milk leading into the season. You don't want Santa getting the shits halfway through his run."

Hill ignored that.

"So is that what we've been doing all day?" he asked. It was meant to sound non-judgmental. He was fairly sure that it didn't, but he pushed on. "Just prank calling Fraser by proxy?"

It wasn't exactly what he'd expected from transgressing the social and spiritual barriers to raising the dead.

"Sure," Davy said as he filled the mug with cold water. "Why not. I gotta get something out of this, since you won't let me kill him."

"This isn't a game," Hill objected. He lifted his hand so Davy could see the hole carved through it, light visible from the other side of the wound. Davy glanced briefly at it as he took a long drink of water, and Hill *aggressively* tried not to notice the way his throat worked as he swallowed. "I didn't defy the Church and do this to myself so you could play games. My dad—"

"Helped cover up my murder," Davy reminded him. He set the mug down on the counter and dried his mouth on the back of his hand. "Don't get me wrong. I've done worse, and I don't hold it against him. But don't expect me to shed any tears for him now he's in the dirt."

That was...a good point, Hill supposed.

He...

For a second he stalled on how to regulate his emotional state without his tried and tested tool kit: deep breathing, a drink so cold it hurt his teeth, a corner to dig his shoulders back into. None of those things would work right now.

Maybe the corner, but...Hill glanced at the nearest one and put *that* thought out of his mind.

In the Beyond, his penthouse apartment—concierge service included in the package—was a derelict, run-down room with cobwebs and mold fighting it out for ownership of the walls. Dead plants haunted cracked pots, and shadows moved constantly in the corners of his eyes. He'd thought they were other ghosts at first, but now he thought they were him. He recognized his posture sometimes, the way he tried to crack his knuckles like his dad had.

So no.

He folded his arms tightly instead, fingers pinched around his elbows, and tried to pull his thoughts back on track. It was easier to do without the static of adrenaline from his body to tangle him up.

Death ain't so bad, the memory of Seb's opening salvo nudged at Hill for his attention.

Hill didn't know about that.

It was easier to keep himself on track, but harder to *let go.* Even though he accepted it wasn't fair to expect Davy to care about what happened to Albie, he couldn't let go of the anger about it. It was like a barbed hook, and he couldn't thrash himself off, no matter how hard he tried.

Something broke, crockery shattering on a hard surface.

Davy had thrown the cup, and that just made him angrier. He was *trying*, and it was—

A tentacle draped over his shoulder and down his chest. The tip curled around his hipbone and then tightened. He could feel the muscles under the pale shadow-mottled skin, long and smooth and tight as they flexed around him. The pressure didn't squeeze the nonexistent breath out of him like he wanted, but it was *there*. It gave him something to work with as he pulled his feelings back under his skin where they belonged.

It still felt...tenuous. Like he had them wrapped up in an overstressed rubber band that would snap the minute he let go of it.

"Feels like blue balls, doesn't it?"

The question caught Hill off guard. He stared at Davy as he mentally confirmed that he was pretty sure he'd not misheard.

He still asked, "What?" just in case he had got the wrong end of the stick.

Davy leaned back against the counter, arms braced behind him. "Blue balls," he repeated.

"I didn't...I wasn't... What?"

Davy stared at him for a second, then dragged up a smirk and a shrug. "I told you yesterday. It takes a while to get used to being dead," he said. "You're used to feeling a certain way in a certain order. It doesn't work that way for a spirit. There's no spent adrenaline hangover when you get mad. You're just angry until you work out how not to be. Or someone distracts you by saying something out of pocket."

Something like "blue balls," Hill supposed. Although that said, the comparison wasn't wrong. His fit of temper did feel vaguely...unfinished...for just having trailed off. It wasn't that he missed that exhausted, sick post-anger feeling, but there should be something.

"I just..." Hill started. He stopped and bit his lip before he admitted, "I don't expect you to feel bad about my dad. I'd understand if you hated him, to be honest. The fact that you don't remember him is what's hard. He was CFO at CIRATTA. He was a husband. He was a philanthropist, sometimes. He played golf with the same people every week. He was *my dad*. He mattered...and then he died, and everyone just couldn't *wait* to forget him. There aren't even any photos of him. Mom kept them for a while, even after she married Fraser, and then they just slowly started to get taken down or moved, or we moved, and now there's just a few I have."

It was more than Hill had meant to say. When he'd started, it had been an awkward apology for being awkward. That was a familiar task. He knew how it went. After all, he had to do it often enough. Once he started to talk, though, the words got away from him.

He blamed being temporarily dead. It was hard to bite back what you were about to say when your teeth were insubstantial.

Davy looked...trapped. His face was hard to read, but his eyes looked uneasy.

"I...um...yeah," he got out, his voice scratchy. "I can see how, um, that would..."

He trailed off. A tentacle patted Hill's head with the clumsy, *heavy* physical version of the empty comfort of "there, there."

Hill reached up and pushed it away. "Thanks," he said.

Davy hitched one corner of his mouth up and shrugged. "You don't want me to kill Fraser," he pointed out. "That and 'there, there' is pretty much all I have, unless you want me to fuck you."

Oh. Yes.

No?

Fuck.

Hill swallowed hard. He licked his lips and remembered the cool grave-dirt and salt-sweetness of Davy's mouth on his. That slow, ed-dying feeling that his brain was *much* quicker to ID as lust rippled through him, dry and slow like sand.

Or ashes.

If the "blue balls" comment hadn't reset his brain, this would have done it.

By comparison, the deer-in-the-headlights look that Davy had been sporting was gone. It was replaced with an amused wickedness that darkened his eyes.

"Huh," he said. "Did not know that was on the table."

Hill bristled half-heartedly.

"What?" he snapped. "I don't read as gay? Sorry. Should I take tips from you?"

Davy cocked his head to the side. "I mean, literally no one has ever questioned it," he said. "So...maybe. But it wasn't that. I just didn't think it was on the menu while I'm, ah, already in you, so to speak."

That was one way to put it, Hill supposed. It was a hotter thought than he'd have expected. Not just Davy's cock in him, thick and solid as Hill squeezed around him, but *all* of him. He shifted his feet and, necessary or not, took a breath.

"You don't look like me," he said. "Not *to* me."

Davy blinked, looked down at himself, and plucked the soft fabric of the T-shirt away from his chest.

"Well, that explains why you blush every time you sneak a look at my ass," he said.

"I didn't..." Hill spluttered the denial. "I haven't looked at it."

Davy snorted. "Please," he said. "I thought you were just really up yourself, but I guess you wanted to be up me?"

"I don't even know if the dead do...if they even *can*," Hill said. The tone of his voice was remarkably prim considering the topic. He didn't seem to be able to fix it. "Fuck, I mean."

"The dead fuck," Davy said. He pushed himself up off the counter and took a step forward. His tentacles squirmed ahead of him, restless and curious. "I fuck."

Hill felt *parched.* Light and hollow and dry with hunger. He thought he might know *enough* about what sex was to the dead. No need to find out more. He ran his hand around the back of his neck, fingers caught in tangled curls.

"Not like it matters right now," Hill said. Despite his very recent decision to be incurious, he felt bitterness like a rock in the back of his throat. "You can't touch me, remember?"

Davy stopped mid-step. He shifted his weight so his legs were apart, soft sweats pulled tight over his thighs.

"Oh, you can touch me. See?" he said as he ran his hand down over his stomach. His fingers dipped under the waistband, went lower, black fleece tented over his knuckles as he wrapped his hand around his—around *Hill's* cock. Color touched his cheeks, the faint spray of freckles on his face floating on top of the flush as he bit his lower lip. His eyes were already dark, black from edge to edge, but it was somehow more intense as his lids lowered over them. A breath swelled his chest, and Hill wondered what *that* felt like after so long dead. Before he could chase the thought, Davy lifted those heavy lids and smirked at him. "And I can touch you. At least, part of me can."

Hill caught his breath in an eager gasp as Davy wrapped a tentacle around his throat. It collared him briefly, tight against his skin, and slid upward. The tip of it—dry and a little rough, not like snake skin but rough leather—traced the curve of Hill's mouth. It pulled his lower lip and slid into his mouth, thick and solid as it pushed against his tongue.

Oh.

When he breathed in, he could taste the cuttlebone and salt of it in the back of his throat.

Under the fig leaf of the sweats, Davy dragged his hand along his cock in slow, lazy strokes. His breath was ragged, his muscles tensed, and he watched Hill's face for a reaction.

Two responses hung in Hill's head and waited for him to pick. Recoil and make his excuses, or wrap his lips around the squirming tentacle and suck it deeper.

The version of him that sat in a pew and listened politely to Father Thomas every Sunday rattled the bars of his cage at the idea that the choice wasn't *obvious.* It was one thing to use the Rite of Invocation, that was...frowned upon, but it wasn't a *sin.*

Not like this. This would be a sin.

This would be necromancy.

That should have made the choice easier, but...

Before Hill had to decide, Davy's phone rang. It was like a switch flipped; the lazy, sultry heat was wiped off Davy's face. He pulled his hand out of his pants and grabbed the phone, answering it with a cool, "I've been waiting."

The tentacle drew back from Hill's mouth, slick and wet. It nudged his mouth shut behind it and then gave his cheek a commiserating pat.

Hill felt like a husk. An echoing, desperate husk. He pressed his fists against his stomach as he tried to pull himself together. It felt like more than want; it felt like a weird sort of hunger.

"You son of a bitch," he said raggedly.

Davy glanced around at him and had the good manners to look apologetic. At least, superficially. He started to say something, paused as he listened to what whoever he was talking to had to say, and then tried again.

"I wish it didn't matter," he said. "But there's consequences for failure."

Hill supposed there would be. It had been hinted at—sidelong, in veiled terms—in a few of his sources. No one had gone into detail. Maybe they'd assumed that anyone desperate enough to call the dead up wouldn't get distracted from their task by their own petty pleasures.

The self-loathing sting to that made Hill flinch a little, but he supposed that pew-Hill had earned the right. He rubbed his injured hand. It didn't hurt, but he remembered when it had.

Everything he'd done to get to this point. The years he'd poured into it—researching instead of living, turning himself into a specter in his own life—and he risked it all being wasted because the dead man had a pretty face.

Despite himself, he glanced at Davy to confirm that, as if he could fool *himself* by pretending to have forgotten. His gaze skimmed over Davy's hard, handsome face and down to broad shoulders and...

...and a great ass.

He grimaced at that, not even sure if it was lust or a bad joke, and turned his back on temptation. Only to stare in dismay at the shattered remains of his plate-glass desk. It lay in shards and splinters on the floor, his monitor smashed in the middle of it. That hadn't been like that before.

"What the hell happened?" he asked in shock as he spun back around to stare at Davy.

He got a shrug, wide innocent eyes, and a confidently mouthed "I dunno" in answer.

That was a lie. An *obvious* lie.

Hill just didn't understand why his broken desk was what mattered enough to lie about.

The ass—Hill admitted to himself as he watched Davy bend over to grab the smashed keyboard off the floor—was exceptional.

Technically, he supposed, Davy was right and that was Hill's own ass. He'd definitely never filled out those sweats so well, though, so...

"And for the record," Davy said as he straightened up. "I might enjoy fucking with Fraser, but that doesn't mean I don't have a plan."

A loose key—the B—slipped between his knuckles and bounced off his shoe. Hill cocked his head to watch it skitter under a nearby chair out of some weird habit, as if he'd care about retrieving it once he had fingers to do it with again.

"So what is it?" he asked as he looked back at Davy. When he got a blank look in return, he bit his tongue in irritation—and how did *that* still hurt?—before he filled in the question. "The plan. What is it?"

Davy dumped what had been, ten minutes ago, a top-of-the-range gamer keyboard into the trash. He picked a bit of glass out of his palm with his thumbnail.

"The first step is to destabilize Fraser," he said, with a cool confidence. "Within the next twenty-four hours he's going to be hit by a series of problems, large and small, that will affect his work, his finances, and his reputation. All within a span of time and time of year that make it difficult for him to respond decisively. Once he's professionally on the back foot, that's when we target his...call 'em moral foundations."

The casual competence was undeniably attractive, but...

"So what you're saying is the plan is to fuck with him?" Hill checked.

Davy cracked a grin. "Yeah," he admitted with a shrug. "Pretty much, but the shits and giggles are just a bonus."

"If you say so," Hill said. He rubbed his hand around the back of his neck and finally said what was really bothering him. "Is there anything I can do? I feel like a spare part just watching you."

Before Davy could answer, someone knocked on the door.

Both of them stopped for a beat. When the knock was repeated, Davy glanced at Hill and raised an expectant eyebrow.

Expecting anyone? he mouthed

Hill hesitated and then shook his head. It wasn't that there was a list of people he had to run through; it was the opposite. He'd spent so long focused on the dead—their wrongs, their invocation—it was only now that Fraser's judgement was at hand that Hill realized his life had flatlined. There was a short list of one who he'd expect at the door, and his mom would be getting ready for the party.

While Hill grappled with the unexpected realization that after Christmas Day, one way or another, he was going to have to find a new focus, Davy padded over to the door. The blithe disregard he showed for bare feet on glass-studded carpet made Hill clench his toes in his sneakers. Davy didn't look through the peephole. He stooped down and peered, sidelong, through the gap underneath.

"What are you doing?" Hill asked. Davy glanced up briefly and brought a tentacle up to his mouth in a "shhh" gesture.

"Why? It's not like they can hear me."

Davy started to retort, stopped, and shrugged an acknowledgement that Hill had a point. Of course, that didn't mean that Hill got an answer, since Davy was audible. Hill sighed and walked over to wait next to him. It was a shame that walking through walls didn't work.

Or so Davy had said, anyhow, and Davy was a liar...

Just to check, Hill poked the door with a finger. He felt it give under the pressure. It felt like taffy, thick and sticky as it reluctantly gave way.

He doubted he could walk through it, but he might be able to push through.

He hesitated at the thought and—

Pain slapped through him like a shock. It sizzled up his nerves from his fingertip to his armpit, then up to jam itself into the base of his skull like a punch. The habit of being alive made him shove his fist in his mouth to stifle his yelp as he staggered back from the door, free hand wrapped tightly around his wrist as if he could strangle the pain.

It didn't work, and when he looked at his finger...

There was enough left that it wasn't *technically* a stump, he thought with queasy, disassociated clarity. A nub might be the right way to describe it. His finger ended just below the nail bed, chopped off in a clean line that leaked a milky...smoke.

Davy looked up at him and pulled an exasperated face. He also thwacked Hill around the back of the head with a tentacle. Hill glared at him as he tried not to hyperventilate.

"My finger..." he spluttered out.

Davy gestured at a tentacle that squirmed under the door and came back with a blob of something...viscous... It held it out expectantly. Hill stared at it. It looked like a bath pearl, the ones his grandma used to have in a big jar in her bathroom.

"Is that my...finger?" he asked. The immediate, eye-watering jolt of pain had faded. He wasn't sure *how,* since he was still short of a chunk of himself.

The tentacle wiggled it at him. The glob of Hill squished down and threatened to pop out of the tentacle's grip. Hill recoiled.

"I don't want it," he protested on autopilot, then reconsidered. "Can it be...reattached?"

It sounded unlikely as he said it, the thing didn't even look finger-shaped anymore, but the tentacle pushed it insistently at him.

This time the knock on the door sounded like hammering. The slap of bare hands against wood made Hill start. He took a step back and, frustrated, just grabbed the bit of...himself with his good hand. It was cool and slippery between his fingers, but he could *feel* his fingertips against it.

"Fine." He closed his eyes, braced himself, and popped the glob in his mouth. Some sort of weird instinct made him try to flatten it against the roof of his mouth, but it was more resilient than it looked. It didn't taste of anything, but...

...warm skin under his fingers...dust and carpet threads and a foot the size of a dinner plate... the faintest flutter of a pulse that was so much steadier than his. Was that...ragged breathing and the shadow against the door as a body leaned closer... bad? Had he gotten it wrong ... warm, wet, and teeth... Fuck.

Hill swallowed, gagged, and looked at his hand. It was still...nubby.

"It takes a minute," Davy said softly. He stood up and finally took a look through the peephole. "It's Reynolds. What does he want?"

Well, since Hill had...in fact...misread his relationship with the man *very* badly, nothing. Unless he wanted to make it clear before the party that Hill was definitely not, under any circumstances, his type.

"I don't know."

"Huh."

Davy turned away from the door to look at Hill. He held up his hand and wiggled his index finger.

"You know, you could have just stuck it back on," he said.

Hill stared at him. "What?" he said. "Are you serious?"

Chapter Eight

Dec 23, 9.40 am

Davy opened the door and looked outside.

No note. No letter. No forgotten Secret Santa shamefully packaged in a 7-Eleven plastic bag.

Just sweaty handprints on the door and the faint, lingering scent of puke.

"You could have just answered the door," Hill said, his voice sour. He was in a mood. "He's a co-worker, not an assassin."

That gave Davy pause. He'd assumed he didn't really need to ask—the answer seemed obvious—but given Hill's optimism about human nature, maybe it shouldn't have been.

"You know what CIRATTA does, right?" he asked.

Hill looked annoyed. "I work there," he said.

Davy waited.

Finally, Hill rolled his eyes and gave in. "It's a military contractor," he said. "I know what they...we...do, but I don't think international assassins buy egg salad sandwiches in the company canteen."

That was a very specific example. Davy felt a scratchy weight in his chest and wished he'd stuck a tentacle further into Renolds' cerebellum. Maybe he could have triggered an aneurysm, not just a migraine.

"What's throwing you?" he asked. "The egg salad or the canteen?"

"Both," Hill said promptly. "He's a consultant, not—"

"Yeah, my fee got put down as that on a few tax returns," Davy said as he stepped back into the room. "And even assassins have to eat, Hill."

He closed the door with a click and tried to put Reynolds out of his mind for now. Maybe he'd been there to get Davy, or Hill, to sign out of the building or pay his share to the party fund. Or something else innocuous.

At the back of his mind, it nagged at him, though. Something about the way Reynolds had hammered the door or the set of his shoulders as he'd headed to the elevators. Whatever monkey was on his back hadn't looked innocuous.

But there was nothing Davy could do about that currently.

And with any luck, the shit show that Davy was about to unleash on Fraser would give Reynolds something else to think about after the holiday season. Davy brushed his hair out of his—

He squinted at the dark hair that still dangled over his eyes. Fuck sake.

He reached up, waved the tentacle out of the way, and raked Hill's hair out of his eyes with one hand.

"You said you wanted to help?" he said.

"I did," Hill said. "I do. How?"

Davy wagged a tentacle at him. "Ask the 'how' *before* you agree to anything," he advised. Then he looked Hill up and down. He didn't mind the view, not at all, even if it did revive the dull ache in his balls from earlier, but... "But first of all, would you say you look anything like your dad?"

The photo was slid between the pages of a book on tort reform.

Davy was glad that the solstice fell during the holiday season. He'd not have wanted to try and pull off Hill's nine-to-five as well as his revenge.

"Dad always said I looked like Mom," Hill said. "Mom said I looked like him, until he died, and then she stopped talking about him at all. But other people sometimes say I look like Fraser, so I think they see what they want."

Albie Rosen. In color.

Davy looked at the photo of the man he'd been trying to place for the last day...

...and he still had no fucking idea who he was.

He couldn't even blame it on it being a bad photo. It wasn't a headshot, but it was a clear enough snapshot of the man as he sat on the front steps of a house with a bright green door, his kid on his lap. Dark-haired, pasty, and fairly hairy in his shorts. He was a bit overweight, but in the way that people get when they're doing well in life. The sort of light flab overlay that Davy had always vaguely associated with white-collar workers and desk officers.

Davy had to disagree with Hill's mom. Hill didn't look much like his dad. If anything, in fact, Davy would have to side with "other people." He could see their point about the resemblance to Fraser, not physically, but in the way they reacted to things.

Luckily, accuracy rarely mattered.

"Did your dad lose a lot of weight before he died?" Davy asked as he turned the photo over to look at the back. The Florida Keys. Two years after Davy died.

"I...how do you know that?" Hill asked.

"People under stress tend to either eat their feelings or starve them," Davy said. "It could have been either, but...I rolled the dice on the one that would be useful."

"How is that useful?" Hill asked. "And what does it matter if I looked like him?"

Davy shrugged and slid the photo back into the book before he reshelved it.

"At this point, it only matters that people *think* you looked like him," Davy said. "Thin, dark-haired, and dead is close enough for our purposes."

"Which is?"

It was important to frame the answer to that question in the right way. Most people didn't care for pragmatism, even when they said they did. Hill wanted to see his stepfather realize what he'd done wrong...because it was wrong.

That was never going to happen.

To get Fraser to repent, Davy was going to appeal to his self-interest. They'd always known they were bad men; it had just always seemed like they had enough time to think about the consequences later. Fraser needed to realize that if he didn't get to work on that now, his afterlife was going to suck.

"I've set the stage for his professional life to start to fall apart," he said. "Once he's on the back foot dealing with that, we need to sow the seeds that it's the result of his own actions over the years. You'll be the ghost of his past sins come home to roost."

That sounded reasonable enough.

Hill seemed to agree, but then he frowned and held up his pale hand. The hole in his palm, Davy noticed, looked bigger. He felt a quick, bone-rotting itch in the flesh version he was wearing and absently dug the knuckle of his thumb against the dressing to squash it.

"How's that going to work, though?" he asked. "He can't see me. Nobody can."

"We're—" Davy started his answer, but before he could get it out, the words clumped up in his throat. After a brief attempt to force them out, he had to clumsily edit what he'd been about to say mid-sentence. "There are ways around that. I can show you a few tricks later."

Hill looked confused, but Davy was the dead man, so he accepted the line with a shrug and a nod.

"Anything else I can do?" he asked. "In the meantime?"

Davy hadn't really expected the second thoughts, so he hadn't prepared a backup. He shrugged and went with the first thing that popped into his head.

"You could talk to some dead people for me," he said. "If you're up to it."

Hill pulled a face. He looked like the idea of that was more daunting than stabbing himself in the hand. He still nodded grimly.

"I can do that," he said. "How will I find them?"

"You said you've spent years looking into Fraser's sins," Davy said. "Local. Dead. Fucked over. That's got to ring some bells."

Hill hesitated as he chewed his thumbnail.

"I was pretty focused on you," he said. "But I have an idea who I could ask."

That couldn't have been a long list to choose from after not even a whole day dead. Davy frowned.

"*Not* the Company man," he said. "The information wouldn't be worth the debt."

Hill gave him a look. "I don't remember you asking my permission for any of this," he said. "But no, not him. I'll need a few hours, though. Are you going to need me for anything?"

That wasn't the problem. Davy hesitated as he weighed how useful it would be to have skeletons other than his own to rattle, against the idea of Hill wandering the Beyond alone.

"Fraser doesn't think I can hack it out in the real world," Hill said. "Don't be like your brother."

Too late for that. That had always been the problem.

Still, Davy gave in with a grimace. Not because he trusted Hill...or any of the dead assholes in the Beyond...but the Company had an interest now. Word would have gone out. That was probably better protection than Davy operating a set of tentacles blind.

"Just don't make any promises," he said. "And don't eat anything that isn't you."

Hill grimaced sickly at that and rubbed his hands together. His thumb grazed the nearly grown-back nub of his finger, and he hesitated as he looked at the door.

"How do I?" he asked.

"There's a knack to it," Davy told him.

His tentacles weren't talking to him.

Davy double-bagged the glass from the desk and ignored their knotted-up sulk. He didn't have the time to deal with them *and* work out why the fuck he'd lied to Hill.

Twice.

He cursed under his breath as he stepped on a bit of glass and had to balance on one foot as he reached down to pick it free from his heel. The splinter glittered between his fingers as he looked at it.

Hill's ash-toned pallor and washed-out silver-green eyes had blanched white. A hollow outline of a person, only a shadow of a panicked Hill visible under its skin. The temperature in the room plummeted, and Davy's breath ghosted into life as it left his lips.

It had been a long time since he'd felt cold. It definitely wasn't as good as food.

The desk broke first, shattered into chunks and splinters of frosted glass.

It felt like it took forever to stop gawping like an idiot at the broken bit of furniture. It couldn't have been that long, because his tentacles were already trying to crawl back inside him, squeezed in tight to his body and braided around each other, when what was left of the computer was smashed into the ground by an invisible something, and the word dropped like lead in his gut.

Polter.

He'd not felt his heart stop for a long time either, but this had *been what it felt like.*

Shit.

The memory made Davy uncomfortable in his borrowed skin, like lemon sting in the back of his throat.

Fight, fuck...and fear. If anyone had asked him, that wasn't the emotion he'd have picked, but he guessed it made sense it was the one that dropped for paywalled users. Luckily, it turned out his panic response was to make a wisecrack about blue balls through his dry-as-dust mouth.

And it had worked. This time. Next time they might not be so lucky.

Orrrrr...the part of Davy that was a full-time asshole nudged at him impatiently...they could roll the dice and find out. Hill wasn't really dead. Who knew if he was bound to the same awful scale as other spirits when it came to the turn?

To the type of man Davy had always been, that made sense. It wasn't his skin in the game, so why not go all in? Polters could manifest in the living world, and even if Hill didn't look much like his dad, it wouldn't take much to convince Fraser that the dark-haired, lean spirit was the dark-haired, lean man he'd murdered.

But Davy had seen the Company's polters rolled out. Just the once, to clear a neighborhood they'd wanted for some obscure, unpopular Company project.

They had shuffled out of the Company trucks in shackles of bone, nothing but shrouds of who they'd been. Burned-out eye sockets and tongues, wet ash on white cheeks. Then, when the shackles were taken off, they'd exploded into shredded skins fluttering over screaming, brutal rage.

Davy didn't want to see Hill like that. He definitely didn't want to be the one who pushed him to it.

The thought gave him an uncomfortable feeling under his skin, and he grimaced as he rolled his shoulders back. Maybe it was just self-preservation of a sort that had made him bite his tongue? The last thing he needed was to learn "guilt." Four emotions were definitely one too many.

He flicked the splinter of glass into the sink and hefted the bag to carry it over to the door. Halfway across the living room, someone knocked at the door.

Reynolds again?

Before Davy could work out a response to that, there was the beep and click as the door was unlocked. It swung open.

"So, you aren't dead?" a pretty blonde, vaguely familiar woman said from the doorway as she brushed snow off her sleeves. "I assumed *that* was why you weren't answering your phone."

Davy drew a blank for a second, then remembered the gross cookies.

Fuck.

"Mom," he said. That felt *fucking* weird. "What are you doing here?"

Chapter Nine

Dec 23, 11am

THE LIVING WORLD FADED the further that Hill got from Davy.

Or more accurately, he supposed, the more distance he put between himself and his living body.

It was still there, but as background noise and shadows. The Beyond was where he had to step sideways to dodge around commuters who managed to be sour-faced over dog muzzles or twitching hare-whiskers and split noses, or jump back out of the way to avoid being run down by a cab with a skull-faced driver.

Company men.

And women, Hill supposed. Davy made no such corrections, but he'd been dead thirty years, and most of Beyond had probably been dead longer. It was probably a safe assumption that being politically correct was a few years behind the living world.

Man or woman, though, most of the spirits on the street wore masks of some kind.

Muzzles, the correction nudged at his brain in that pointed voice that Davy used when he *wasn't* going to say anything. Hill tried to pretend he'd not heard it. There was too much implied in that word for him to unpack right now. The less-weighted "masks" moved on more easily in his head.

That left him room to wonder why the only person he saw with stigmata like Davy's was a ragged beggar, his disorientingly lumpy body hidden under rags and cut-up blankets.

Instincts of a city kid told Hill to avoid eye contact and keep moving. He hesitated, but stopped instead.

"Do you know—" he started to ask.

The man raised his head, and Hill inwardly recoiled. Runnels of loose flesh covered the man's face like lumps of melted plastic, sealing his eyes shut and twisting his mouth into a tooth-baring grimace.

"Change?" the man slurred, his voice rough and clumsy. The blankets slid back from his body as he stuck his hand out, a jar of thin tin coins clutched in fingers that looked like warmed wax. "Have some pity, man."

Hill patted himself down out of habit. "I'm sorry," he said. "I don't..."

The beggar reached up and dug his fingers into the skin over his eyes to claw it back. A sharp blue eye peered out at Hill for a second before the skin dripped back over it.

"Fuck sake," the man said. His voice was still thick, but it was harder now. "The wet dead walking the streets. Get the fuck away from me. Go on. Piss off."

He kicked at Hill with a booted foot and then spat at him when Hill didn't move on fast enough.

"I don't...what?" Hill spluttered as he backed up. "Sorry?"

A hand caught his arm and tugged him away.

"Pay no attention to him," the woman said as she tossed a distasteful look toward the beggar. "The Hounds will move him on soon enough."

Hill looked back over his shoulder. "Why?"

"Nobody wants to come out of work and see that," the woman said. She gave a delicate, mannered shudder as she glanced back over her shoulder. "We're all dead. Some of us just still want to better ourselves."

The question "*for what*" was on the tip of Hill's tongue. He took a proper look at the woman before he asked and completely forgot what he'd been about to say.

"I...Aunt Hen?" he asked, his voice stuck halfway between surprise and uncertainty.

The tall brunette chuckled and squeezed his elbow with something like affection.

"And there I thought you'd forgotten me," she said through the short, pointed beak of her pre-death namesake. The fleshy lobes of bright red wattles swung against her neck as she looked up at him. She still wore glasses, Hill noticed with distant interest, and her eyes crinkled around a smile her beak couldn't form. "Last time I saw you, you were only six or seven? Now look at you, all grown-up and dead already."

"Do you want a coffee?" Hen asked as she pulled her purse around to the front of her body and stepped into the queue for the small kiosk.

Hill glanced at the menu. A Depresso Espresso was four scrip. An In Love Latte was six.

"I don't—" he started to demur, with Davy's tossed-off directive not to touch the food at the forefront of his brain. Except he'd already broken that, hadn't he? So... "A Latte, please?"

"Iced?" Hen asked as she pulled a thin metal card out of her wallet. The logo on it was of a pair of scales and a feather.

"OK," Hill said.

He thought better of it immediately, or at least doubted himself, but it was too late to change his mind as Hen stepped up to the counter. As she put the order in and scanned her card, he just hovered awkwardly next to her and looked around.

Everyone in the shop was masked. Some of them didn't have the grafted muzzle like Hen and Seb. They just had static masks in wood or cloth. One man had a skeletal hand tattooed over his mouth.

"So, how have you been?" Hen asked. She pointed at a donut through the glass screen and nodded approvingly when the barista picked it up with a pair of tongs. "What are you up to these days?"

It was strange to interact with someone you'd last seen dying in a hospital bed. She'd called him a slur then, in the same upbeat tone, and his mom had dragged him out. She'd covered his ears, although it had been far too late, and told him Hen hadn't meant it.

She'd been sick.

Hill wondered what that meant for her spirit. Davy was who he'd been when he died. Hill felt the same. Was Hen still the person the cancer had turned her into, or had death undone the tumor's work?

"Being dead is taking up a lot of my time," Hill said. "How did you find me?"

"I was looking for you," Hen said. She tucked the card back in her wallet and shooed him toward a table by the window. "You're a person of interest for the people I work for."

"The Company."

She clucked her tongue. Hill stared at her over a napkin dispenser and tried to work out if that was meant to mean something or was just a noise she made.

"They're the only game in town worth playing," she said. "I know it sounds pretentious, but it could be worse. Back in Europe, so I hear, they still have Courts. Well, not over here. We're dead, but we're still American."

She chuckled, wattles wobbling with amusement. Hill really wanted to ask whether her lifelong nickname had influenced her choice of animal, or did she get a vote. He wasn't sure if it would be rude or not. The decision tree he usually ran through to work that out didn't have the options he needed for his current situation.

Hen was done with the joke, anyhow. She wiped the corners of her beak with her thumb and forefinger. Hill was surprised at how familiar the gesture was, the memory of a dozen lunches he'd sat through with his mom. Although before, the gesture had always been accompanied by a crustless sandwich and a smudge of her signature red lipstick left on her fingertips.

"But yes," she acknowledged. "I work for the Company, and while you're still weighing up their offer, they want me to help show you some of the advantages. A familiar face, and all."

She caught the edge of an order being called and turned to look. When the man with the skeleton hand shushing him picked it up instead, she heaved an annoyed sigh.

"How did they know you knew me?" Hill asked.

Hen shrugged. "They're the Company," she said, as if that was answer enough.

"Have you seen my dad?" Hill asked.

The ache in his voice made his chest hurt and flicked the living world briefly back into hi-res around them. Instead of a coffee shop, they were perched on the windowsill of a daycare. One of the kids playing on the ground nearby shivered abruptly despite his "Santa's Favorite Helper" sweater and started to cry.

Hen looked alarmed as she pressed both hands flat on the faded-out sketch of the Beyond's table.

"Who?" she said.

"My dad?" Hill said. "Albie. Albert Rosen. Your best friend's husband?"

"Doesn't ring a bell," Hen said. She looked around, the jerky movements of her head starkly birdlike. "What is this? Who are they?"

An elf on the shelf fell off its perch and bounced off the ground. Its plastic face grinned maliciously at the ceiling as the rest of the toddlers joined in with the first one. As the daycare providers ran over to calm them down, the living world faded back to sketch lines and background noise as Hill stared at Hen.

"You remember me?"

"Of course," Hen said. She smoothed her hair fretfully with one hand, preening it tidy with her nails. "You're my godchild."

"You remember my mom?"

"Lisa?" Hen gave him a bewildered look. "Why wouldn't I? She's my best friend. I can't wait for her to die so I can catch her up on everything. Oh...tell me..."

She reached over the table and put her hand on Hill's. It felt odd. He could feel the weight of it, even though he supposed that was just imagination,

"Does she still look good? It can be fixed, but it's better to die looking...well...in your prime. Like me." She gestured at her face, fingers brushing the sharp edges of her beak.

"You didn't look like that when you died," Hill corrected her. "You'd been sick for months. You were bald."

She stared at him and then reached up to touch her hair. "What are you talking about?" she said. "I spent a fortune at the hairdresser's. One thin spot and she'd have had me upside down applying the best treatments from Europe."

Hill bristled, ready to argue, but...

He'd expected Davy to remember his dad, but it had also seemed in character when he didn't. Aunt Hen, who'd lived with them for two months with her Yorkie after a spiteful ex had flushed Orbeez into her condo's plumbing, didn't have that excuse. And she'd not died suddenly. It had been months of illness and hospitals.

She could just be in denial, but it wasn't that. It was like when he'd asked what Davy's real name was, like the answer should be there but wasn't. The hole had to be papered up with something.

"It doesn't matter," Hill said.

Hen's frown stayed etched between her eyebrows as she stared at him. Before she could say anything, though, the barista called her name. She tried to lift her hand to shush him, but he just yelled the order out again.

"All right," Hen huffed as she got up. "I'm coming."

She went over to grab the cups, throwing a thin, tin-dull bit of coin into the tip jar. When she brought the coffees back and set them down, foam oozed out from under the lid of Hill's and ran down the side to puddle on the table.

"Do you remember Fraser?" he asked as he pulled a napkin out of the dispenser to wipe the foam. "My...mom's husband worked for him."

Hen still looked uneasy, but it passed as she leaned back and nodded.

"Of course," she said as she popped the top off the cup. She added sugar and jabbed it down through the foam into the coffee with her straw. "Fraser Jones. He was a robot in the sack. Businesslike, but got the job done."

That was...that was more than Hill had ever wanted to know. He took a second to try and aggressively NOT write that into his long-term memory. To give himself a second to recover, he took a drink of his latte.

....his chest hurt and his eyes stung. He couldn't breathe, and he never wanted to again.

The attempt to compose himself failed as laughter and coffee snorted down his nose. He fanned himself with one hand and...OK...it was fine. He could do this.

He glanced across the table at his friend's miserable, mortified face and... Nope.

The more they cringed, the funnier it was.

Hill coughed on the memory of meanness. He wiped foam off his lips on his crumpled-up napkin. He shouldn't have gotten iced, maybe.

"That's not really the sort of...information I need," he said. "Maybe this isn't a good idea. I was going to CIRATTA. The receptionist there, the dead one, had to have seen a lot over the years. She—"

Hen rolled her eyes at him and gestured over her shoulder with one finger.

"How much of the living do you see?" she asked. "A lot? A little? Nothing?"

Hill knew what she meant. He looked anyhow. The living world had, if anything, faded back more since that quick, shock flash of solidity. If he squinted he could see them, just as blurred shapes that passed to and fro.

He clung to the idea anyhow. "Fraser isn't an...affable man. There have to be spirits that want to haunt him. That'd be the first place—"

What he was about to say was muffled as Hen pressed a finger to his mouth.

"Don't use that word in public," she said. "What next? Call us...ghosts?"

She muttered the last word under her breath and then looked around quickly, offering an awkward smile to a nearby table that frowned at her.

"Sorry," she murmured, making a placating hand gesture. "Sorry."

Hill wiped his mouth. "I didn't know that was—"

"Well, it is," Hen said. She took a drink of her coffee and swallowed whatever rage was brewed into Mad at You Mocha. "And the odds of anyone who hated Fraser dying, reaching the Beyond, *and* escaping the gauntlet—"

"You mean the men with snares?" Hill asked.

Hen clicked her beak shut and went a funny color. Even her wattles blanched, the red lobes fading to a dull burgundy.

"We don't talk about them," she said sharply. "What if they hear you? And to the living it might seem Fraser had a lot of enemies, but among the dead it's a drop in the bucket. A drop in the bucket with no map. Whereas I have all the resources of the Company, and a remit to show you just how invaluable that is."

Hill twiddled with the straw in his cup. The ice cubes clattered against each other.

"Was he afraid of anyone?"

"His brother," Hen said immediately. "They were both dangerous men, but Davy could charm... Fraser could never understand that, and it bothered him."

Hill felt the hollow lack-of-heat flush through him as he thought of the way Davy's eyes crinkled when he was pleased with himself and the blunt nudge of a tentacle against the seam of his mouth. He reached for his coffee and took a sip.

The sharp tang of meanness cut through the honey-sweetness of the smooth roasted beans. Hill licked the mockery off his lips. He'd always assumed that sort of crowing meanness was performative, to make the victim feel bad. Whoever's coffee this had been was...genuinely having a good time.

"Is there anyone else? Anyone that worried him or put him on edge?" he asked. Hen wrinkled her brow as she thought about it, obviously stumped. Hill stirred his drink and thought about the real delight brewed into it. What would Fraser's coffee order be like? He tried again. "Anyone he gloated about getting one over on?"

That struck a chord with Hen. She started to smile before she answered him.

"I don't know, this is maybe stupid," she said. "But there was this deli—umm—Delilicious? The everything bagels were to die for. I went there all the time, but Fraser wouldn't even drop me off outside to pick up an order. I remember when the place got closed down by the health department, he was so smug about it. He took me to eat at one of their competitors the night they were closing down. Spent a fortune. It wasn't—"

Someone hit the door into the shop hard, nearly tripped over their own feet as they fell over the threshold, and shoved the door shut behind them. Hen put her coffee down and stood up. She came around the table to peer out into the street. When Hill twisted around to see what she was looking at, he was surprised to see the pavements were nearly empty. The few people left on the street looked nervous and on edge. A black Buick drove down the road, stopped, and a lean man in gray got out. He had a muzzle, but it wasn't living. It was a carved bone dog skull, yellowed and scored with cracks repaired with a dull, grayish solder.

"What did you do?" Hen asked.

"Me?" Hill said. It wasn't a protest; he was genuinely confused. "I don't...I didn't do anything. I don't know HOW to do anything."

She put her hand on his shoulder and squeezed hard, her nails digging down into the muscle.

"You did," she insisted. "I felt it. When we saw the living and they...did they see us?"

"I didn't think they..."

She shook him. "Did they see us?"

He focused on the flash he'd seen, red-faced toddlers on a snowflake mat, and the elf as it bounced off the floor. The one toddler's shocked face before it screwed up into a howl.

"I guess the baby might have?" he said. "Maybe? I don't..."

Hen dragged him to his feet. "Idiot," she hissed. "Come on. We have to get out of here."

She dragged him behind her as she headed toward the back of the store. A sort of uneasy muttering built up around them.

"Where are they going?"

"Haunting..."

"He said something about ghosts..."

"He's wet. The kid's still wet. He's not been stripped."

What started as private murmurs began to pick up volume as chairs were pushed back and people stood up.

"What's going on?" Hill asked.

"Great things," Hen snapped at him. "Good things. This is going to do my career absolutely no harm."

The barista stepped up from behind the counter to block them. His mask was cheap, wood pieces carved together so the dog's teeth clacked against each other when he talked.

"Is that about you out there?" he asked.

"Get out of the way," Hen said.

"Is it about him?" The barista pointed.

"It's not just a patrol," someone yelled over their shoulder as people jostled for position at the window. "That's a whole pack. I think there's a fucking Handler."

Hen clacked her beak and glared at the barista. "I work for the Company," she said. "Get out of my way or I'll—"

The barista grabbed her shoulders and shoved her back. "You're just one of the birds," he said and jabbed his finger toward the window. "They're *Hounds.* I know who I'm more scared of."

"Maybe she's a traitor."

"They'll give you her muzzle if she is. That's what I hear."

Hen made a low clucking noise in her throat as she looked around. The only way out was the door or the back room.

"I thought you said the Company wanted me on their side," Hill hissed at her in protest. "You said they sent you."

She swung her head around and glared at him. "They did," she snapped. "And someone else sent the dogs in after you."

That...didn't sound good.

"Fuck fuck fuck."

She sounded a lot like a chicken in that moment. Inappropriate laughter hitched at the back of Hill's throat, but he managed to control it.

"I've been dead a long time," the barista said as he tightened his grip on Hen's shoulder. "Maybe it's time the Company gets to see what I can do."

Hen's grip on Hill's wrist tightened.

"This is nothing to do with me," she said in a tight, controlled voice.

"Why don't we let the Hounds decide that?" the barista said.

His mouth was hidden behind the clacking wooden teeth, but the smirk was in his voice. He shoved them back a step and half-turned to catch the attention of the customers.

"One of you go and tell the Hounds we've got them," he said. Nobody moved. Their enthusiasm for the detainment suddenly dried up as they shifted uncomfortably. "Go on! She's—"

Hen snapped her head forward and...*pecked*...at him viciously. The scissor-sharp jab of her beak carved long worms of flesh out of the barista's face and cracked his muzzle. The tip caught his eyelid and peeled it back until it ripped.

There was no blood, just dribbles of smoky-wet *stuff* that clotted as it dripped.

The barista let go of her and fell back with a shriek, hands clapped to his savaged face. His back hit the counter, and he slid down it, his heels kicking the ground in pain. The rest of the customers drew back.

"How do you feel about me being 'just one of the birds' now?" Hen spat as she stepped over his legs. She dragged Hill with her. The spilled "blood" was tacky under his feet as he stepped through it.

"You won't get far!" the other customers warned from behind them. "We'll tell the Hounds what you did."

None of them managed to work up the courage to actually try and stop them.

Hill staggered along behind Hen as they cut through the narrow galley kitchen at the back of the store. It smelled of sour milk and even more sour water. A mop stood in a pail of stagnant-foul water by the back door. Hen shoved Hill out into the alley and then—in a flash of petty that showed she was still his Aunt Hen no matter who she remembered—kicked the pail over to flood the kitchen.

"What's going on?" Hill asked again. "You *said* the Hounds would move that beggar on soon enough. What made you think they're here for me instead?"

Hen rolled her eyes at him. "They don't send a *Hunt* to roust some unaffiliated beggar," she said. "You're important enough to try and help, my little roadblock? You're important enough to someone else to hurt. Now come on."

She gave his arm a yank hard enough to make his shoulder hurt to get him moving. Hill didn't have any satisfactory answers, but he could hear the sound of breaking wood and yelling out on the street. It didn't seem like the time to dig his heels in.

They made it two steps.

The Hound appeared at the end of the alley before they could get any farther. He didn't just have a mask (*muzzle)* on. The dog graft covered his whole head, right up to the pricked, darkly pointed ears that stuck through human curls. When he opened his mouth it was just a dog's growl that rolled out.

Hen took a step back. A discarded paper bag crinkled under the sharp heel of her expensively impractical shoes.

Did the dead shop?

Did they have wardrobes? Peer pressure.

Did they recycle human fashion, like they did food, or were there dead fashion designers putting together shows?

It didn't *matter*, Hill howled at the inside of his brain in frustration. The clatter of inconvenient noise didn't go away, but it dimmed enough that he could think over it.

"How bad is it?" he asked. "At the Company."

Hen didn't answer him. She just let go of his wrist. "The deli guy," she said.

"I...what...do you...Are you talking about Fraser?"

Hen nodded. "I can't remember his name, but it was the Mother's Meat Deli. He was just the deli guy. I don't know what Fraser's problem was with the guy, but there was one. The place closed, and you'd have thought he'd closed a deal with the US government. I don't know if that helps, but if it comes to it? Tell the Company it did."

The Hound pulled a short, hooked stick out of his belt as he stalked into the alley. His eyes weren't human. That was disconcerting.

Hen stepped away from him. "What were you thinking about in the cafe when we saw the toddlers?"

Hill glanced at her and then back at the Hound. He took a step backward and then another. Part of him wanted to pretend he couldn't answer her immediately. It felt like the "normal" thing to say.

"My dad," he said. "I did all this for him and—"

"Yeah, whatever, I'd think about him again," Hen said. She reached up and ripped the muzzle off her face. Under it was bone, the flesh neatly carved off and the skull notched to hold the muzzle in place. She tossed it to Hill and broke into a limping, exaggerated run that ended with her throwing herself at the Hound. He staggered at the impact and made a futile effort to shake her off the arm she'd wrapped herself around. Hen clutched him tighter and looked up at him with that half-flayed face. "Oh, thank God you're here! That one...that dead man, he tried to make me go with him to the living world! I don't understand what's going on!"

Her voice pitched up into a wail as her knees gave way. Some instinct made the Hound grab at her with hands that were tipped with thick, black, padded claws. He snarled in frustration as she limply hung off him.

Hill looked down at the muzzle. It was just a chicken's skull, smeared with coffee and the sticky plasm that passed for blood here. He closed his fingers around it, the ridges of the eye sockets sharp against his skin, and backed up as he scrambled for that feeling.

How do you get *angry* on cue? Now that he wanted to, Hill couldn't even remember what it felt like.

Hot? Staticky?

It made him bounce his knees?

Hen's hysterics had lost their impact. The Hound pulled her off him and shoved her into a wall. She bounced off the brickwork and caught herself. For a second, as she gathered herself, it looked like she was going to try again, but instead she gave Hill a quick apologetic shrug and ran.

"They're in there!" she yelled, waving her arms and pointing in what—in a generous interpretation—could have been one last redirection towards the coffee shop. "One of your men has him!"

The Hound's eyes narrowed as he glanced back that way; then his attention was back on his target. The dead man flicked the hooked stick in a brisk, wrist-loosening maneuver and then pointed it at Hill.

"Run, I hurt you. Fight, I hurt you," he said. It didn't sound human, or easy, the voice that scraped out of his throat. It was a snarl chopped up and clumsily stitched back into words. "What's left?"

It wasn't a question. It was—unintentionally—an answer.

Hill didn't need to be angry. That was just where he ended up. What he needed was despair. The heavy, leaden weight that dragged him down into knowing he'd spent his life—spent all the kisses he'd not gotten, the dates he'd avoided, the friends he'd not made—on revenge so empty that no one but him even knew who it was for.

Now he wouldn't even get that because...

The world fractured into white, and a cat, tail bottle-brushed out, stared at him for a second and then ran—

...some idiot who'd taken his fursona too far...

The lid of a rusted green dumpster slammed down, and it slammed back into the wall. Sharp metal edges cracked the cheap plaster.

...thought he was funny.

The door on the car parked in front of the alley suddenly buckled. The glossy hunter-green paint cracked, and the window shattered in. As the alarm was jolted on, it pulled a handful of people out onto the street. They commented uncomfortably on the chill as they tried to work out what had happened. One man, a crucifix around his neck, crossed himself quietly.

There was no non-sequitur from Davy to break the spell this time, no weirdly comforting tentacle to lean on. Hill just had to claw his way back out on his own.

He was on his knees.

Hill stared at his hands braced in the dirt and tried to remember how they worked. They felt thick and clumsy, like he had shoved them into a pair of gloves wrong. He managed to get them to work enough to push himself upright and...

The walls of the alley were broken, rents clawed in the plaster and stucco like it was butter, and the ground under him was cracked and pitted. Blood—and even if it was milky and viscous, he *knew* what it was—splattered the walls. The sound of alarms and slow, rattled voices were drawn out and muffled by the rattling in his ears.

A dog's skull lay on the ground in front of him, close enough to touch. Half of it anyhow, the crack where it had broken scoured smooth and the teeth blunted.

Hill reached out to touch it, but changed his mind.

He scrambled to his feet and took a step backwards. He felt something under his heel just in time not to put his weight on it and glanced down to see Hen's chicken skull there in the dirt. It looked clean, tiny scratches worked into the bone, but it was intact.

She'd *tried* to help.

Hill bent down and grabbed it. He fumbled it for a second as he tried to work out where to put it. He finally just clutched it in one hand as he ventured out of the alley and down the street.

The Hounds were still there. He might have—whatever happened to that one in the alley—but the rest had just been knocked on their backs. They were already pulling themselves back together as Hill tried to work out what to do next.

One near him that Hill hadn't noticed grabbed his foot, thick pink nails scraping his ankle, and Hill kicked out at him to get free. Despite everything, he felt a little jolt of guilt as the heel of his foot jammed into the dog's eye. Stupid. It wasn't a dog, but...it still felt bad.

The Hound's hand slipped free, and Hill ran.

He didn't know where. It just needed not to be here.

Chapter Ten

Dec 23, 1pm

Hill's mother took her long peacock-blue coat off as she stepped into the apartment. Melt dripped from the ends of it as she looked around for somewhere to hang it. With the sigh of a person who was going to give Hill a coat rack for Christmas, she hung it over the back of a chair already half-covered with dumped outerwear.

"What am I doing here?" she parroted. "Lovely way to greet your mother, and if you'd answered your phone then you'd know."

"But since I didn't, you're going to have to tell me," Davy said.

She looked taken aback at his tone. He supposed he could understand that. Hill seemed to have a much better relationship with his mom than Davy had with his. The guilt-trip routine probably didn't put Hill's back up quite that much.

"Sorry," he said. "I...ah...think I've lost my phone."

That actually wasn't a lie, he realized as he glanced around the apartment. The only phone he'd seen was the burner that Fraser had...

Davy's brain skipped the track mid-thought as his eyes fell on the money, guns, and ID still laid out on the coffee table.

Fuck.

It was hidden by the back of the couch for now, but as fig leaves went, it was precarious. Davy mentally scrambled for a solution as Hill's mom sighed.

"Again?"

"I might have left it at work," Davy lied on autopilot as he assessed his options. "I dropped by there this morning to pick something up before the party."

Hill's mom raised her eyebrows at him.

"You're coming to the party?" she said suspiciously. "That's new."

"You invited me."

"I invite you every year," she pointed out. "And every year you say no. What's changed? And where was the last place you saw your phone?"

She started across the room toward him, with the clear intent of helping him look. Davy cursed to himself and quickly met her halfway to intercept. He put a hand on her waist and dropped a kiss on her cold, damp cheek as he turned to keep his body between her and a good view of the coffee table.

"It's somewhere," he dismissed the phone. "Do you want to go and get breakfast with me?"

She looked surprised, and then, in quick succession, delighted. Her smile crinkled the corners of her eyes and made her look...if Davy was being a dick, "her age," and if he wasn't, "more approachable."

"Of course," she said as she reached to touch his cheek affectionately. Her neatly arched eyebrows pinched slightly together as she then turned her hand to check her watch. "Although we might have to make it brunch?"

Davy shrugged. "As long as I get something to eat."

She continued to look bewildered. Davy had a feeling he was *not* knocking his Hill impersonation out of the park. Since she didn't want to look the gift horse in the mouth, though, it worked in his favor.

"Then *that's* why I'm here, I guess," she said with airy good humor. Then she stepped back from him and lifted a "just a minute" finger as she said, "Just let me use your bathroom first."

She headed in that direction, a cloud of soft floral scent left in her wake.

Davy put his hands behind his back and stayed where he was until he heard the door click shut. Then he let his breath hiss out between his teeth as he turned on his heel and headed over toward the table. He swept the money and IDs off the table and into the duffel bag they'd come from. Then he reached for the gun, but hesitated with his fingers on the cool metal.

If he wanted to destabilize Fraser, that would work.

Whatever his little brother could feel these days, he'd be on edge that anyone could get that close to him. It would put him on the back foot even before the rest of the dominoes that Davy had set up started to topple.

It was a solid move...and he'd done worse.

So why not? He picked up the gun and hefted it briefly. His body wasn't familiar with the weight of it, but *he* was.

Hill wouldn't be happy, but by the time he found out he wouldn't be Davy's problem anymore.

That thought made something big and ungainly move behind the paywall in Davy's brain.

The toilet flushed. Davy tightened his grip on the gun and then dropped it in on top of the money. He shoved the bag under the couch…along with any emotions attached to it.

Davy straightened up just as Hill's mom came back into the main room.

"So?" she said with a bright smile. "Where do you want to go? Oh, what about that cafe down by Riverside? They had some good vegan options, didn't they?"

Huh. Davy forced a smile and nod that slipped from his face as he helped Hill's mom put her coat back on.

Shit. He grabbed a hoodie from the chair to shrug it on.

He'd forgotten about the vegan thing.

Trudy.

That was Hill's mom's name, courtesy of her calling ahead to book a table. Trudy Jones, Davy supposed. His sister-in-law.

That was still a weird idea to wrap his head around. Fraser had never liked people much. Although being a family man did convey a certain respectability in some circles. Politicians and criminals alike preferred their contractors to have something to lose.

"How are your eggs?" Trudy asked as she came back to the table from greeting her third random acquaintance of the meal. She pulled the chair back from the table to sit back down.

There was a beat as Davy poked at a lump of egg substitute on the plate with the tines of his fork. It resisted being pierced.

"They're better if you don't think of them as eggs," he said.

Trudy shook her head. The legs of the chair scraped against the tiled floor as she scooted back in and picked up her abandoned knife and fork.

"You used to love eggs," she said. "Then...I swear, you turned vegan just to avoid them."

Davy watched with mild envy as she tucked into her Eggs Benedict. It was probably cold by now, but still better than his plate of beetroot, negs (not-eggs, it wasn't as cute as the menu thought), and fried potato.

The potato *was* OK, but Davy wasn't going to give much credit for that. It was hard to fuck up a potato.

"So," Trudy said. She took a bite of a dripping bit of muffin and looked at Davy curiously. "You're going to show your face at your stepdad's Christmas party?"

One of Davy's tentacles responded to his envy and snuck up over the edge of the table. It squirmed between her glass and plate and dipped itself into the hollandaise sauce. Technically, it wasn't touching it, but it still made Davy's mouth twitch.

He'd grown up hungry enough, often enough, that he didn't like to fuck with people's food.

"I just...I've been thinking about Dad a lot recently," Davy said. He gave the tentacle a kick to knock it off the table and ignored the offended slither of it to back around his feet. His heel caught the leg of the table as he pulled it back, and he couldn't tell if Trudy's frown was a reaction to that or to what he'd said. "When he was my age..."

He trailed off to give himself a chance to do some quick math in his head. Numbers had never been his strong suit, and after a while, he'd lost track of the years in the Beyond. But he was fairly sure that when Albie Rosen had been around Hill's age, he'd already buried a man in the foundations of a starter house and had a son.

Trudy mistook his attempt at adding up for some sort of feeling. She put her fork down neatly on the side of her plate and reached over to cover her hand with his. Davy's elbow twitched at the contact as he resisted the urge to pull away.

"What is it?" she nudged him. "You know you can always talk to me."

The rest of Davy's body—Hill's body—felt like it had gone numb as all sensation crowded down past his wrist to focus on the sweaty weight of her hand on his. His eyelid twitched as he tried to focus on where he wanted the conversation to go.

The food wasn't good, and he'd decided not to kill Trudy, so if he wanted to get anything out of the last hour, he needed it to be making Fraser's domestic environment uncomfortable.

"He didn't know it, but he'd lived most of his life," he said. "And when he died, what was left behind?"

Trudy looked confused, but after a breath she squeezed Davy's hand and said gently, "You?"

"And what will I leave behind?" Davy asked and waited for Trudy's expression to soften with pity before he jabbed. "I don't even have a best friend to marry my widow and take over my life."

That caught Trudy by surprise. Her eyes widened and she drew back.

Something in Davy's gut—the muscle memory of filial duty, he supposed—felt queasy at hurting her. Mostly, though, he was glad to have his hand back.

"I didn't mean it like that," he lied. "I know that you—"

Trudy shook it off. "I know. It's OK," she said. That was a lie too. "You aren't like your dad, Davy. Your life isn't half over, and you aren't going to kill yourself."

Wait. What?

Davy had to hesitate as his brain record scratched off track to take in that information. Albie had *what-the-fucked* himself? Before he could pry for more details, there was an insistent *bzzt* from Trudy's coat pocket.

"Oh, for..." she muttered in annoyance as she twisted in her chair to hunt through her pockets. She finally produced the phone from an inner breast pocket and sighed at the screen. "It's Fraser. Give me a second, sweetheart, it's probably something to do with the party. Every year it's like he's forgotten we've ever thrown one before. If he suggests we save money on catering and make the sandwiches, I...I'm not going to be responsible for what I say."

She swiped her thumb over the phone and lifted it to her ear.

"Fraser, what—" she started to ask, then paused with a frown as she was interrupted. The volume was too low to pick up words, but from the sharp tones Fraser wasn't in a good mood. She heard him out as a confused frown knit her eyebrows together. "Our accountant? I don't know. If he's not answering his phone, it's probably because he's on holiday. He's not at his house? *Fraser*, you can't go by the man's house to doorstep him on the holidays. I'm not going to call his wife, either. She's...Fraser. *Fraser!* Fine. Fine. I don't think I have her number, but Jo might. Yes. Now. Fine!"

Tax man or mafia don, Davy wondered as he listened in. He raked a chunk of fried beetroot in the crust of salt on the side of the plate before he ate it. The food here really wasn't that bad.

She hung up and pulled an apologetic face at Hill over the table.

"I have to go," she said as she pushed her chair back. "Our accountant isn't answering the phone a few days before Christmas, and obviously, the only reason for that is he's dead in a ditch with his whole family."

Davy wiped a bit of beetroot off his lip, his thumb smudged purple-red where it smeared.

"Why does he need an accountant?" he asked. "Have you gone over-budget on the party by that much?"

"If I'd gone over-budget, he'd be calling a divorce lawyer," Trudy said dryly. She buttoned up her coat and came around to drop a quick eggy kiss on his cheek. "No, it's something about taxes? A friend of his gave him a heads-up about an audit or something? Don't worry about it. I'm sure it's something and nothing. And our accountant is just day-drinking at his in-laws'."

Huh. Davy's money would have bet the Mafia would have been the first to respond to him chumming the water. He supposed it wasn't surprising that an organization with that much Catholicism baked in lagged on the holidays.

"I hope so," Davy said. "With everything that's been going on at work, I'm not surprised he's worried, though."

He really was good at being an asshole.

Trudy caught the inference enough to look worried, but she didn't ask. At a guess, after ten years of being a military contractor's wife, she'd learned ignorance helped her sleep at night.

"Anyhow," she said, changing the subject awkwardly. "I'm still going to see you at the party?"

Davy nodded and...well, why the hell not. It was worth a shot.

"If there is going to be an audit, maybe you should get the wheels on that divorce lawyer moving," he said, with a smile to make it obvious it was a joke. "How much would it cost to make it into a costume party, do you think?"

Trudy rolled her eyes. "The only one who'd hate that more than Fraser is you," she pointed out. "You don't even like wearing a suit."

Davy shrugged. "Tell you what," he said. "Make it a masked ball and I'll wear a costume. If I'm lyin', I'm—"

Trudy shushed him quickly. "No," she said and pointed a finger at him. "Not even as a joke. Not during Solstice."

She left, coat billowing behind her. Davy watched her go and then reached over the table to swap their plates. One of the other diners gave him a disapproving look. He ignored them as he tucked into the leftover muffin.

Social engineering had always been Fraser's side of things, not his. But he thought the little bit of poison he'd dripped could bear some fruit.

He probably wasn't going to get his masked ball, but there was a good chance Fraser would end up sleeping alone tonight.

Which could be useful...*if* Davy used Hill.

Davy sopped up some hollandaise and egg with the muffin and took a bite. He still wasn't sure it was worth the risk, although he refused to think it further through than that.

"Three dollars," the cheerful, sweaty man behind the kiosk counter said as he held the Baby Ruth chocolate bar out. A battery-powered Santa jiggled merrily on a bench behind him.

He waited, blissfully unaware of the tentacles trying to shoplift their own treats off the counter. It wasn't even candy. They poked at a chewed pen and dipped into the change jar to try and stir the pennies.

Davy stared at him. Then he shook his head, gave up on the "in my day" rant that was welling up, and handed over the well-washed five he'd found in a pocket. He got less change back than he'd been expecting, but it wasn't like it was his money.

He tore the end of the wrapper open with his teeth as he walked away. The first bite was gooey, sticky, satisfying non-caroby goodness, but it turned to dirt and worms on his tongue. It was stupid, but for the first time since he'd crawled into Hill he felt ...out of place.

Not his time.

Not his life.

Not his fucking candy.

Davy grimaced to himself and stashed the half-eaten confection in his pocket. It was stupid. He knew he was dead, long dead. Time passed differently, or at least *felt* differently, in the Beyond. The dead still saw the living world move and change without them.

Hell, Davy was wearing the very attractive body of a man who'd been an egg in someone's ovary the last time Davy had taken a breath. It was what it was.

But the price of a *Baby Ruth* threw him for a loop? Davy took a deep breath that didn't help as he fell into step with the rest of the seasonal shoppers. Make it make sense.

The uneasy feeling crawled down his spine and got into his tentacles. They hackled up around him, restless and insistent as they lashed out at the empty air. Davy assumed there *was* something there, in the Beyond, but since he couldn't see whose space the tentacles had decided to invade, it wasn't his problem. It was a refreshing break from any accountability for their behavior...not that he'd ever taken much of that.

Then something grabbed hold of one and *yanked* hard enough that Davy felt it. Not Hill's skin and bones, *Davy* himself. He was crushed against the inside of Hill's body, suddenly aware of the sharp edges of bone and tangles of nerves.

Another yank and he felt something *tear*. The...pain?... It wasn't the same as the hot, nerve-ending battering of Hill's physical pain, but it wasn't anything that Davy had gotten used to in the Between either. It was deep and wet and felt like someone was trying to pull his cock out through his spinal column.

Davy clenched his jaw against it and hung out as his tentacles mobbed whatever it was. Little jabs of pain pattered over his body—a bruise under his knee, a fingernail dug in that caught in the hinge of his jaw—but nothing like the original agony.

He—well, the bits of him still in the Beyond—finally managed to wrench free of whatever had grabbed him. Davy staggered at the release, his knees weak as he tried to remember where they went. A passerby grabbed his arm, her face concerned under a Santa hat, to steady him. He grimaced out a pro forma "thanks, no, I'm OK" as he got his balance.

The concerned stranger didn't look convinced, but after a searching look reluctantly moved on with her bags of shopping.

Davy gave his head a brisk shake—didn't help, never did, fuck knew why he always tried—and straightened up. His veins felt as dry as his mouth, and his heart was doing double-time against his ribs. It felt like the aftermath of a fight, even if it wasn't the one he'd been after.

"The hell was that?" he muttered.

His tentacles were an agitated tangle around him, except for the injured one. It sagged around his feet, heavy and sluggish, ectoplasmic skin bruised and punctured.

Davy crouched back down and pretended to tie his laces as he examined it. He grazed a hand along the length of it, his fingers sinking through the torn flesh until it touched *him.*

The dead didn't *heal*, not exactly, but they didn't care to be changed either. An injury was something gone forever, but it didn't leave a scar. You were just...less. Usually, anyhow. The Company had a way, or so he'd heard, but that was proprietary information. Even most of the dead at the Company didn't know anything other than that it existed.

That or the ones that Davy had cultivated were better liars than he'd thought.

Davy gave the tentacle a pat and straightened up...just in time for Hill to barrel into him. Instinct made him try and catch the man, but he barely had time to register the panic on Hill's face before they passed through each other. The chill cut down into Davy's bones and dug sharp fingers into the muscle of his heart.

The clutch at his chest, his fingers tangled into his T-shirt, made another passerby slow down to look at him with concern. Apparently, everyone today wanted to be a good Samaritan. Davy glared it out of them and grabbed for Hill with his uninjured tentacles, wrapping the whip-thin ends around Hill's chest and arms.

Hill struggled against the tethers for a moment and then visibly relaxed as he realized who had him.

"What's wrong?" Davy asked as he reeled Hill back in. "Are you OK?"

Hill looked at him, and Davy felt a brief, hard pang of something that made his chest hurt, and then, when he didn't have the emotional nous to deal with that, made him angry. It was efficient if nothing else.

The lively silver-green shade of Hill's eyes had faded, down to moss-green in one and completely gone to pewter in the other. His cheeks were marked with unmistakable smuts of greasy soot.

It was what passed for stigmata with a polter.

"What did you do?" Davy amended the question, his voice tight and frustrated. His tentacles picked up on his mood and gave Hill a quick, angry shake.

Hill grabbed them and peeled them off his arms. It didn't do much, as they squirmed back in to cling to his thighs and around his throat.

"I don't know," he said. His voice pitched up an octave towards panic as he dragged the tentacle from around his throat with frustrated, clawed fingers. "I don't understand any of it. It doesn't make any sense, and— Leave me alone!"

The words burst out of Hill. He wasn't looking at Davy, though. His attention was focused, wide-eyed and desperate, over Davy's shoulder. Whatever he saw...

Around Davy, the temperature dropped enough that the last-minute shoppers shuddered and hunched down into their coats, not placing the "goose walked over their grave" chill. His breath smoked as it left his lips, and the Veil thinned. It didn't lift, and it was still thick enough to hide all but the shadows and shapes on the other side, but it was enough.

Even as a silhouette, there wasn't much you could mistake a dog-headed dead man for.

The Company had let the Hounds out of their kennels.

"Fuck," Davy said, with feeling.

Chapter Eleven

Dec 23rd, 1.30pm

FEAR WAS NOT THE same as despair.

Hill sank his teeth into his lower lip as he clawed at the inside of his own mind for the hollowing *drop* that he'd felt before he did...what he'd done. It was gone, replaced by the staticky need to run.

He grabbed at Davy's tentacles to try and squirm free. It didn't work. They tightened around him, one tucked under his chin as it turned his head to look at Davy.

"Is it after you?" Davy asked, then clarified. "Specifically, after you? You weren't just a target of convenience during a sweep?"

"No, it was..." Hill started to explain, then stumbled to a halt. He'd been going to say "it was the same thing that happened in the apartment"...the thing that Davy had lied to him about. The lie wasn't a surprise; it was the sort of thing the man Hill had spent years researching would do. It was the "why" of the lie that made Hill bite his lip and hesitate.

Davy didn't bother to try and look hurt. He just rolled his eyes in exasperation as he hustled Hill into a loping walk, a tentacle at the back of his neck and slung around his waist.

"I get it, I'm an asshole," Davy said. "But I'm *your* asshole, remember? God himself handed you the leash and said, 'sic 'em.' Is this really the time to question God's judgment, before his kid's big day?"

The laugh hiccupped out of Hill, more from surprise than amusement. It got one sharp "ha" out before panic throttled it back down into his gullet.

"You lied to me," Hill said. "You knew what happened to my computer."

The brief look of...regret? guilt?...that crossed Davy's face surprised him. It didn't last long, gone in the time it took Davy to look over his shoulder, but it had been there.

"It happened again," he said.

Hill supposed that was all the acknowledgement he was going to get. He opened his mouth to answer, but before he could, Davy stepped off the curb and into traffic. A lifetime of road safety lectures made Hill try to dig his heels in. It didn't do much good. The tentacle around his waist tightened and yanked him unceremoniously along in Davy's wake.

A festive green Ford screeched to a halt inches from Davy's legs. Hill was the one who flinched at the thought of what might have been. To be fair, though, they *would* be his legs again at some point...and he'd rather they not be in bits.

The driver of the Ford stared at them, eyes huge and face pale, from behind a swinging Xmas Tree air freshener. A dozen tiny LED lights cast multi-colored shadows on her face. Davy waved vaguely in her general direction and kept on dodging cars.

"What are you doing?" Hill objected as he tried to twist around to check on his pursuers. He'd lost track of them, and he scanned the crowd—of dead *and* living faces now he was back in close proximity to Davy—for sharp ears and bloodied muzzles. "They're going to catch up."

"The Company has two big rules," Davy said as they reached the other side of the road. "Do what it tells you, and don't get in death's way."

Hill screwed up his face. "What?" he said. "I don't—"

"If it looks like death might be imminent, when someone plays live-action Frogger, for example, the Company's operatives keep their distance," Davy explained. "It's like they always say, don't speed when you have a body in the trunk."

"No one says that," Hill snapped.

"They should," Davy said. "It's good advice."

"So is don't play in traffic," Hill said. "You didn't listen to that...and flirting with death is only going to keep those..."

"Hounds."

"...Hounds away for so long."

The tentacle around Hill's waist gave him a possessive squeeze, the end of it curled around his thigh. Davy turned and gave him a quick, wicked smirk.

"We'll see," he said, with a wink of one hard-to-read pitch-dark eye. "I'm a really good flirt."

"And you have a plan?"

"Working on it," Davy said.

He paused briefly to look up and down the street. Hill took a breath to argue and then let it out raggedly.

"Maybe I should hand myself in," he said. "You didn't see what I did back there. I'm dangerous. I'm—"

"An idiot," Davy finished for him. "Shut up and keep moving."

If he'd meant the offer, Hill could have argued. Instead, he felt a wave of gratitude at Davy's gruff rejection of it. Without thinking, he reached down and took a tentacle, the skin of it velvety as it curled around his fingers.

They pushed through the crowds on the street. Anytime the Hound drew closer, Davy rolled his ankle and fell off the curb into the street, or got into someone's face with convincing drunken aggression.

Hill cringed as Davy got bounced off a wall by a furious boyfriend. He mouthed "sorry" to the offended woman on the way by, and then to the outraged bystanders who watched his body stagger down the street.

"Is the plan to get arrested?" he asked.

"Still working on that," Davy said. He wiped blood off his—Hill's!—lip with his thumb. "But probably not."

Hill glanced back again. For a second he didn't see the Hound; then it pushed through a giggling cluster of schoolgirls. They shivered, breath visible, and the joy visibly drained out of them. One of them teared up, another rolled her eyes in annoyance and snapped something as she chafed her hands together.

Then another Hound, this one lean and beaky with a Doberman's streamlined snout, joined it. The two dead men moved in eerie lockstep as they wove through the crowd.

"There's another one," he said. Davy muttered a guttural curse under his breath. "They're going to work out this isn't *Final Destination* soon, aren't they?"

Davy hitched one shoulder. "Eventually," he said. "But the Company isn't forgiving, and they aren't that bright. So not just yet."

That wasn't much comfort.

Davy paused at an intersection as his gaze darted across the nearby buildings. He squinted and then made a frustrated noise under his breath. The tentacle that Hill was still clutching squeezed his fingers as Davy pointed across the road.

"Is that the Hood and Noose?" he asked.

"I—" Hill stared blankly across the street as his brain drew a blank on how to identify a business. In the end, it was the surprisingly adept bit of graphic design on the front window that flicked the switch in his brain. A "hooded" crow on a gibbet, all etched out in one swirled blood-red line. "Yes. Yes? Why?"

Davy grinned and lifted his hand, fingers curled into a loose fist, up to his shoulder. One of his tentacles dapped him.

"The dead are like water," he said. "They find their own level, and Murderer's Row is mine."

"No one looks happy to see you," Hill said under his breath as he shied away from the glare of a woman who had thick black bear paws for hands. An old man with a scarf wrapped over his lower face pulled the folds of wool apart enough to spit on the ground as they passed.

A tentacle jabbed out and grabbed the tasseled end of the scarf. It gave the length of wool a yank hard enough to spin the old man around, bony hands flapping. Hill stammered an apology as he grabbed the middle of the tentacle and reeled it back in.

"You surprised?" Davy asked as he looked back over his shoulder, one eyebrow cocked. "I'm not a nice man."

Hill supposed that the evidence backed that up. It was just...he'd been nice to Hill. And snarky, impatient, and unnecessarily dramatic about oat milk, but in between that, he'd been nice. The wave of relief that had crashed over Hill when he'd fallen into Davy's arms on the street...even if they were tentacles...was still very clear in Hill's mind.

"So I guess the plan *isn't* to ask for help?" he asked as he half-tripped to avoid a crack in the pavement. Habit made it seem stupid, but under his current circumstances he didn't want to dismiss any superstition out of hand.

Davy sniggered his appreciation of Hill's "joke" as he hesitated for a second at a corner. The tentacles decided their route as they reached out and grabbed a leaflet-papered post to drag them in that direction.

"Ask, no," Davy said. "We're going to depend on them acting in their own self-interest. Are they still there?"

"Ummm..." Hill hedged as he twisted around to look over his shoulder. Dread cramped in his stomach when he saw only one of the Hounds behind them. "I can only see one of them. He's getting closer."

Davy narrowed his eyes and then made an annoyed sound as he scrubbed the back of his hand over them.

"It's like looking through milk," he muttered and then shrugged it off. "But it doesn't matter. I don't need to see to out-think a fucking Hound. If they're going to try and cut us off, they'll do it at Barrowland. Might as well get it over with and meet them there."

He turned abruptly and broke into a run.

Hill had seen himself run before. It wasn't an efficient process, but it got him to where he needed to go faster than walking. There wasn't much more he could expect from it, in his experience.

Somehow, Davy took the same set of bones and joints and made a spring into something loose-limbed and natural. Hill would have been frustrated if he had the time. Instead, he was dragged along in a loping stumble as the narrow tenement-shabby alley in the Beyond queasily shifted in jolting increments to accommodate the passage of someone both living and dead.

Ahead of them, people saw Davy coming and prudently decided it was none of their business. They grabbed laundry—and seriously, even when *dead?* The random thought flickered irreverently through Hill's mind—or stalls and slammed doors behind them. Curtains whisked across windows, but Hill saw a few fingers hook the fabric back enough for the owner to peek out.

"Is the dog keeping up?" Davy asked.

He used Hill's body to dodge around a rusty skip in an alley and boost himself over a chain link fence that didn't exist in the Beyond. The two worlds glitched and folded around each other, with no one on either side apparently aware of it.

Except Hill.

It was just layers, he told himself in a desperate attempt to quell the existential nausea, *just Adobe Undead.*

He took a quick glance back over his shoulder and saw the Hound drop to all fours as he lurched into a graceless, efficient run. It wasn't quite the same locomotion as a canine, but closer to it than seemed possible with more or less human anatomy. Slaver dripped, pink-tinged and frothy, from the narrow, scarred muzzle and splattered the ground.

Hill flinched into a misstep. His foot slipped off a low step and pitched to the side. Davy caught him with a tentacle under the arm and one under his ass. A rough shove from both straightened him out and propelled him after Davy.

"He's catching up," he said in a thin, tense voice.

"Good," Davy grunted.

Hill gave the back of Davy's neck a confused glare. "Good?" he spluttered out a challenge to that statement.

A tentacle snapped out and grabbed a nearby pole, pale flesh wrapped tight around the tar-dark, splintered wood. It tensed into a yank, and Davy gave a quick, uncomfortable shudder before he turned that way. He saw the pole just in time to throw his hand up in front of his face, but it came apart before he could touch it, ripped like paper, and stitched itself back together again behind him.

Just in time for Hill to nearly end up floored by it. He just about managed to dodge past it, swapping one set of supportive tentacles for another.

"Asshole," Davy muttered as he swiped one hand at the tentacle without breaking stride. Some of the other tentacles joined in, a knot of pinching and pulling flesh. While they worked out—whatever that was—Davy headed on down the narrow alley. His voice was ragged and breathless as he tossed an answer to Hill over his shoulder. "And yeah. Don't want him to catch up, but don't want him to fall behind either. Sweet spot of about...ten feet."

"How do you feel about six?"

The truth was somewhere in between, but a sour part of Hill wanted Davy to feel the same wet twist of fear drag his stomach toward his asshole. All he got was a grunt and a tentacle in the small of his back as Davy shoved him out in front.

"In that case," Davy told him, "move your ass."

Hill grimaced but did his best. He was pretty sure that his view had been better than Davy's, but fear and the lack of lactic acid were on Hill's side. A ragged, stained sheet flapped from a loose line strung over the end of the alley. He slapped it aside, the fabric clammy and sour, as he staggered out onto the next street and almost bumped into the Hound.

They *both* recoiled from the contact, and the Hound flattened its ears as it flicked its pale tongue over snagged teeth and black lips. For the first time, it occurred to Hill that the Hounds had good reason to be scared of him too. It didn't make him feel any better.

He froze for a beat, his legs no longer taking instruction from his brain, but the tentacle in his back shoved him unceremoniously into the street. Hill tripped down the curb and into the path of a black hearse-like car. He flinched at the blare of a horn and fell on his ass before he realized the helpful tentacles had abandoned him.

Shit.

The driver of the car started to open their door. Hill got a glimpse of a heavy, sour-looking face that somehow managed to look florid even in the undersaturated light of the Beyond. Something about the thickness of the skin and the shape of the nose gave the impression he'd have been choleric in his coffin. Before the scowl could be fully deployed, the Hound slammed a thick, paw-like hand flat on the window and shoved it shut. The edges of it crushed the man's finger and split the skin. He started to scream, then saw the big canine head turn his way, and choked the noise back.

During the brief distraction, Hill scrambled to his feet and bolted.

It would have *helped*, he thought as he dodged between cars that braked and those that tried to keep going out of the area, if Davy had given him any idea what the plan was.

If there was a plan yet, he supposed.

He glanced back and saw both Hounds behind him now, and an overtaken Davy lagging behind them. They had a brief shoving match, culminating in snapped teeth and snarls, to establish who took point as they moved to cut him off.

What happened, Hill wondered for the first time, if there was no spirit to put back in his body once the Invocation window closed? Would it just drop, like a puppet with its strings cut? Or would Davy, in lieu of any other claimant, just get to keep it?

The notion probably should have scared him, but...

Maybe *that* was fair. Whether Davy held a grudge or not, Hill's dad had been party to cutting his first life short. What better compensation for that than a second chance? And, if Hill was honest, Davy would probably make more of Hill's life than Hill had to date.

The dragging self-pity in that thought tickled the corners of Hill's brain with the static white rush that had leveled the cafe. Unfortunately, the flash of relief he felt at that banished it again.

Great. That was a fucking useless power.

Hill caught a glimpse of something gray-white and emphatic out of the corner of his eye. A glance that way showed Davy's tentacles raised as he gestured emphatically toward...

Another alley.

More running? So far, that didn't seem to have done much good. They'd not gained any ground on the Hounds; if anything, they'd lost it. But since Hill didn't have any better ideas, he scrambled in that direction.

He dodged a woman coming out of a butcher's shop, a haunch of something wrapped in dripping brown paper cradled in her arm, and threw himself into the alley. A lifetime of movies and TV shows had primed his brain to expect to see a startled arch of a cat or a spooked rat scurrying for cover.

Except he'd not, he realized, seen an animal since he got here. Just the muzzles.

That probably would have puzzled him more if he wasn't preoccupied by the wall at the end of the alley.

It was a dead-end.

Hill turned on cornered instinct to bolt back out of the trap. It was too late. The Hounds were already there, broad shoulders and sharp teeth blocking his exit.

"Not bad," the one with the sharp, bony muzzle growled out. "You got...pretty far, dead rabbit."

The other one, hairier and bulkier, curled black lips back in a strained-looking smile. "Not far enough."

They both laughed at that. It looked like Davy had been right about one thing at least; they weren't bright.

Big, though, he thought as they stalked toward him. The bulky one pulled what looked like a bridle made of wire and bone out of his jacket. It rattled as it dangled from his hand.

Hill clenched his fists and tried to remember all the self-defense classes that Fraser had sent him to over the years.

Except *that* wasn't going to do much good, was it? Hill had never been great at taking the lessons from class to...well...most of the time back to class. And that had been against other children. He didn't fancy his chances against whatever the Company had made into their Hounds.

He backed up, feet scuffing over cracked concrete and gravel, as he tried to *give* up.

Why was it so *hard*? Hill's mouth twisted around the old, sour reminder as it bubbled up. It was in his DNA to throw in the towel. Why fight that now?

Self-pity wasn't despair either, it turned out.

Hill took one more step back, and his shoulders hit the wall. He stopped with a little grunt of surprise as if...as if the world might have reshaped itself to suit him. Just this once more. It looked like he only got one of those in a lifetime, though.

He took a deep, unnecessary breath and squeezed his eyes closed. If Davy got to keep his body—he thought, generously under the circumstances—he hoped he did something spectac—

The sharp, sliding whistle cut through what Hill had expected to be his last thoughts. He snapped his eyes open and flinched back from the bridle hung in front of his face. Hard enough that the back of his head hit the wall.

The bit was made of teeth.

Both Hounds had flattened their ears at the sound. They turned and stared at Davy. The confused, in-unison head cock as they tried to make sense of him was so canine it read as cute despite...everything else.

Hill stifled a choked laugh against his fist. His arm brushed the bridle as he raised his hand, and the strung bones clattered against themselves. Amusement faded quickly as he noticed something.

The bit, Hill corrected his earlier thought grimly, *was made of* sharp *teeth.*

The thought made his stomach turn unhappily.

While he absorbed that, Davy grinned at the Hounds and uncurled his tentacles from behind his back. Twelve of them. One of them made what was somehow a clearly rude gesture at the Hounds, while the others lashed out to the sides.

"You fuckers spoil dogs," Davy said.

He pressed his tentacles against the wall, the tips picking at the mortar and at the texture of the bricks as they crawled upward until they lashed around the rusty bottom step of a fire escape.

Oh.

Hill glanced over at the other wall and saw two tentacles latched onto the struts that propped up the bowed wall of the butcher's.

Oh! *That* was the plan.

Davy braced himself and pulled. The long ropes of his tentacles tensed into wiry bands of sinew and muscle, the soft, dappled skin pulled taut. Metal creaked, and brick made a raw, surprisingly organic sound as the nails ripped out of the walls. The fire escape came down first in a rattle and clash of metal, and then the struts gave way with a wet spray of splinters.

Hill dropped to the ground and covered his head with his arms.

Dust and bits of metal stung the back of his neck and exposed arms. The bone-and-tooth bridle hit the ground in front of him, two of the teeth breaking as a brick landed on it.

Without thinking about it, Hill reached and grabbed the strap that would have gone over his head. He meant to throw it away. That was the reason for grabbing it that occurred to him once the warm, wet leather was gripped in his hand, anyhow. He never got around to it, though.

The Hound dropped in front of him, one ear hanging by a bloody, ragged string, and jaw kicked wonky. One eye was caked shut with blood and brick dust and hair, the other was bloodshot, and the pain made it so uncomprehendingly animal-like that Hill felt guilty for a second. Like he'd kicked a dog.

His ears were ringing, and he could barely see from all the dust and debris that hung in the air like smoke. But someone yelled something.

"...the...fucking id..." The words filtered through the high-pitched thrum that bounced between Hill's eardrums. It didn't sound flattering. He shook his head, chunks of mortar falling out, and tried to make it out anyhow. "...muzzle! Get the fucking muzzle."

Hill's first thought was the bridle he still clutched, but then he looked at the Hound and realized what Davy meant. He hesitated. How did that even work? Hen had just plucked it off, but that had been—

Before he could work out a plan, the Hound reached up to scrape the scab off its eye and then just rip its ear off like a hangnail. Blood dripped from its still-broken muzzle as it tried to push itself up. It failed, but that obviously wasn't going to last.

Hill swallowed shakily and scrambled up onto unsteady legs. He'd work it out, he guessed as he lunged forward and grabbed hold of the Hound's head. His fingers dug down into fur, and into the wet hole where its ear had been, and the smell of it made him gag.

Dead dog smelled worse than wet dog, it turned out.

He hauled on it as hard as he could and felt it shift slightly, like a sealed jar. Before he could try again, the Hound lashed out at him with one arm. It caught him across the torso, and he felt his ribs give with a weird internal *pop* as he was flung backwards.

One hand slid loose, caked with grease, dust, and dog hair, but he managed to hang on with the other. That might have been a mistake. The Hound grabbed him by the shirt and dragged him in, until he could smell the sourness on its breath.

"...peel you," it gargled out of its broken jaws. "Slice you. Sell you to the hollowmen for *laces*."

All Hill meant to do was put something between his face and the Hound's rank, fanged jaws. He just used the hand he'd slung the bridle around. It slid down over his wrist and clacked against the Hound's teeth.

Bloodshot eyes dilated until they looked almost human again. Human and afraid. It let go of Hill.

"...don't..."

The voice that came out of that ruined mouth sounded almost human, too. Hill didn't know if that should make him feel worse or not. Either way, he couldn't afford for it to stop him.

He shoved his fist, bridle still clutched in one hand, into the Hound's mouth. Broken teeth scraped over the back of his hand, ripping the skin over his knuckles. He bled sticky memories onto the Hound's tongue as he jammed the toothy bit back as far as it would go.

The Hound fought him, ripping its tongue and the soft meat of its cheeks on the ragged yellow canines. Hill got half-stunned by a glancing head-butt, pain radiating back into his sinuses, but he managed to grab the strap and twist it around the back of the Hound's head. It wasn't properly fastened, but close enough.

The Hound stopped.

Hill staggered backwards from it and fell onto his ass. He grabbed hold of a broken bit of fire escape, rust rough against his fingers, and stared at the Hound. It stared back with frosted-over eyes and a dull expression.

He hit it with the rail anyhow. Better safe than sorry.

Then he turned to look for Davy.

Chapter Twelve

Dec 23rd 3:30pm

It wasn't the fight that Davy had *wanted,* but he supposed you had to take what you could get.

Or, he thought dourly as he fumbled blindly with his tentacles, fucking *find.* He edged to the side of the street and leaned against a car, hands in his pockets as he tried to look like someone who didn't need an intervention to the passersby. From the worried look an older man gave him and the way a young dad power-walked his baby's stroller past Davy, it wasn't working.

A stab of pain raked through his chest, like teeth scraping the gristle off his ribs. He instinctively yanked that tentacle back, losing a chunk of meat and splattering plasm up the wall, and swung another in low. If the teeth were up *there*, after all, there'd be a leg down...

There it was.

He wrapped the tentacle twice around the Hound's calf and yanked. The leg bent but didn't shift, and he didn't snatch it back quickly enough. A hand grabbed it, clawed fingers digging down into the dense muscle, and something cold and sharp and...hollow...stabbed through it and into the ground.

Davy staggered as the chill sucked on him. The Beyond was set at cool, but this was different. It was a numb, deadening cold that sucked the energy out of him. His tentacles felt heavy and sluggish, like it was too much of an effort to lift them up.

So he let them drop.

One tentacle might not have been enough to move the Hound; all of them dropped on him at once was a different matter. Davy sagged down onto his knees, his hands braced against the ground, as he groped out a map of the Hound. It got another chunk of him, claws ripping rents into pale flesh, but he jammed a tentacle into its ear and pushed another against the wet, hard grape resistance of its eye. Another tentacle wrapped twice around its throat and squeezed enthusiastically.

Every time, Davy thought groggily. The dead didn't breathe, but his tentacles still always *tried* for a strangle. It did make it difficult for the Hound to get at him with those teeth, so he let it be.

A yank made the Hound howl. Even sheltered in Hill's meat, Davy *felt* it hit him, an atavistic jolt of fear that went from the back of his skull down to clench his balls. The rest of its pack would hear it too.

It would still take them too long to get here.

That was what passed for Davy's plan, anyhow.

He twisted his tentacle down farther into the Hound's ear, stretching it out as thin and wiry as it would go. The labyrinth of the inner ear was clammy and sticky with wax as he drilled down. The eardrum popped like a balloon as he jabbed it.

The Hound writhed and threw its head back as it realized what he was doing. It grabbed hold of his tentacles and yanked, twisting them around its forearms like rope as it tried to pop him out of Hill like a mussel out of its shell.

That was a new sort of pain. Davy didn't even know what to do with it. It was like hitting his funny bone with a hammer made of acid, only all over.

If nothing else, it helped fight the sluggish exhaustion from whatever still pinned him to the ground. He jammed his tentacle into the corner of the Hound's eye until he felt something give—wet and slick—and he could hook the end of it around the edge of the socket.

"Down, boy," he grunted as he yanked as hard as he could.

For a beat nothing happened. His heart dropped into his boots in dismay and his brain scrabbled for another plan, only to come up blank. Before he could try anything desperate, he yanked again, and this time the muzzle gave. It slid free with a wet ripping sound, like skin being peeled off. The Hound howled again, only for it to choke off into a human shout of pain.

The muzzle in Davy's grip was suddenly lighter and colder, just bone and teeth instead of hair and muscle. He tossed it blindly at what was probably a wall. The Hound in his grip wasn't done yet, though. He stamped on whatever it was that nailed Davy's tentacle to the ground. The pain read as pins jammed up under all of Davy's fingernails at once, and he retched, bile splattering from between clenched teeth and out his nose.

Someone in a pair of nice leather boots took a quick step to the side and then quick-stepped past him. At this point, "someone who's fine" had clearly left the building. The best he could hope for was that he looked more like someone who needed a paramedic than a cop.

Then it all stopped.

Well, most of it. The dull, chewed-rib throb of the skewer in his tentacle persisted.

Davy spat out a mouthful of hollandaise and lifted his head.

Hill, a dented length of metal gripped in one hand, stood over what, when Davy squinted, he assumed was the Hound. His face looked even paler than usual.

"Are you OK?" he asked.

Davy shrugged an answer to that. It felt *odd* inside Hill, but he had no context to decide if it was going to be a problem or not.

He got his elbow under him.

"Vultures anywhere?" he asked.

Hill looked up at the sky. Fair enough, Davy supposed. He wrinkled his nose and sniffed hard. "Scavengers. Bad men with knives and forks come to clear the plate."

Someone touched his shoulder.

He swung on them out of instinct before the "Are you all right?" sank in. The woman fell back with a startled cry, one gloved hand up to her face. Blood splattered over the back of the cream leather.

Fuck. That was the cops, then.

"Yeah," Hill said nervously as he looked around. He swallowed, his Adam's apple prominent against the line of his throat. "A couple. Should I...stop...them?"

He had the good sense to sound like he wasn't sure that was going to work.

Good Samaritans had pulled the woman that Davy had cold-cocked away. She had tissues pressed to her nose and older women clucking over her. The less nurturing among them went for dragging Davy to his feet and slamming him against a car.

"You think 'cause the solstice is past, you don't have to worry about payback?" the ruddy-faced man in a mid-tier suit demanded as he hoisted Davy up onto his toes. Pain tore through Davy as his tentacle stretched out, ripping around the Hound's skewer. He let the other tentacles fumble with it—the handle stung like nettles as he gripped it—and work it out of the ground. The man gave Davy a shake. "The spirits aren't the only ones who can hurt you."

Huh. Looked like he'd get that fight after all.

Davy spat out the last of the sick in his mouth. It splattered over the man's jacket, and instinct made him draw back.

"Let them clean that up," he said. The Hounds would come back—the Company had a retention clause—but it would take a while once Murderer's Row's best broke them down for parts. "Get out of here before anyone sees you."

The man holding Davy hesitated as his expression tried to decide between confusion and disgust. Before it could settle, Davy solved it for him by punching him in the face. As the brawl kicked off—messy and highly charged and packing the area full of living, breathing bodies to push the Beyond back—he saw a brief glimpse of a shadowy, predatory press of bodies that faded away as Hill made himself scarce.

Then someone slid a punch through his guard and split his lip. He focused back on the problem at hand.

Being arrested as a rich kid was a *whole* different experience from being arrested as gutter trash. They'd given him a sandwich and a Starbucks, for fuck's sake.

Davy would rate it 10/10. He would be arrested here again.

The desk sergeant handed his wallet back to him. "...and tell your dad thanks for the donation to the Widows and Orphans fund," she said. "We appreciate his continued support."

"Thanks," Davy said as he tucked the wallet into his back pocket. He scrawled something that would probably pass as Hill's signature on the papers handed to him, playing on the bruises on his ribs to explain anything weird. "He appreciates everything you do for the city."

Bullshit, obviously. Fraser appreciated everything they did for him, or he'd not keep paying them to do it. Most people would rather pretend they were being generous than admit they were bought and paid for, though.

The desk sergeant smiled and nodded as she shuffled the paperwork back together.

"Don't worry about this," she said. "It was obviously just a misunderstanding."

Davy nodded. "Give the lady who got hurt Fl...our lawyer's number," he said. "We'll make it right with her."

Why not, after all. It was one jab at Fraser, and, well, Davy didn't feel great about the woman's nose. If it had actually been Hill in need, she'd have been doing a good deed. It wasn't her fault she'd got a hair-trigger asshole instead.

"I'll do that," the sergeant said, her mouth tucked in an approving smile. "Happy holidays."

Davy took his jacket and shrugged it on as he left. As he walked out, he saw Hill sitting on the bottom step and Reynolds on the curb, in front of a black SUV from the company fleet. He paused on the steps under the pretext of fixing his collar as he weighed how he wanted to play this.

"Fraser asked me to pick you up," Reynolds noted as he pushed himself up off the door. He looked haggard, with a twitch under one eye and his collar wrinkled, but he sounded normal enough. Hill looked up and bolted to his feet in surprise as Reynolds came into focus for him. He glanced up at Davy for direction, and Davy did his best to communicate "play it chill" without looking weird. Reynolds didn't seem to notice the slight gesture of his hand. "He'd have been here himself, but...apparently, there's a few unseasonal fires he needs to put out."

It was hard to be annoyed with someone who came bearing good news.

Davy took the last three steps down.

"That's new," he said, and took a punt on what portion of the world could still be volatile enough to be relevant decades on since he'd been involved. "The oil fields?"

He realized his mistake when Hill, hovering behind Reynolds's shoulder, gave him a puzzled look. That wasn't something Hill would have been involved in, apparently. Fraser did seem invested in keeping his stepson unsullied by the...illicit side of things.

Davy would have to check and see if Fraser was setting Hill up to be the unsuspecting patsy for something.

Luckily, Reynolds was too busy looking aggrieved to register the slip.

"No, that's all in hand," he said. A frown pinched his eyebrows together, and the tic under his eye got worse, the nerve visibly squirming under the skin. "He told me it wasn't anything to worry about. It was being handled."

Huh. It looked like Reynolds was in Fraser's good books if he was surprised at being kept in the dark. Not that Fraser hadn't had secrets from him—Davy's brother would have kept secrets from *himself* if he could—but he'd made the effort to make sure Reynolds didn't know that.

Which could be useful.

"I had lunch with my mom," Davy said. Behind Reynolds's shoulder, Hill looked surprised at that news and mouthed "*what*?" Davy ignored him. "She said their accountant was having some sort of family emergency. Maybe it's that?"

Or the Mafia had caught up with the IRS. Who knew? Davy had set a *lot* of small fires earlier.

"Maybe," Reynolds said. He rubbed the frown off his face and gave Davy a once-over that was...hungrier...than the last time they'd talked. "Your mom the one who got you drunk? Or did you, maybe, hook up with someone after? If they gave you something to get you...to get you to do something, I can deal with them."

That was a little off, but that didn't mean he couldn't be useful. It might help.

"Blood sugar." Davy didn't bother to put much effort into selling the lie. "But I could do with a drink now. How about you?"

Reynolds swallowed hard.

Hill went "*WHAT*?" still silent but more emphatically.

"I could do with a whiskey," Reynolds admitted. "It's been a long day, and your mom just sent an email that it's a costume party tomorrow. So I need to find one."

Davy didn't have to fake his surprise at that. He'd not expected that Hail Mary to pay out, but—other than the Hounds—all the cards he'd played were paying off. It made him wonder if the universe hadn't done Hill a favor by letting Davy out of the Beyond...or maybe it just had it out for Fraser.

"Perfect," he said. "I can help you brainstorm something."

Reynolds waved a finger at him absently. "You can't say that anymore," he corrected on autopilot. "And where do you want to go? There's a bar around the corner."

"Why not back to your place?" Davy suggested. He took a step forward and smirked cockily. "Unless you don't have any liquor in the house?"

Both Reynolds and Hill looked like the wind had been knocked out of them. Presumably for different reasons.

Apparently the liquor tolerance went with the body.

The back of Davy's throat burned as he swallowed the mouthful of whiskey, and his eyes wanted to water. The disapproving angel on his shoulder—or perched on the edge of the coffee table—muttered something about "you deserved that" under his breath. Davy ignored Hill's mood and pretended he wasn't in pain as he leaned back and stretched his legs out in front of him. It was hard to look casual on the aggressively minimalist...and underpadded...couch, but he pulled it off.

"I didn't know you liked whiskey," Reynolds said. He'd already tossed back one tumbler. Now he poured himself another. His hand shook a little, enough to clink the neck of the bottle against the rim of the glass. The tremor made him pause and stare at his hand.

"I'm trying new things," Davy said vaguely. He gave a snorted laugh and lifted the glass to rub it over his forehead. "Before I die...so not much time?"

Reynolds finished the pour and turned to look at Davy. "Is something wrong?"

"Maybe," Davy said. "I...um...might have gotten a bit free with the company credit card when my blood sugar was low."

Hill rolled his eyes. "Oh yes, that's a well-known side-effect of hypoglycemia. Dizziness, sweatiness...*fraud.* It's in all the diagnostics."

He got ignored again.

"Shit," Reynolds said. "That's going to be fun to explain."

Davy nodded. "Especially with the current IRS problem... Shit. Forget I said that."

He wouldn't. No one would. That was the point.

Reynolds raised his eyebrows. "Shit," he said. "I guess the tax man doesn't even take Christmas off."

Davy tapped his fingernail against the glass as he watched Reynolds take a gulp of whiskey. The golden spot was tipsy enough to be suggestible, but not so drunk that he had enough liquid courage to make whatever move he was working up to.

"I'd break into his phone and claw back the charges," Davy said. "But...my stepdad isn't a well-meaning preacher man. And just when you think there's no drawbacks to being a military contractor's kid, huh?"

Reynolds chuckled sympathetically and sat down on the couch next to Davy. He took another drink.

"And your mother is one of the top security architects in the state," he said. "They got you coming and going."

That was news to Davy. He hadn't asked, to be fair. Good for Fraser. He'd married the sort of girl who was smart enough to have second thoughts if she'd met their mother.

The hook was baited. Give it a pull or not?

Ideally, he'd give it more time, let it sink in, but the Invocation had set the deadline, not him. Davy faked a sip of whiskey and leaned forward, putting one hand on Reynolds's knee.

The motion made Hill look panicky as he glanced from Davy to Reynolds and back again.

"What are you doing?" Hill demanded. It was a shame he'd remembered that no one but Davy could see him. He tried to slap Davy's hand away. It was distracting enough that Davy grabbed his wrist with a tentacle to put a stop to that.

"I don't suppose you could go to the costume party as a cat burglar and steal his password for me. Just to sell the bit?"

He grinned around the suggestion, because of course he wasn't serious. There was no way he could be. Right? And even if he was, it was a family thing...not industrial espionage.

With any luck, that or something like it was the train of thought behind Reynolds's surprised hesitation.

"Hey! Hey!" Hill spluttered his objections as he tried to pry the tentacle off his arm. "Don't. What the hell? Davy. Davy! That's *my* body."

Davy gave Hill an absent-minded pat on the shoulder to reassure him and squeezed Reynolds's knee.

"Kidding," he said, and lightly touched Reynolds's forehead with his tentacle. It stroked across, slightly through, the skin and made Reynolds shiver. He leaned into it, like he knew what was about to happen on some level. "I mean, if you did, I'd do anything for you...but it would be stupid."

Reynolds had started to agree—or that's what the shape of his mouth looked like—when Davy flicked Reynolds's brain. The static jolt of pain dug into his molars this time, a throb that spread through his jaw. Meanwhile, Reynolds's jaw snapped shut, the click of his teeth painfully loud.

...Hill's mouth moving, all lips and tongue, and he wanted him. Want want want want. The brief thought that it wouldn't be bad *for his career as he looked at Hill's cautiously hopeful face and the sour 'No' that scratched out of him. Shame—he wanted to fuck him, crawl into him, up him—but it was Fraser's fault he couldn't, that he hadn't, and he'd remember that.*

The stream of consciousness felt the same, but different. Davy tried to hang on to more this time, enough to get an idea of what had happened. It spilled through his fingers like sand. Once it was gone, the only impression it left was that the memory had...cramped up?

Reynolds leaned in for a kiss, his lips parted.

It could have sealed the deal, and Davy had done worse for less, but... Davy's breath misted around his lips, a chill that pinched at his mouth, and there was a sharp crack from somewhere. He glanced at Hill. The expression on the other man's face was a mixture of disgust and unhappiness. It made Davy feel weird in his gut, like he needed a bath or something.

"Sorry," he said as he pulled away before he could taste more than Reynolds's breath. He shook his head and scrambled to his feet. "That was inappropriate. I don't think my taste for whiskey is quite acquired enough. I shouldn't have said that or done that."

Reynolds stared at him, frozen on the way to a kiss with his lips still parted. He blinked and then scrambled to his feet.

"No," he said as he reached out to grab Davy's arm. His fingers dug into the bicep a little too hard, and the nerve under his eye had more of a pulse than a tic now. "I should have. I've not been able to think of anything but you. All day it's just been—"

He stopped and pressed the knuckles of his free hand to his forehead.

"It's been you. I can't stop thinking of you and..." He trailed off as his face took on a grayish cast and his mouth twisted. He took a gulp of air, muttered, "I have to...I've got to..."

He staggered off toward the toilet as the side effects hit. Davy watched him go and then wrinkled his nose as the sound of retching filled the apartment.

"You were right," he said to Hill as he turned to go. A tug of his tentacle got the other man up onto his feet and dragged him along behind. "I did *not* want to be kissing him when that hit."

Hill made an annoyed sound and shook Davy's tentacle off.

"How about you don't kiss anyone while you're in my body?" he said. "For a start. And what was that? What can't he stop thinking about?"

Davy let them out into the hall and closed the door behind him before he answered.

"OK, but hear me out before you get all self-righteous," he warned Hill. "I didn't know that sticking a tentacle in his brain would fuck him up."

Chapter Thirteen

Dec, 23rd 6.30pm

THE DEAD COULD GET headaches.

That was good to know.

Hill stood in the middle of his apartment and rubbed the heel of his hand against his forehead. It didn't help. The breathing exercises he usually did weren't cutting the mustard either. The familiarity of it was a comfort, but without the physical pressure on his lungs, it just didn't have the same impact.

"So, you think that...interfering...with John's brain—"

"John?" Davy said dubiously. "Who's John?"

He knew the answer to that. It was clear from context. He was just being difficult to try and dodge responsibility.

It was probably the same reason he'd stripped down to fitted black boxers the minute the door had closed behind them. His shed clothes were left on the floor behind him where they'd dropped. But if he thought that was going to distract Hill, he was wrong.

Hill hesitated mid-righteous denial as Davy padded past him on his way into the kitchen. Bruises stippled his ribs and the small of his back. Others stained the smooth gray surface of the tentacles that dragged tiredly along behind Davy. The bruises shifted shape as Davy stretched and muscles moved under his skin. Or when the tentacles contracted or stretched out. Hill's mouth went dry as the thought of kissing them better flitted through his mind.

OK, he wasn't entirely wrong. Hill wasn't about to admit that, though.

"Reynolds, then," he corrected himself, unnecessary though they both knew it was. "You think interfering with his brain with your...tentacles..."

He hesitated as he said that and glanced at the tentacles. The physical presence—metaphysical?—of the tentacles didn't throw him anymore; even their casual handsiness didn't, but for some reason the word always got stuck on his tongue like oatmeal.

Tentacles. How could he talk casually about that? It seemed impossible, but Hill made himself press on.

"You think that's what made him fixate on me?"

Davy shrugged. "It makes sense."

Did it? Hill had not gotten that memo.

"It does?" he asked.

Davy opened the fridge. He hitched his shoulders up in a shudder as the cold hit him and then reached in to sort through the juices. Most of them, apparently, didn't meet his standards.

"I saw it happen once," Davy explained. He picked out a bottle of kombucha to regard dubiously. After a second, he shrugged to himself and twisted the lid off. "Back when I was alive. This sniper we were working with got the shit kicked out of him by some kid's family. He ended up being cycled through the docs, the shrinks, and finally the priest. Apparently, it was some sort of half-assed possession. He'd crossed paths with a spirit who had enough in common with him that his brain got confused between what was *him* and what was *it*."

"And you think you and Reynolds have something in common?" Hill asked. He wasn't sure who the dubious note in his voice insulted. Probably someone.

Davy took a swig of juice and then wiped the back of his mouth on his arm. He gave Hill a lazy once-over and then smirked slowly.

"Oh, there's a couple of things," he said.

At this point, Hill had accepted that the dead could blush; he just wished it wasn't so easy for Davy to make him flustered and hot. He had to clear his throat and take a moment to shuffle his thoughts back on track. Once he did, he remembered why he was annoyed.

"Oh, right, so it's a thing," he said and stalked forward to glare at Davy. If he could have poked him in the chest, he would have. "And you thought it was a good idea to *stick your tentacle up his nose again*?"

Davy looked thoughtful.

"Yeah," he said after a pause. "Either he goes off the rails and Fraser has to deal with that, or he wants in your pants enough he gets us the password...and Fraser has to deal with that. Win-win for us."

He swigged from the bottle and then lowered it, holding it out so he could frown at it.

"This is disgusting," he said. "Why do I want more?"

"That's how I feel about you," Hill said sourly.

In isolation, in his head, it was cutting. Once he'd *said* it out loud...

Davy grinned. "How I got laid alive, too," he admitted.

It was... Hill gave up. He sat down on the floor and buried his head in his hands, fingers twisted through his tangled hair. There were no chemicals to give him the familiar come down from the panic and flight and rage. He kind of missed them. The emotional hangover was worse.

Where the hell was he supposed to start? He pressed his thumbs against the side of his nose as he thought about it. Which of the moral or practical problems he had with what Davy had just done needed to take pole position?

Something cracked somewhere. A second later kombucha and glass splattered over his knees.

Through, technically, and all over the floor. It looked like he'd soiled himself in some sort of horrendous way. He stared at it for a second and then looked up at Davy, who was holding a jagged stump of bottle in one hand.

"I didn't..." Hill fumbled over the horrified apology. He remembered the bloody alley and the scoured-clean muzzle of the Hound. He glanced back down at the splattered vinegar and tea and imagined it in red as his stomach twisted. "You...are you..."

"Shit, if it means that much to you," Davy said as he crouched down. A tentacle slid under Hill's chin to tip his eyes up away from the mess. "I'll not complain about what's in your fridge again."

Hill laughed. He caught himself and rubbed his hand roughly over his face.

"Don't," he said. "It's not funny. I could hurt you."

He ignored Davy's skeptical snort at that and pressed on. "What you did to Reynolds, it could hurt him. What if it causes a brain aneurysm or a stroke? I wanted...I wanted justice. I wanted Fraser to make things right. Not for more people to get hurt."

The tentacle stroked a stray curl out of Hill's face. It was gentle, the brush of it against his temples soft as velvet. Hill reached up to push it away, but couldn't quite bring himself to reject the touch.

"I mean, considering who you brought back," Davy said. "I think we're doing pretty good. No one's dead. Well...no one new."

Hill turned his face into the curve of Davy's tentacle. The gash from earlier caught his eye, a jagged line thick as his thumb. It wasn't bleeding, but it hadn't healed either. The skin was puckered and raw. On a whim, he brushed his mouth over it to kiss it better like he'd imagined earlier.

Davy hitched in a startled breath in reaction and closed his eyes for a moment. He reached for Hill with one hand, fingers cupped for the nape of his neck. A frustrated "fuck" escaped through clenched teeth as his palm swiped through Hill's throat instead.

"Is this part of what we're meant to learn?" Hill asked ruefully. "Not to want what we can't have? To not waste our life wanting the dead?"

"I know I've said this before," Davy said. He braced a tentacle against Hill's chest and pushed him down onto his back. Another tentacle crawled up his leg and hooked around the waistband of his jeans. The quick tug made Hill gasp and then laugh in confusion. "But they brought the wrong dead man back for that."

A tentacle grazed over Hill's stomach and up along the slats of his ribs. The pulled-fine tip of it flicked against a nipple and then wrapped around it. The pinch made Hill gasp and squirm, a quick jab of pleasure zapped straight down to his balls. His cock felt thick and heavy under his jeans.

"How does it...how can we—"

A tentacle covered his mouth. Davy crawled on top of him, weight braced on his arms and knees in the mess of glass and kombucha.

They weren't, Hill supposed, touching, but the proximity and the squirming weight of tentacles made it feel like they were.

"It just works," Davy said. "Don't worry about how."

Hill screwed up his nose. "Why not?" he asked from behind the tentacle gag.

Black-on-black eyes crinkled at the corners. A tentacle cupped Hill's cock through his jeans and kneaded the bulge. The strange, thirsty pleasure of the dead clutched at Hill's balls and twisted in his stomach. Davy leaned down until his mouth *almost* touched Hill. Close enough Hill could pretend he could still taste the memory of that first old bone and grave dirt kiss.

"It might stop working."

Oh well, Hill did not want that. He reached up to graze his fingers along Davy's jaw and was intercepted by a tentacle. It toyed with his fingers, cool and velvet soft, and then pinned his hand down to the floor.

The restraint made something in Hill's chest catch. It was part arousal and part nervousness, all tangled together until he wasn't sure where one started and the other stopped. Davy cupped his chin with a tentacle. It traced the curve of his mouth like it was the only thing they had to do, and then slid up to give his earlobe a tug.

"Is this what you want?" Davy asked.

Hill squirmed on the floor. He arched his hips to press the jut of his erection against the tentacle laid over his hips.

"What do you think?" he said pointedly.

The corner of Davy's mouth tucked in a smile. That unexpected dimple, the one that was only a suggestion when he smirked, made an appearance again.

"I get your cock is all in," he said. The tentacle curled tenderly against the nape of Hill's neck to lift his head up. "What about you?"

Hill huffed out an annoyed breath. "I'm autistic, not an addict," he said tartly. "I know they start with the same letter, but I don't have any trouble with 'no' if I don't want this."

He *wanted* to pull Davy down into a kiss to underline that statement. He *wanted* his fingers wrapped around the back of Davy's neck and his leg hooked over a lean hip. It felt a bit...greedy, maybe...to want more than the heavy, prying caress of Davy's tentacles, but the frustration at not being able to touch skin and hair and cock still yanked at his gut.

"Yeah, and usually that'd be enough," Davy said. "But..."

He trailed off and looked nearly as frustrated as Hill felt. Then he pushed himself up and sat back, his hands slack between his knees. Most of his tentacles pulled back with him, laid over his thighs, or slung over his shoulder. Only the ones on Hill's thigh and curled around the back of his neck stayed where they were.

"You saw how I played Reynolds," Davy said abruptly. The tease was gone from his voice; it had gone flat and unemotional. It felt like the opposite. Maybe that was just a way for Hill to lie to himself, though. Davy scratched the back of his wrist and frowned. "I could do that to you. Use you, what you can do, to get what I need. It wouldn't be hard anyhow, but this would make it easier."

"So why tell me?" Hill asked.

Davy made a sour face. "I don't know," he said. "I guess I don't want to."

"So don't."

"Yeah, easier said than done," Davy said. "When it comes to the crunch, I'm an expedient sort of asshole. If using you makes sense, I'll try."

"I'm not that easy to—"

The tentacle on his thigh squeezed and then pushed up between his legs. It was thick and firm as it pressed against his ass, the narrow end of it hooked into the waistband of his jeans. Hill's stomach hitched, and the words got all tangled in his throat. He clenched his jaw and closed his eyes, his fingers digging down against the floor. His cock ached as it pressed against the confinement of his jeans.

"What was that?" Davy asked. "You're not that easy to...?"

Hill swallowed hard and lifted his head off the floor. He reached up and grabbed a handful of tentacle to untangle it from his neck, the bulk of it cool and heavy as it twisted and wriggled against his palm.

"I want to fuck you," Hill said. "That doesn't mean I trust you."

He did, though. It might not be smart, but he did. That discussion, however, would definitely take longer than he wanted right now.

Hill wrapped his fingers around the tentacle, tight enough he could feel the muscles flex under the fine skin, and hesitated a second. He wasn't actually sure if what he was about to do was hot, or...well...not. There was only one way to work that out, though.

He lifted it to his face and wrapped his lips around it.

The tentacle was cool against his tongue. It tasted of *blood, whiskey, and regret* as it filled his mouth. He swallowed out of surprise—he'd not considered it might have the same effect as the Beyond's food did—and that dragged a very satisfying groan out of Davy.

Hill glanced up through his lashes at Davy. The other man had tilted his head back, the line of his throat drawn taut and long, and dug his teeth into his lower lip. His hands were braced against his thighs, blunt nails dug into the lean, clenched muscles.

Whatever this was, somewhere between a kiss and a blowjob as Hill worked out what pulled those small, hungry sounds out of Davy's mouth, it was definitely hot. And Hill could, at least a bit, touch Davy back.

He ran his hand down the tentacle, the thickness of it straining his fingers as he got closer to the base, and tangled his tongue around the section of it in his mouth. After a moment, he pulled back, jaw aching and the tentacle wet and slick as it slid from his lips, and gave Davy a challenging look.

"And I didn't carve the Beyond open from the goodness of my heart," he said. "I'm using too, remember."

Davy took a ragged breath, and Hill weirdly kind of missed that too, and dropped his chin. It should have been hard to read arousal in his eyes without dilated pupils to use as a gauge. Somehow, between the hooded lids and a swallow-him-whole deepening of the black, it wasn't. The quiescent tentacles stirred and stretched out to Hill as they came back to life.

"Yeah, fuck it, that's good enough for me," Davy said. "Who am I trying to fool, anyhow?"

Tentacles curled around Hill's legs, under his knees and ass, and tucked under his armpits. Hill couldn't stifle a yelp of surprise as he was hoisted off the ground and suspended in midair. He supposed he should have realized after he'd seen what they did in the alley, but he'd not realized how strong they were.

Or how undignified it felt to just...dangle.

"Umm..." he hedged as he tried to shift his weight. "Can we..."

The words trailed off as Davy stood up and stripped efficiently out of the briefs that were all he had on. It wasn't the first time that Hill had seen, or lusted over, Davy's naked body. It was the first time that he'd seen Davy's cock thick and ready as it hitched up towards his flat, hard-slatted stomach.

His mouth dried up, and for the first time since he'd been shucked out of his body, he *felt* the lack of air in his lungs.

Had he been about to say something? He couldn't remember. Right now, he wasn't sure if he was still verbal or not.

"Oh," he said.

That didn't really clear up the "verbal" question. It was more of a sound than a word.

"What should I do?" Davy asked.

"Huh?"

Still not a word, but closer. Hill tried to brace an elbow on nothing and then gasped as a tentacle slid up under his shirt. It wasn't *rough*. The tentacle's surface was cool and fine, softer than fingers as it rubbed against Hill's stomach and up over his collarbone. There was still a texture to it that he could feel rasp against his skin.

"It's your body," Davy reminded him. He hooked a thumb into the corner of his mouth and dragged it along his lower lip, the exposed skin wet and pink. As Hill watched, a tentacle curled up from the neck of his shirt, fabric stretched around it, and repeated the gesture on his mouth. Davy waited till it was done to repeat his question. "If you were the one wearing it, what would you do? Tell me how you'd fuck me."

The answer was easy. It was getting it out of his parched, thirsty mouth that took Hill a moment.

While he waited, Davy plucked at the sleeve of Hill's T-shirt with a tentacle. Another grabbed at the hem, pulling it up, and between them, they quickly stripped it over his head. Hill blinked as the cotton was pulled up over his nose and shook his head to get his hair out of his face.

"I'd give you—"

"Wait," Davy interrupted. He strolled across the room, his tentacles hauling Hill along with him, and flopped down on the sofa.

A stray, unhelpfully prosaic part of Hill's brain took a second to be distracted at that. There was a towel somewhere. If Davy had asked...

Shut up, he told it firmly, *shut up, shut up.*

"I'm a kinesthetic learner," Davy said. He paused, head cocked as he waited. When Hill didn't chip in, Davy prompted him. "Most people like to compliment me on knowing a big word like that."

"Why?"

It was the real smile again, slow and warm and dimpled. Davy tilted his head to the side, fingers buried in his hair, and chuckled. Something about the gesture felt so intimate that Hill made a quick, deliberate attempt to absorb all the details, from the creases on Davy's wrist to the scuffed skin on his knees. For...for later, when it was over.

"Never mind," Davy said.

Hill tucked the memory away somewhere safe in his brain. He looked at Davy curiously.

"I'll be honest, I thought my...appreciation...of this, of you, was already clear without any more compliments."

"I mean, everyone likes to hear they're pretty," Davy said. He raised an eyebrow and dragged a tentacle along the bulge under Hill's jeans. Hill hitched his hips up into the contact, but the tentacle flicked away after a quick tease of a grope. "But yeah, that is pretty flattering. So, back to business. Like I said, I learn by doing. So clear step-by-step instructions so I can follow along. Detail is always good. Where do I start?"

Part of Hill wanted to skip straight to the good part, but he'd been given a social cue detailed enough he couldn't misinterpret it. So he probably should acknowledge it.

"Put your hand on your collarbone," he said.

Davy did as he was told. If Hill had wanted to be pedantic, he could have pointed out he'd not said which shoulder. He'd also not said for

Davy to do it seductively, rubbing his thumb along the sharp jut of his collarbone and licking his lips.

This once he'd let the improvisations slide.

"Like that," he said, and then the words stuck on the back of his tongue as Davy repeated the gesture on him. A tentacle brushed gently along his collarbone and then...waited. So did Davy. Hill bit his lower lip and nodded. "That's it. Just like that. Now run your hand down your chest to your...your nipple."

Davy ran his hand down to his nipple. He grazed his thumb over it and mimicked the gesture on Hill's with the flat of a tentacle. Breath or not, Hill's lungs hitched in his chest, and his muscles tightened. Meanwhile, other tentacles stripped off his socks and sneakers, dropping them to the floor.

It briefly occurred to Hill that he could well spend the rest of Christmas naked, depending on how clothes worked in the Beyond. They'd "died" with him, but could they persist without him being in contact with them?

He supposed he'd find out. Tentacles wrapped around his feet, the tickle of them against his soles and around his bony ankles making him curl his toes. His cock ached, that increasingly familiar hollowing ache of lust in the Beyond.

"Pinch your nipple," Hill managed to choke out. He groaned at the same time as Davy did, the stretched-thin tendril tip wrapped all the way around his. Davy rolled both of their nipples until they hardened, tight and puckered, under the attention. He clenched his fists. "Tighter."

Hill stumbled through the next few steps of the seduction. The perfectionist in him demanded he put together a well-structured, logical guide, but his thoughts were scattered with lust and hunger. His own and the groans and lip-bitten reactions from Davy. Hands moved down and spread over lean, hard stomachs, combing through the short trail of sweat-matted hair under his navel. Davy's cock thrust up between the V of his thumb and fingers as he waited. The grubby square of the gauze that covered his injured hand looked stark against tanned, bony hands.

"Touch yourself," Hill got out, the words dry and stuck to the end of his tongue.

Davy smirked at him. "How?"

The image was in Hill's head, long, competent fingers cuffed around the thickness of the shaft as the thin skin creased with each slow, steady pump. The way it slid, slick with come, against the palm as Davy's hips fucked up into the tight grip. Except it wasn't just *technically* Hill's hands in the fantasy; he could feel the heat and heartbeat of the erection against his skin and tighten his grip without having to input the directions.

It was raw and immediate, and he couldn't break it down into easily followed steps. Not with his own body hollowed out and tight with his reaction to the attentive caress of Davy's tentacles.

"If you don't know," he said, "I'm not sure you're the one taking advantage of me."

Davy caught his upper lip between his teeth and shrugged. His tentacles pulled Hill closer and lowered him until he was almost sitting in Hill's lap.

"Oh, don't worry," he said as he reached out. His hand grazed through the air a few inches above Hill's waist, and the pressure of the tentacle that *actually* touched him wasn't that far off if he closed his eyes and pretended. He twisted the buttons off Hill's jeans, one after the other, with a precise flick of a tentacle. "I was just warming up."

Chapter Fourteen

Dec 23, 7.00pm

Davy peeled Hill out of his jeans and dropped them unceremoniously to the ground.

He already knew what Hill looked like naked, having spent the last two days in the man's body. There were no surprises in the bony shoulders and lean, wirily muscled body that Davy supported in midair. Not even in the decently sized cock that lifted from the sparse nest of wiry hair between Hill's legs.

It still felt *better.*

Maybe it was just that Hill knew how to wear the body, or the way he looked at Davy with that open, eager expression. Like he trusted him.

There weren't enough acting lessons in the world for Davy to pull off that look. He was too much of an asshole for that; it always shone through.

And Hill might be an idiot to trust Davy, but it was kinda hot.

Look at that. Nearly half a century, living and dead, under his belt, and he'd finally found his kink. Who could have guessed it would be dumbass?

He curled a tentacle over Hill's hip bone and spread it down over the tight skin of his abdomen until he could wind it around Hill's cock. For a second, he was taken aback at the lack of a pulse. It was funny how quickly he'd gotten used to that. The low whimper that scraped out of Hill's throat as Davy gave a brief squeeze confirmed that pleasure didn't need a pulse.

"I don't know who's going to get fucked more thoroughly," he said as he sprawled back on the couch and spread his legs wider. He wrapped his/Hill's fingers around his/Hill's cock, and there it was, the steady throb of something alive in his grip. "You or the universe's plans for me to learn anything."

Hill had squeezed his eyes shut. He opened them now to give Davy a dry look.

"Is that what passes for dirty talk in the spirit world?" he asked.

"You can do better?" Davy asked.

Hill opened his mouth, closed it, and then admitted, "Not right now."

That...was kinda flattering.

"That's what I thought," Davy said. "Besides, Fraser did the talking—"

The mention of Fraser made Hill screw up his face. "Not wanting to think about him right now."

Yeah, Davy probably didn't want to think too hard about that either. He pushed on to get back on track.

"I'm more hands-on," he said as he stroked his fist along his cock in time with the tentacle that dragged along Hill's. And his brain was a *lot* better at mapping pleasure than it was with pain. Instead of the roll of the dice body part being on fire/dipped in acid/chewed, it took what his tentacles felt and dropped it where it seemed to make the most sense.

In this case, anywhere from Davy's cock to his asshole, with the occasional jangled nerve pop of electric pleasure in his fingertips or on his lips.

Right now, he could feel Hill's fingers on his cock *and* Hill's cock in his hands. The feedback loop of it fired off nerves he didn't know he had. His balls pulled up tight and eager between his legs, heavy with come and heat, as he thumbed the foreskins on two cocks to reveal the flushed, wet heads.

Hill groaned and sprawled back against the support of Davy's tentacles, the muscles on his arms and legs taut as he thrust his hips up against the tight, smooth grip of flesh around his shaft. The feedback made Davy groan and press his shoulders back against the couch cushions.

Because it wasn't *just* in his fingertips. It felt like their cocks were tangled together, squeezed around each other. It was a weird visual, but it felt fucking good.

It didn't help that the tentacles he'd not focused on were still busy with Hill's body. They squirmed around his throat and thighs, knotted through his eager, clutching hands, and swiped across the soft, wet line of his mouth. Pleasure and a little pain, as Hill's fingers dug into Hound-caused bruises or scraped the barely scabbed cut from a Hound's knife.

That chilled Davy a little, even through the flood of sensory overload that clenched his thigh muscles and plucked at his taint like a wire. He'd lost something there, and it had been something important. Not that he could tell you how he knew that, but he did.

It was gone, though, and there was no way to bring it back. So Davy shoved that cold bit of knowledge down under the wet wrap of Hill's mouth around a tentacle/cock/tongue and the hot, heavy pleasure that dragged at his cock and ass with every stroke.

One of his tentacles ran up the back of Hill's thigh, tracing the knots of tight muscle, and flicked along the crease of lean ass. The caress made Hill moan, the sound strangled as it struggled out of his stretched-taut throat and pleasure-slack mouth.

Davy hesitated. He'd never...

Obviously, he'd grabbed the occasional grope and stuffed a tentacle into some dead man's willing mouth to muffle an inconvenient whimper. When it came to fucking, though, he'd always fallen back on his cock. Why wouldn't he, after all? It had the experience, he'd never had any complaints about it, and...it wasn't the physical embodiment of his sins.

He'd always assumed they were mostly murders. Although he *had* killed a lot more than twelve people, so he wasn't entirely sure.

One of Hill's legs sagged down to the floor as Davy's tentacles responded to his distraction. He pressed the ball of his foot against the floor to brace himself, the muscles in his calf and thigh defined under pale skin. On a whim, Davy withdrew his tentacles, slick with sweat, spit, and come, to let him stand up. Hill staggered as he took his full weight and went down onto his knees.

Everything in Davy's body clenched in visceral reaction to that.

He licked his lips and dragged his hand away from his aching-hard cock to try and hang onto control for just a little longer. Meanwhile,

Hill had tilted his head forward, tangled hair falling over his face as he pulled himself back together.

"Is that enough?" Davy asked. He tucked a curve of tentacle under Hill's chin to tilt his head up. Mismatched eyes, the green still faded down to pewter shades, stared at him as Hill pressed his knuckles against bare thighs. "Or do you want more?"

Hill gripped the tentacle under his chin, the rough scrape of his fingers a ghost-sensation that made Davy's cock throb painfully, and kissed it.

"I want you," he said. The tentacle slid between Hill's fingers to nudge at his lips. Hill pushed it away for a second as he looked at Davy. "All of you that I can get. While I can still have any of you."

That was right. Davy clenched his hand into a fist to remind himself. His fingers pressed against the gauze that covered the raw gash in his hand. It didn't hurt. It *had*, but the dead flesh had spread across most of his palm now. They were under a—literal—*dead*line.

"I'm not worth it." It took a second for Davy to realize that was *his* voice and *his* words. It didn't sound like him, but now that he was paying attention, he could feel his mouth saying it. "You know that, right? I was never worth much, and now I'm just...someone else's dead."

"Fuck you and forget you?" Hill said. "Is that it?"

Davy slapped a tentacle against Hill's ass cheek. The sound was ironically fleshy, considering the topic of discussion.

"Be realistic, you're not going to forget me," Davy said. "I'm fucking you with tentacles, you're going to be 102 in a nursing home and bring that up. But...if I were alive, I'd fuck this up. If you were dead, I'd fuck it up. So you don't need to be sad or feel bad."

Hill wrapped his hand around the tentacle and stroked his fist down it. The reflected touch made Davy's balls twist in the sac and forced a low grunt out of him as his diaphragm clenched.

"I'm the invoker," he reminded Davy. "You don't tell me what to do."

It shouldn't have mattered. Davy was used to it not mattering. He had no concept of how to react to the fact that, for some reason, it suddenly did.

He'd be missed. So what? Why did he care?

There was no precedent here for Davy to follow, so he fell back on the old, familiar standbys. Fight or fuck...and he'd already laid the groundwork for one.

A bead of come dewed on the head of Hill's cock. Davy flicked it up with a tentacle, then wrapped the long, sinewy length of it around Hill's leg from balls to knee. Others wrapped around Hill's chest to scrape over his nipples or stretched up to slip between his lips and fill his mouth.

It all poured back into Davy, the overwhelming sensation settling into his balls like a weight. He swore raggedly under his breath and wrapped Hill's hand, bandage and all, around his cock.

Like when he was a kid and he'd sat on his hand so he felt numb when he jerked off.

Tentacles pushed between Hill's ass cheeks and traced the pucker of his hole. The taste of it filled Davy's mouth, soap and the distinct musky earthiness, and he hitched his hips up off the couch as he fucked his hand. Sweat beaded on his stomach and trickled down his back into the crack of his ass.

Davy folded his lower lip between his teeth and watched through hooded eyes as he pushed the spit-slick length of himself up inside Hill. He could feel the tight clutch of Hill's ass around him, layered over the rough grip of his fingers. He had to bite down until it hurt to throttle the knot of want/pleasure that pulsed in his gut and balls back down.

"What does it feel like?" he asked as he slid a tentacle out of Hill's mouth. It slid over his shoulder and down his arm, a trail of damp left on his skin. The chill of it prickled a line of goose bumps along Davy's arms in sympathy.

Hill made a ragged noise as he arched his back, stomach muscles pulled tight and long under his skin, and clenched his fingers around the tentacles that shackled his arms. His mouth opened and closed as he groped for the words.

"Too much," he said, then licked his upper lip and clenched his ass around Davy's tentacle. The jolt of *that* fed back a rough grab to the balls that tipped over into that prickling zone where pleasure and pain were the same thing. "Not enough. Fuck me."

Hill *was* the Invoker. Who was Davy to second-guess him?

Tentacles wrapped around Hill's back and under his arms to hold him in place as Davy fucked him. He shoved his hips up against his hand with each stroke, fingers rough as they squeezed around his cock in time with the tentacle that lashed around Hill's flushed erection. He felt each jerk in his ass, like Hill was fucking him as he fucked Hill.

He wrapped the tip of his tentacle around the smooth lump of Hill's prostate and caressed it. The touch dragged a raw groan from Hill, his fingers spread to clutch the air. At the same time, Davy used the rest of the muscular length to spread Hill wide. The muscles in Hill's stomach and thighs twitched with each thrust.

Davy came first, come spilled warm (he'd forgotten what *that* felt like) and sticky over his knuckles. He twisted his fist up his cock to wring the last milky drops out of it as he slouched back against the cushions. Sweat dripped onto his lips, salty and a bit sweet where he licked it.

He watched Hill as he wrung the last drops out of him, too, tentacles squeezing cock, balls, and prostate all at once. Hill arched his back, mouth open as he choked on his own howl of pleasure, and room-temperature come splattered over Davy's tentacles.

At the same moment, Davy saw his breath mist from his lips and felt the couch rattle under him. He grabbed the arm, fingers dug down into the soft fabric, as glass shattered and a chair flew through the air to smash into a wall. The quake of pleasure rippled out from Hill until the orgasm was done with him and he went limp in Davy's tentacles, head lolled back and face slack.

"Fuck," Davy muttered. He wiped sticky come off his hand onto his stomach as he looked around the apartment. The windows were crazed with cracks, and the wall was dented where the chair had hit it. The plaster was cracked and paint had flaked onto the carpet.

Once he'd taken it all in, he looked back at Hill, cradled naked and boneless in a hammock of thick tentacles. His cock lay limp against his leg, and his hand dangled limply until one of Davy's tentacles dipped under it to lift it up. The movement made Hill stir and lift his head, squinting in dazed appreciation at Davy.

The pewtery mismatch of his eyes was gone, leaving them that bright silvery green again.

Davy was pretty sure that was something the Company didn't know about.

Hill poked an insubstantial finger at the window. It didn't do anything, but Hill made an aggrieved noise anyhow. The view had been better before he put his clothes back on.

"How am I going to explain this?" he asked.

Davy bent over to grab a chair and set it back on its feet again.

"You're rich," he said. "Why bother?"

"I'm not rich," Hill corrected him. "Fraser's rich."

"Same difference."

Hill turned around to frown at him. He apparently disagreed, but he let it go.

"Are you always in a bad mood after sex?" he asked.

"No," Davy said. He leaned on the back of the chair as he thought about it for a moment and then shrugged. "Maybe. Now I have to get back to work. Why didn't you tell me that your dad killed himself?"

Hill started to answer and stopped. He looked down and rubbed the back of his neck, picking out the tangles in his dark hair.

"He didn't," he said. "Fraser killed him. Even if Dad...even if he did pull the trigger, it was Fraser who made him do it. The things Fraser made him do."

Davy shook his head. "Fraser doesn't make people do things," he said. "He just...finds the things they're willing to do."

"Does that make it any better?"

He had a point, Davy supposed. It was *different*, though, but not in a way that Davy wanted to explain to a dead man's upset son.

"I hope whatever force governs the Invocation agrees with you," he said.

Hill shrugged stiffly. "It knew what happened when it let you out of the Beyond," he said, and then grimaced. "Or I assume it did, unless it forgot him like everyone else."

There was a broken plant on the ground. Davy considered it briefly and then kicked the broken pottery and already dead spider plant under a chair.

"I never had a good memory for faces," he said. It was a lie, but the gap in his memory bothered him like a missing tooth. He didn't want to think about it.

"Hen didn't either," Hill said.

Davy looked at him, one eyebrow cocked, and waited for context. He didn't get it as Hill just frowned and fiddled with something in his pocket. The one-sided stand-off lasted a few seconds till Davy gave in and asked.

"Who?"

Hill blinked at him. "Hen. Henrietta Bennett. She was my mom's best friend, until she died. It was after you, but before Dad. She found me."

"That's...coincidental."

"Not so much," Hill said. "She worked for the Company. They sent her to try and convince me to take their offer."

Davy sighed. It wasn't his business, but...

"You didn't agree to anything, did—"

"No," Hill said. "But that's not... That's not the point. She knew Dad. They worked together. They had dinner parties. She didn't remember him. Mom. Me. Fraser..."

Hill paused to make a face—not the usual frustrated one either—as he mentioned Fraser. Before Davy could ask, Hill pushed on with what he was saying.

"Not Dad," he said. "Not even a little. It was like she just papered over the gap where he'd been."

That was...

Davy rubbed the back of his neck and poked dubiously at the Albie-Rosen-shaped hole in his memory. It was stupid. So he didn't remember one of Fraser's little lapdogs, who the *fuck* cared?

And why did it make Davy so mad?

He didn't know.

"The dead are only what we remember," he said and absently reached down to rub his fingertips over the wound that carved through his tentacle. "Cut a bit off and whatever memory was there is gone, but even the Company doesn't know how to carve out one particular memory. Even if they did...why? What was so special about Albie Rosen?"

It was, Davy registered a moment too late, a cruel question to ask a man's son.

"Nothing," Hill said bitterly. "Nothing at all. Ask anyone. Even me."

They stared at each other awkwardly, and then Davy reached out and patted Hill's shoulder with a tentacle. Hill reached up to cover it with his hand, the brief, grateful squeeze making Davy bite the inside of his lip.

The tentacle-to-cock transfer was still in play.

He cleared his throat, retrieved his tentacle, and tried to redirect the conversation to something he *could* do something about.

"You said she remembered Fraser?"

Hill shuddered. "In disturbing detail," he said. "Apparently they...you know...before my dad died."

OK, Davy did know. He wasn't going to ask any questions. It was probably less disturbing to think about your little brother fucking than your stepdad doing it. It still wasn't something Davy wanted to dwell on.

"So the slip from memory has nothing to do with the Invocation," he said. "Maybe—"

Hill missed that. He snapped his fingers and then slapped his palm against his forehead.

"She gave me a name."

"What?"

Hill flapped his hand in the air as he looked around. His gaze skimmed over where his computer had been, and then he patted down his pockets.

"I need a phone," he said. The words tripped over themselves as his voice sped up with excitement. "Or a laptop. Something—"

"Who are you going to call?" Davy asked. "Death? The Hounds?"

Hill took that in and gave him an exasperated look. "Fine. *You* need a phone. Do you still have the burner?"

"I don't know how to tell you this," Davy said as he headed into the kitchen. The last place he'd thrown the burner had been into the cutlery drawer. "But polters and tech tend to—"

He fished the lime-green Samsung out and held it up. Or rather what *had* been a lime-green Samsung; the case was blackened and partially melted, the screen cracked and smoke-glazed.

"Urgh," Hill said in frustration. "If I'd remembered earlier, but she told me just before the Hounds and I forgot. Fuck."

Davy dropped the phone back into the drawer, bumped it shut with his hip, and headed over to the couch. He leaned on it, the cushion still sweaty and warm from his ass, and dragged Fraser's duffel out.

"It's Christmas," he said as he pulled the bundle of cash out and flashed it at Hill. "I assume everywhere still stays open late. We can buy a new one. I need to get a costume for tomorrow's party anyhow."

Chapter Fifteen

Dec 23, 8pm

"You never did tell me how you pulled the costume party off," Hill said. He poked the bag at Davy's feet with his toe. It didn't crinkle with the contact.

Opposite him, Davy swore under his breath as he pried at the melted casing of the burner phone with his thumbnails. The tip of his tongue was caught between his teeth as he worked at it. His scowl was in direct contrast to the piped-in Christmas music on repeat through the mall's speakers.

"It was easy," Davy said. "I just told your mom it would make me happy. Happy brother-in-law, happy Christmas blow-out. Right?"

His tentacles snuck up onto the table, over the arms of the chair, and poked at the phone. Or tried to. Davy made an annoyed noise under his breath as they blocked his view. He shooed them back off the table.

They slunk back down. Hill could feel them sullenly coiled under the table, loops of heavy undead flesh draped over his shoes. He tried not to think about what they had, recently enough that he could still feel the ache of it, done to him.

It had been...

He wasn't ready to think about that, actually. So he frowned at Davy instead.

"You didn't tell her..."

Davy looked up long enough to give Hill a deadpan stare. "You really think if I told her..." He paused, glanced at the couple at a nearby table, and reached up to push the earbud more securely into place. "Told her the truth, her reaction would be to throw me a party? No, I didn't. She just thinks the therapist you've been seeing about feeling suicidal suggested it."

It took a second for Hill to recover from that one. He finally pulled himself together enough to shut his mouth and scrubbed his hands over his face. It was his own fault, he supposed. He should have just thought about the tentacle sex.

"The Per Se," he said. "It's just around the corner from where I ran into you, isn't it? My mom took you—me—to brunch?"

"She seems nice," Davy said. "Fraser was punching up."

He finally popped the back of the phone off. The already damaged plastic cracked in half as it came apart. Davy swept it off the table into the bag at his feet and pried the SIM card out. He turned the narrow wafer of plastic and circuitry over on his fingertip as he checked for obvious damage.

Hill stifled the urge to strangle him and twisted his fingers in the cuffs of a hoodie he'd found hanging in the Beyond's version of his wardrobe.

"That's what Dad always said, too," Hill said. "Everyone did, but Mom...Mom always said she was lucky to have him."

Davy paused halfway through slipping the card into the new phone. He gave the cafe's plate glass window a wary look and then cocked a silently questioning brow at Hill.

"It's fine," Hill said. "I'm not going to...it takes more than just being sad."

Probably. He said that like he knew, and he really didn't. It was good enough for Davy, though, who finished installing the sim and depressed the power button with his thumb. While he waited for the phone to run through its start-up, he took a drink of coffee.

Hill reached over the table without thinking to turn the phone so he could see the screen. The display flickered as his fingers grazed over—and a little through—the glass, but that was it. Hill made a frustrated sound in the back of his throat and curled his fingers into a fist. The table rattled under them. Davy cursed as he spilled the coffee he'd just set down. The eavesdroppers next to them put their hands on the cutlery and looked around.

"Like being useless," Hill said. He held up both hands in surrender and slumped back in the chair as he tried to feel nothing. "That will do it too, I guess."

Davy waited to make sure there weren't going to be any aftershocks. Then he grabbed a napkin to sop up the puddle of coffee on the tabletop.

"Don't get too attached to that idea," he said. "I've got plans, once we finish here, that depend on your being useful."

Hill straightened up in the chair. "Really?" he said. Despite it being what he wanted, nerves almost immediately set in. He cleared his throat. "Are you sure? Is it safe from the Hounds?"

"It should be," he said as he tapped at the keyboard with both thumbs. He typed like he was his actual age. "As long as we move fast. What was the name of the restaurant? Delicious?"

"Deli-licious," Hill corrected him. He got up, stepped over the loosely coiled tentacles, and moved to look over Davy's shoulder. "Hen said that Fraser had a real grudge against the owner. She thought he'd had them shut down. I suppose they're lucky he didn't have them killed."

Davy shook his head absently. "No," he said. "Getting them shut down is on brand. Fraser didn't like killing people. He can't keep making things worse for the dead."

At the table next to them, the man snorted out a laugh and muttered, "Like your sister" to the woman opposite him. She glared at him and took a resentful bite of her croissant, crumbs scattered in front of her.

The search results finished loading on the phone. A vintage Facebook page, a defunct Tripadvisor entry, a handful of food reviews, and a food blogger's reaction to the closure. Davy flicked down, back up, and then tapped the image tab with the side of his finger.

A man grinned, arms crossed over his compulsory artisanal black canvas and leather apron, from in front of the Delilicious. He had short red hair, a birthmark on his jaw, and a wedding ring that glinted gold from one finger.

"I know him," Davy said. He snapped his fingers as he tried to pull something up out of memory. "Trevor? Thomas? Something with a T."

Hill gave him a sour look. "You remember the guy who made your bagels, but not my dad?"

"I thought we'd agreed that was the Company's fault," Davy said. He tapped one of the images and bounced his heel impatiently as he waited for the information to load. "And I didn't know he had a deli, I was just fucking him."

At the table next to them, the woman sniffed over her croissant. "Now that sounds like *your* sister."

They glared at each other. Hill felt briefly guilty at being the unheard cause of contention, but then got distracted as Greg Tannenbaum—and yes, he was a bit smug that Davy had been so wrong about the name—appeared on the phone.

"I...um...didn't expect that," Hill said. "Was it serious?"

Davy glanced up at him, raised an eyebrow, and then went back to the phone.

"You've met me," he said. "What do you think?"

Hill braced himself for that to sting worse than finding out Davy used to have a thing for a guy that would call his restaurant "Delilicious." After all, it wasn't like Hill had thought Davy was a virgin. If he dismissed someone he'd actually been with like that, though, what did it mean for some sad little orphan he couldn't even touch?

It should have hit Hill in every nerdy, neurodivergent, never-fitting-in insecurity he'd built up over the years. Except...

You don't need to miss me.

Because Hill had met the man, and that was up there with "I know" on the declaration of feelings by the emotionally incompetent scale.

Whatever the force that approved or denied opening the Veil had expected this to be? It wasn't nothing. Probably a tragedy, and definitely time-limited, but it was still more of Davy than Greg Tannenbaum had gotten.

Hill leaned on Davy's shoulder—well, on a handily placed tentacle in the same general area—and squinted at the screen.

"I *meant,* was there any reason for Fraser to think he mattered?" he said. The tentacle he was leaning on curled up his arm and along his shoulder. It idly caressed his jaw as he talked. "That you'd have told him something? Or he saw something?"

Davy snorted. "I'd be fucking offended if he did," he said. "It wasn't like we were dating. We just fucked sometimes."

He paused and glanced over at the eavesdroppers next to him. "Now you either commit to the fight and bring up someone's mother, or get the fuck up and go pay your bill."

The man bristled. His partner had the good sense to think better of it and grabbed his arm. A quick glare and a tug at his sleeve gave him enough time to decide she was right. They got up in a huff and stalked off.

Davy stared flatly after them to make sure no one had second thoughts. Then he went back to flicking through web entries on Greg while he picked up his phone. Hill glanced at him and then after the cowed couple.

It was times like this that made it hard to remember that, to the rest of the world, that was Hill. *He* could see Davy's lean body and heavy, brutally handsome face. All they saw was Hill...a man who'd never successfully intimidated anyone unless it was over the Erie doctrine.

Apparently, the spirit did make the man.

"Maybe Fraser was jealous," Hill said.

"Of Greg?" Davy said skeptically. "I doubt it. Fraser didn't bother with his dick much, but when he did, it liked smarts and pussy."

Oh.

OK, there was the horrific price that Hill had to pay for violating the natural order. Those words were not going away.

While Hill swallowed bile, Davy frowned over the phone. Then he made a rude noise and swiped the screen closed. "There's something there. You were right about that," he said. "The man's house burned down. That's a bit too much bad luck to be natural. But we've only got a day left, so there's no time to dig into it. I'll see if I can get Gallagher on the job."

"You told her you only wanted one thing," Hill said.

"I lied," Davy said. He drained his coffee cup, head tilted back and throat working, and grabbed his bag as he stood up. It got slung over his shoulder, whatever costume was inside straining the plastic handles. "I do that. You should try it. In fact, why not start now?"

He smirked and headed off across the forecourt. Hill tried to hesitate, but the tentacle already had hold of him, so he just got hauled along for the ride.

Hill paused on the street and stared at the flat facade of his stepfather's brownstone.

It had been a few years since he'd last been here, so he'd not noticed before, but... The house his stepfather lived in wasn't that different from the one his brother had been buried under. It was in better repair and was in a better neighborhood; the bus driver hadn't hesitated to let Davy disembark at the nearest stop.

Still a strange coincidence.

"Is your mom going to be here?" Davy asked. He snapped a pair of blue gloves over his hands and forced the circuit box on the side of the building open. As he looked at the breakers inside, he made a pleased noise in the back of his throat. "I love old buildings."

"No," Hill said. "Mom moved to the lake house full-time during Covid...I mean, you missed it, but there was—"

Davy cut him off. "We didn't get to work from home," he said. "But trust me, the dead don't miss a pandemic."

That made sense. Hill hunched his shoulders and shoved his hands into the pockets of his hoodie. The card that Seb from the Company had given him jabbed up under his thumbnail on one hand, and he barked his knuckles on the sharp eye sockets of the bird skull Hen had given him.

He'd forgotten about those. It was lucky they'd not fallen out when he was—

Hill glanced at the tentacles. They were currently hackled up as they tossed the makeshift shelter of the unmuzzled spirit that had been squatting back there. He—she?—had made themselves scarce without needing to be told when they'd seen Hill. The tentacles had unearthed a sickle-bladed knife from the bedding, which they passed between themselves, while two others pulled out a mildewed book and hung it up by one corner.

Well, earlier.

"Yeah," Hill said as he tried to get back on track. "Anyhow, she lives out there full-time now. Fraser stays here during the week and goes to visit on weekends. He'll be here. He's usually alone."

"Good," Davy said and flicked the breakers.

If Hill had been asked, he'd have said the building had already been in darkness. He'd just edited out all the little power lights and chargers and the faint glow from a TV left on standby. Hill hadn't realized the cumulative glow they generated. When they all cut out at once, the shift to *absolute* darkness was noticeable.

"Are you going to tell me the plan?" Hill asked.

Davy straightened up, stripped his gloves off, and stuck them in his pocket. He wiped his nose on the back of his hand and looked up at the second floor of the building.

"I think it's time that my brother gets a visit from your dad," he said. "And since we've had no luck tracking him down..."

He trailed off. A tentacle pulled Hill's hood up over his head and tugged it down until it nearly touched his nose.

"But he can't see me," Hill said. "None of the living can."

The tentacle pushed the hood back again, enough so that Davy could meet his eyes. "They can't see spirits," he said. "They can see polts...some of the time."

Hill couldn't even pretend to be shocked. He tried, but he didn't even fool himself. The minute he'd broken that table, Davy had started to work up to this.

"I don't...I can't control it," Hill said. "I could hurt someone. I could knock down another building. I could hurt *you*."

Davy cupped the side of his face in a tentacle. The tension in Hill's stomach untwisted, just a little, as he turned his face into the caress.

"Don't flatter yourself."

"Asshole."

The tentacle gave the end of Hill's nose a tweak. "See?" Davy said. "You do know me. And we don't need you to unleash the full experience, just...crack the door for Fraser. Let him get a glimpse under the curtain. Like at the cafe. Or when I made you come."

A tentacle grazed suggestively along the small of Hill's back. It dipped down under the waistband of his jeans and delved briefly into his crack. He reached back and pulled it out.

"What if I lose control?"

Davy thought about that for a moment as he used his tentacles to zip up the hoodie.

"Try not to, but if you do—" He put two tentacles on Hill's shoulders and turned him around. "Face away from me."

Power cut or not, Hill knew the brownstone had a backup security system. In the living world. In the Beyond, once he got away from Davy's grounding presence, it was a tenement with stories stacked up until it needed to lean against the building next to it for support. A woman with a short seed-cracking beak and overalls with a name embroidered on them gave him an annoyed look as she pushed by him in the hall.

"Sorry," Hill muttered as he shuffled to the side.

"Wet dead," she said, like it was a slur. At the door, she paused, sighed, and looked back at him. "You know anyone? Family? Friends? Ex who died in a horrible car accident?"

Hill shuffled his feet on the cracked tiles. They were the same in the living world, although the colors were brighter from restoration and they were covered with an expensive rug his mom had picked out. She was never there, but she liked it to still remind Fraser of her.

"My dad," he said.

She raised her eyebrows at him, glanced at her bare wrist, and clacked her beak together. "And is your 'dad' in the building?" she asked.

"I'm looking for him," Hill said.

He didn't think it was that convincing. It was good enough for a dead woman with places to be. She visibly marked off her brief concern for him as "resolved" and let herself out.

"Don't leave any doors open," she said and slammed the door behind her.

Hill rubbed his chest.

"It's the walls you should be worried about," he muttered and poked at the hollow in his chest.

It did nothing.

If Hill felt anything about this—the childhood home his dad's killer had made for him—he couldn't get to it. Habit, practice, the shape of his neurodivergence? He didn't know which to blame or how to get around it.

Except that was a lie. He might be able to bury—or not be able to *un*bury—his feelings, but he'd never had much luck ignoring logic. Nearly every time he'd used his *polt* abilities had been triggered by a taste of the living world.

He slid his hand into his pocket. The cookie he'd taken from Seb's office was crumbs in a greasy napkin at this point. He pulled it out and tipped its debris into his palm. A few chunks of chocolate and smears of cream fell between his fingers and bounced off the floor. The taste of it, when he licked his palm, was sweetness undercut by the stale texture of the cookie and a burst of breathless, uncomplicated joy that was so pure it nearly gave Hill a headache.

A kid, he realized, *happy with her cookie and the taste of her own socks as she pulled one canary-yellow foot up to her mouth. The nappy, dry texture of the wool on her gums and...*

It had just happened every other time. This time, Hill clung to the feeling and used it like a lodestone to find something similar in him.

It was socks. That was...vaguely embarrassing in a way Hill couldn't explain. The memory still felt painfully fresh, almost raw.

It had been a month after his dad's death that Fraser spent the night for the first time. He'd slept on the couch, his bare feet in expensive socks the first thing that Hill saw when he came downstairs in the morning. At the time, he'd not thought anything of it, other than being glad to see his uncle.

Later...

Now...

When had Fraser first looked at his mom and thought, "She's smart and she's got—"

The walls either side of Hill cracked. Plaster dust splattered the floor underfoot as the tiles cracked and crunched to powder. He flinched back as the world shattered white, and he saw the still-familiar hall of the brownstone, dimly lit by the light of the moon through the uncurtained front windows. Frost spread over the pictures hung on the wall, cracking the glass and blistering the ink that chronicled Fraser's perfectly acceptable life and family. The antique Tiffany light fitting—another addition of his mom's—swung violently from side to side.

Hill reached up without thinking to try and steady it. If it broke, his mom would be devastated. She'd gotten it at some Virginia swap meet and— The glass clipped through his fingers and *popped.* The spray of glass studded the blandly cream wall with fragments of color.

That hurt *too* much. Maybe it had been throwing in that little bit of disgust at the end.

He shouldn't have brought his mom into it. It wasn't like he didn't know that he couldn't cope with thinking honestly about that.

He *never* thought honestly about that.

Hill didn't think he could put it back into the bottle now, though.

The stairs creaked as he climbed them. The varnish on the banister bubbled, and the spindles cracked, top to bottom. Under his feet, the fabric of the carpet frayed and stained.

Face it that way, Davy reminded him in memory.

He was downstairs, in Fraser's office next to the kitchen, as he looked for anything they could use. Hill just had to trust that Davy wouldn't get him arrested—again—and not look that way.

Hill got to the top of the stairs and headed toward the master bedroom. The closed door stymied him for a second, until he remembered trying it once.

The handle rattled but didn't open. Hill gave it a shove and, on the other side of it, heard his mom giggle.

"Give me a second," she said, breathless, and then muttering something he'd not caught to someone else. "I needed a nap."

Hill flinched away from the memory like it stung him. The *white* that bleached out the world made his eyes hurt.

Couldn't he just stick to *sad*, he thought irritably? Did he have to go for psycho-sexual trauma on top of it?

It did work, though.

The handle of the door was crumpled, a child's fingerprints crushed into the metal, and it swung open.

Fraser still liked expensive socks.

His stepdad lay on top of the bed, still dressed and with paperwork stacked on the bed next to him. He was already awake, and he squinted at the door as he sat up.

"Trudy?" he said.

There had been a plan, the rough outline of a script. It hadn't been as detailed as Hill would have liked, given the short notice Davy had given him, but he'd done his best. The problem was that when he'd come up with it, he'd not factored in the gutful of despair and grief.

"He was your friend," he blurted out instead. "She was your friend's wife. I was his son!"

The papers were blown off the bed, and Fraser was forced back against the pillows. He cringed back and threw his hand up in front of his face.

"How do you do it?" Hill demanded. "Just get up and kiss your friend's wife and say goodbye to your friend's son and go to work at your brother's company? When it's your fault!"

The headboard of the bed cracked in half. Fraser rolled onto his side and grabbed for the drawer. He yanked it open and pulled out a gun.

It shouldn't have been—Hill knew who Fraser was and what he'd done before—but it was still strange somehow to see him hold the gun like he knew how to use it.

"Everything you have is built on death," Hill spat. "You put the people who love you in the dirt and take what they had. Now you have to pay. You *have* to, that's how it works. That's what makes things right."

Fraser swung the gun up. His finger hovered on the trigger as he squinted at whatever he could make out of Hill, through the Veil and the black hoodie.

"Mark?" he said. "Is that you?"

"You killed my dad!" Hill screamed.

The windows shattered, and the alarm went off.

"What was I supposed to do?" Fraser yelled. He scrambled up onto his knees and lowered the gun. "You went dark, and I didn't know why. Was it him? I ruined him., Every fucking night, I ruined him. Isn't that enough? What else do you want?"

He didn't know.

It was too ridiculous to even despair over. All that anger and grief just ran out of Hill like someone had opened a tap in his gut. The living world faded away, his last glimpse of it Fraser throwing his gun at the wall in frustration, and he sank to the ground in the wreckage of someone's studio apartment, among the broken furniture and torn-up clothes.

Everything he'd done, all the sacrifices he'd made, literal and figurative, and whatever the Invocation would cost him in the long run?

Fraser thought it was all for someone else.

For everything Hill had done, it looked like death wasn't so different from life. It didn't matter how hard he tried to be seen, to fit in, to prove his worth. No one saw him. Not really. Not the *him* that was under the skin and the diagnosis.

Hill buried his head in his hands and laughed at the absurdity of that until he cried.

He might have just cried; there was no one there to confirm that, though.

Chapter Sixteen

Dec 23, 11.10pm

DAVY BRACED HIMSELF AGAINST the wall as a crash made the glass rattle in the windows.

He glanced at the ceiling, cracks spiderwebbed through the expensive plasterwork, and then checked the time on his phone. He ran a few timings through in his head on how long it would take the Hounds to get there.

They still had time.

Just about.

Probably.

It would be different if it were just dead-on-dead crime. He could estimate to the minute by neighborhood how long it would take the

Hounds to show their snouts. Polt activity always involved the living, though, and that would light a fire under their hairy asses.

Davy grabbed a handful of sweets from the stash in the drawer. He unwrapped a blue Jolly Rancher, popped the candy onto his tongue, and crinkled the cellophane wrapper into a ball between his fingers. The sugary pop of flavor on his tongue was almost sickly. He tucked it into his cheek as he flicked through the handful of irritably scrawled Post-its on the desk.

By the time he picked up the phone, he had sucked the candy down to a sliver. He cracked it between his teeth as he navigated his way through the menu to the call log.

He didn't know most of the numbers.

There were a handful of missed calls to Gallagher. It looked like she'd decided to keep her distance from whatever was going down. Smart. She'd always been a canny operator. There were also two to Davy's old number, so some of the breadcrumbs he'd dropped had gotten back to Fraser.

Shame the Invocation didn't give him more time. He could have gone back to his grave and dug up his old phone. It was probably still in his pocket. He'd been on his way to the club before—

Davy paused as he caught the tail end of that thought as it breezed through his head.

Had he been? His memory of the night was blurred with trauma and the gap between the memory being recorded and it being mapped over onto his spirit. The few he had of those last few years were snapshots at random, filed away in no particular order.

You didn't have to do this...

That one he assumed came from just before he died, but he hadn't been on his way to the club. The door had been... Davy flexed his fingers as he tried to scrape any more details from the memory. It had been a front door, slick green paint under his fingers. Not his door. Not Fraser's.

He'd never been to Greg's house, but there'd been a Mrs. Tannenbaum, apparently. So it seemed unlikely they'd hook up there. It felt domestic too. Davy would have run a mile from "domestic" back then.

Not now, though? He snorted at himself, but let that go. There wasn't time to chase it down.

He redialed a handful of the numbers at random and got mostly voicemails. The accountant, his wife, and an actual person who answered with the angry retort, "He's not here! I told you. I'll call the police!" Davy assumed the accountants' in-laws. There was also the Truisi Waste Management company, a few states over, and an Irish pub with a vaguely familiar name.

Davy hadn't had a chance to stir things with the IRA, but maybe Fraser wanted to make sure there weren't going to be any surprises on Christmas morning.

A nagging sense of seconds passing made him check the time again. He grimaced as he realized how badly he lost track of it. Whatever haunting Hill had planned needed to wrap itself up.

But first, Davy had one more card to play to throw Fraser off balance.

He reached into his pocket and pulled out a folded photo. The only photo that Hill had of his dad. Davy stared for a moment at Albie's face as he tried to dredge up some shred of memory about him. He drew a blank.

"When I'm dead again," Davy muttered as he started to slide the photo into the desk drawer, "I'm going to work out how you managed to do that."

He thought better of it at the last moment and pulled the photo back out. Sentiment had never been his vice, but the photo mattered to

Hill. It was all he had left, and Davy realized that's not how he wanted Hill to remember him.

Davy put the photo back in his pocket and then nudged the office chair into place with his foot. He grabbed another candy from the stash and shoved the drawer shut with his knee. As he turned to go, the raw sound of the security alarm cut through the dark silence of the house.

Time to go. He might be fairly confident about how quickly the Hounds would get here, but he was 100 percent certain that Fraser paid for a prompt response. Davy tucked the candy in his pocket and headed out.

He met Hill in the hall as he came down the stairs at a run.

"How did it go?" Davy asked.

Hill grimaced and rubbed his hand over his face. "I scared him," he said. "But he's—"

Before he could finish, Fraser appeared at the top of the stairs. His eyes passed right through Hill and landed on Davy. Between the darkness and Davy's black clothes, it didn't look like Fraser recognized him.

That came with its own problems, of course.

"Who the fuck are you?" Fraser asked as he raised his gun.

Fuck. Davy bolted for the door. A bullet hissed by his ear and chipped a chunk of the door jamb. Splinters caught the side of Davy's face as he half-fell, half-jumped down the stairs. Habit made him throw out a tentacle to catch himself with. It didn't work, and he fell down the last two steps. He skinned his knees on the pavement, cursed under his breath, and scrambled back to his feet.

Behind him, Fraser threw his front door open. He wasn't the only one. As doors opened and witnesses appeared along the street, he grimaced and tucked his gun behind his leg. Davy cut over the road, vaulted a fence, and dodged the side of a house—ignoring the startled protest from the owner—to cut through the back yard.

A dog bolted up out of its sleep to snarl groggily at him as he ran past. It would have been more threatening if it weren't for the festive red velvet and gold bells collar that jangled around its neck. Before it could do more than grumble at him, Davy hauled himself up onto the roof of the kennel and over the fence.

As he dropped down on the other side, knees bent to absorb the impact, he slowed to a walk. A quick yank unzipped his hoodie and stripped it off. He lifted the lid of a bin as he passed and tossed it in on top of bags of rubbish and a chicken carcass.

He'd dropped back to a relaxed saunter as he stepped out onto the road. No one headed to see what was going on around the corner bothered to give him a second look.

The few hours sleep that Davy had grabbed should have been more than enough, but apparently Hill's body expected more from his shut-eye. Davy sat in the pew and tried to keep from yawning too widely as the sermon dragged on.

" For as John says in his gospel, 'light (that) shines in the darkness, and the darkness overcomes it not,'" the tall, stocky priest said from the pulpit. He shuffled through his notes to check something, and then shuffled back to the place he'd marked with his finger. "That is the message and measure we should take from the solstice..."

Davy sat on the hard wooden bench next to his murderer and the boy whose body he'd stolen's mother and tried to look like he was paying attention. His tentacles, uncomfortable on hallowed ground, squirmed sheepishly around his feet as they tried to stay out of sight. He tried to discreetly check the time to see how much longer this was likely to last.

Fraser reached over and put a hand on Davy's forearm to push it down. He tugged Hill's sleeve down over the watch. It took everything Davy had not to react by slapping his baby brother across the back of the head.

"Pay attention," Fraser murmured to him. "You might learn something."

Davy glanced sidelong at him. He couldn't really picture how Hill, who hated his stepfather and yet wanted to redeem him, would interact with Fraser. He could have looked to Hill for answers, but Hill had shied away from the family pew and lingered at the back of the Church.

"Like what?" he went with.

"That's up to you, isn't it," Fraser said mildly. He picked up the hymn sheet and flicked idly through the cheaply printed pages. It was Trudy's turn to take that off him and tuck it under her leg for safekeeping.

Davy smirked to himself as he leaned back against the hardwood pew and folded his arms.

It looked like they were *both* going to be paying attention to the rest of the sermon.

It would have been useful if Hill had been a smoker. Since he wasn't, Davy pretended to be occupied with the gravestones. He stood, hands in pockets, on the narrow path and studied the names etched on the snow-topped granite.

"I thought he might at least have a sleepless night," Hill said bitterly. He leaned on Marie De Luca's memorial, hands loosely crossed, and watched his family over Davy's shoulder. "Do you think he gets visited by the spirit of his wronged dead every year?"

Davy shook his head. "He'd have moved the breakables," he said. "Besides, you're wrong. He's off balance."

"Really?" Hill asked. "He looks like it's business as usual."

Davy turned to look. In fairness, Fraser didn't look like he was under spiritual—and financial—attack. He stood, his arm around his wife's waist, as he spoke to the priest and a few of the other well-heeled parishioners.

"He was fidgeting," Davy said. "He only fidgets when he's pissed off."

Hill snorted. "Yeah, well, he's pissed off at the wrong person," he said. "I hope Mark appreciates us doing his haunting for him."

That part actually wasn't ideal. "We could still work with it if we knew who Mark was," Davy said.

"And we could work with Tannenbaum if we knew what he'd done," Hill pointed out. "But we don't have time to find out."

True.

"It's not like we can ask for an extension," Davy pointed out. "We'll just have to hope that Mark would have wanted Fraser to better himself, too. Come on."

He offered Hill a tentacle.

Hill glared at it for a second and then grabbed it as he stepped over the low wall around the grave.

"What happens if we fail?" he asked. "If we don't get through to Fraser by tomorrow."

Nothing good.

Davy supposed he should lie about that, but it would hardly be convincing. Hill had seen enough of the Beyond to know that Death wasn't a forgiving place.

"Whatever it is," Davy said as he curled a tentacle around Hill's waist, "the last thing you'll hear before it happens is that you should have just let me kill him."

"I don't know," Trudy fussed as she picked at the edges of the gauze dressing on Davy's hand. "Maybe you should see a doctor."

Davy took his hand back. "It's just an allergic reaction," he said. "It'll be cleared up by New Year's."

That was very probably the truth, one way or another.

"He probably caught something, lurking around old churches," Fraser said as he stepped away from his tense conversation with the police and joined them. "There's a reason they close the gates at night."

Trudy glanced at him and then at Davy. A pale eyebrow lifted interrogatively.

"Is anyone going to normalize giving context?" she asked. "Or is this a boy's club only?"

It would, Davy thought as he glanced sidelong at Hill, help.

Hill leaned in to murmur in his ear, which wasn't necessary, but Davy enjoyed it, so he didn't point that out.

"I was at St Januarius last night," he said quietly. "It's where Dad is buried. I wanted him to think that's who I wanted to use the Invocation for."

"I take it someone saw me?" Davy asked.

"Saw you where?" Trudy poked for an answer.

"I went to see Dad," Davy said. It rarely bothered him to lie, but that felt weird on his tongue. He had to fight the urge to look apologetically at Hill. "I wasn't going to...I didn't expect to get in. It just felt bad not to try."

Trudy sighed and gave Davy a look that was more disappointment than anger.

"Again?" she said. "Oh, Hill."

"I can understand that," Fraser said. "But you should take Father Thomas' advice. You don't want to see your dad like that."

He sounded genuinely grim. Davy wondered what he thought he'd seen last night when Hill had confronted him. Before he could try and pry, Fraser's phone rang in his pocket. He fished it out, glanced at the screen, and pulled an apologetic face at Trudy.

"I need to take this," he said. "I'll see you at the car."

He turned and walked away through the gravestones. Snow crunched under his expensive loafers as he took a shortcut off the main path.

Trudy watched him walk away and then turned back to Davy. "I should go with him," she said. "Something is bothering him, and that's when he fires people. I'm still going to see you tonight?"

"I have a costume and everything," Davy confirmed.

She nodded and left, picking her way precariously through the snow in heels. When she caught up with Fraser, they exchanged a few words, and then he turned to come back over to them.

"I'll send a car to fetch you tonight," he said and held up his hand. "No arguing. There's been some unexpected tensions with some of our business associates. It's best to play it safe for a couple of days. Understood?"

The last thing Davy wanted to do was lie. The Dudley bus system could have been worse, but it also could have been a motorbike. He knew which he'd prefer. Unfortunately, that was Davy, and he could, out of the corner of his eye, see Hill bristling at the offer.

"I don't mind taking the bus," he lied.

"I mind," Fraser said. "Just take the car. I don't want to worry your mother."

Hill was still gesturing no, but Davy had made his pro forma protest. That would have to do.

"Fine," he said. "But that's your birthday present."

Fraser looked amused and satisfied. Before he could go, Davy stepped forward and looked at him intently.

"Is there anyone you'd want to talk to?" he asked. "With the Invocation?"

Fraser gave a startled, not very amused chuckle at the question.

"If you'd asked me last week..." he muttered, then shook himself. "No. Nobody. The dead should stay dead. It's kinder. On them and on us."

He shoved his hands in the pockets of his overcoat and hunched his shoulders up towards his ears. The expression on his face was troubled as he turned and stomped back over to Trudy.

"You were right," Hill said. "It looks like Mark, whoever he is, struck a nerve."

Davy hung his fancy dress costume in its garment bag on a hanger and hooked it over the top of the wardrobe door. He had just turned away to go into the bathroom when his phone rang.

There were only a few people it could be. Davy picked the phone up and waited in silence to find out which of them it was.

"If Davy's really back?" Gallagher said after a moment. "Tell him to fuck off. I've sent you what I could find on Tannenbaum, and that's it. We're square now. No more debt."

"And the new ID?"

"With the courier," Gallagher said. "They're on schedule to deliver tonight, at the party, like you asked. I had to use some age progression software on the photo I had of him. Hope he doesn't mind, but I made him bald."

She hung up.

Davy reached up with a tentacle to touch his hair. Although he supposed it was *Hill's* hair, so he couldn't claim any of it officially. Not that he'd needed to. He'd died with a full head of hair, so that wasn't going to change now.

Besides, he shared at least 50 percent of his genetics with Fraser, and Fraser had a good head of hair.

While Davy struggled with his unexpected insecurity about his hair, he opened his email program and waited. It had already been sent, according to Gallagher, but it was only when he opened the app that the email appeared at the top of the list. No tone. No notifications. It just arrived.

He opened it and flicked down and across, sliding the unresponsive PDF back and forth on the small screen to get all the details. It was a thorough report—Gallagher had her pride—but Davy just skimmed it.

All he really needed was the Cliff Notes version, and Gallagher delivered. The highlights of Tannenbaum's last thirty years popped off the page for him.

Debt.

Bankruptcy.

Insurance fraud.

Divorce. Two of those.

His house was foreclosed on. His parents' house burned down.

He was on the no-fly list.

Hell, apparently he'd been the victim of a home invasion in the early hours of this morning. He was going to spend Christmas in a hospital.

It was a lot of misfortune for one man, but the sticking point was that Tannenbaum didn't seem worth all that effort. He was politically moderate, socially neutral, and he drove at the speed limit. There was nothing about him that seemed like the trigger for a decades-long harassment campaign.

Fraser had been called a sociopath before—as had Davy, although that hadn't been in a therapeutic environment—but he wouldn't spend resources on something like this without a reason.

He didn't have a green front door. Davy checked. It had been red.

His tentacles had been draped around the room while he read: draped over the back of a loveseat, slung bonelessly over the handle of the bathroom door, curled up on the bed like a cat. They suddenly stirred and picked themselves up.

Davy turned as Hill walked into the room. He looked...tired? He did, but that wasn't it exactly. It took a second, but Davy remembered the word his mom had always used for people she didn't care for.

Drawn.

He looked drawn, like someone had just sketched him in. Last night had drained his eyes to a dull greenish gray and left shadows at his temples and collarbones. Or maybe that was just the Invocation, a supernatural reaction to being somehow *wrong*.

"You look like shit," Davy said.

"Thanks." Hill reached out and stroked one of the tentacles absently. The brush of his fingers against it still mapped straight to Davy's cock. It seemed crass to bring it up right now, though. He shifted his weight awkwardly instead. Before he could think of something to say, Hill spoke up. "I'm sorry."

"For what?" Davy asked.

Hill gave a humorless little laugh. He reached up and stuck his finger in his ear, wriggling it briefly.

"For whatever is going to happen if Fraser doesn't redeem himself," he said. "You were right. I should have just let you kill him."

"I know."

This time Hill's snort of laughter was genuine, and hard enough to make his eyes water.

Davy waited until he finished.

"I was definitely right," he said. "I want that on record, but...I'd rather you were. It's not the real world, but I like your world better. In your world, *I'm* better somehow."

Hill sniffed and wiped his eyes with the heel of his hand. "But you still wish I'd just let you kill Fraser?"

"*So* much," Davy said. He put a companionable tentacle around Hill's shoulder. "But you didn't, so we've got to convince Fraser to make right a lifetime of wrongs with a masquerade ball and a spirit with a mistaken identity."

"By midnight."

Davy checked the clock. "Five hours," he said.

"You really think we can do it?" Hill asked dubiously.

"No," Davy admitted. "But if all else fails, I'm just going to kill him and hope for the best."

The rite clamped down on his jaw in punishment for that blithe threat. It felt like prongs being driven down into his jawbone, like how he'd always imagined muzzling to feel. But it made Hill laugh again, so he'd bear it.

Chapter Seventeen

Dec 24, 8.10pm

HILL HADN'T EXPECTED A party on his side of the Veil, but there was one. The dead thronged among the living around the lake house, decked out in clothes that ranged from Prada to…whoever a famous Gilded Age designer was. Butt cracks and bustles were on equal footing.

All of them were muzzled.

Dogs and birds. Cats and rats. One woman in a dress that was just two translucent plastic hands that covered her boobs and her bits, and who had an insect's flat green mandibles instead of a mouth. As he watched, a frilled proboscis flicked out to lap at her drink.

Even the servers who dodged in and out, between the living and the dead, had short finch-like beaks.

In the middle of it all, Hill felt oddly self-conscious about his lips and teeth. He tucked his chin down and pulled the zipper of his hoodie up.

"Is the lake house on an old burial ground or battlefield or something?" he asked Davy.

Davy stopped in the middle of the hallway as he puzzled over that question.

"How would I know?" Davy asked. "Why?"

"There's a lot of dead people here."

"There's a lot of dead people everywhere," Davy pointed out. "There's more of us than there are of you."

One of the staff hired for the party gave Davy a confused look. Whatever he thought of the man talking to himself, though, he didn't ask any questions. Or rather, only one.

"Can I take your coat?"

He could. Davy shrugged the heavy jacket off and handed it over. Under it...

Hill briefly forgot to be self-conscious about his chin as he gawped in confusion at the...toga. He supposed there was nothing wrong with that as a costume; he'd just expected something sexier. It was possible he should feel bad for that.

"You're a—"

Davy shook the costume out, grabbed part of it, and dragged it up over his head, giving the front of it a tug to get the eye holes in the right area. The folds fell into place as he gave his shoulders a quick shimmy.

"You're a ghost?" Hill course-corrected on the question.

Davy pulled the edges of the sheet back from his wrists. His tentacles squirmed out from under the folds, the material thin enough that they could pass through it without any problems.

"It seemed on brand," he said.

The man who'd just taken Davy's jacket just nodded. "I've only seen five," he said, damning it with faint praise.

He gave Davy a ticket for the coat and stepped away to hang it on the long rail that ran along in front of the staircase. Davy headed on into the party. He grabbed a glass of champagne from a passing server and moved through the crowd.

"Don't worry about the dead," he said. "Just think of them as another department, one that doesn't get out much. Just stay close to me."

He lashed a tentacle around Hill's wrist to make sure he did as they pushed through the dead and people *dressed* as the dead. It occurred to Hill to wonder if the dead might not care for that, but there was no point in asking Davy. He wasn't the sort to care what other people cared about...except maybe what Hill did. Which was...heady.

"Do you have any sort of plan?" Hill asked.

"Sort of," Davy said.

"Is it 'wing it and see what happens,' or are there actual steps?"

Davy freed his arm under the ghost-sheet to gulp his champagne. "Sort of."

Someone had queued up Bloodhound Gang on the sound system. It pulsed through the air as Davy quartered the party efficiently on a hunt for Fraser. No sign of him in the foyer or the main dining room. Someone had given Davy a strange look when he'd asked if they'd seen Fraser, but after the double-take had pointed him toward the kitchen.

When they got there, a frazzled member of staff had shooed them back out and directed them to the gardens.

Strung fairy lights hung from trees and decorated the rose bushes. They didn't provide much light, but enough to walk over the manicured lawn without breaking an ankle. Hill wished there'd been a little less light, as he caught a few unexpected glimpses of the dead trysting out here.

Hill could hardly judge, he supposed, but some of them made tentacles look quite tame. He was a little bit annoyed by that.

They found Fraser by the glowing light of the cigar he had just lit. He glanced at them through the cloud of blue-gray smoke that drifted from pursed lips.

"Don't tell your mother," he said.

Davy paused a beat and pulled the hem of the costume up over his head to drape his shoulders. He scrubbed a hand through his sweat-flattened hair.

"How did you know it was me?"

"I've known you since you were a toddler," Fraser said. "And I recognize your shoes."

Davy looked down at his damp Converse. He wriggled his toes.

"Fair play."

Fraser laughed. He took a puff of the cigar and tapped ash onto the grass.

"You got that from me, you know," he said. "I've not been much of a stepdad, but I guess there's that."

Davy hesitated at that opening. He scratched his lower lip with his thumbnail and glanced sidelong at Hill. All Hill could do in reply was shrug in confusion. It was, he supposed, the sort of self-reflection they wanted. He had just thought the various war crimes and a few murders would have been where the doubts set in.

"I guess it wasn't something you set out to be," Davy said. "I mean, who does?"

"Perverts."

That got another quick check-in glance with Hill. Davy raised his eyebrows in a "Well?" expression. When it dawned on Hill what he was asking, he shook his head in a violent no. Fraser had been...

He'd never been a bad stepdad, Hill supposed. Detached, reserved, and sometimes disinterested, but Hill realized that had been his best. It was better than some got. If Fraser hadn't killed his dad, Hill might even have been grateful.

"I appreciate you weren't," Davy said. "That would have sucked."

Fraser puffed smoke like a dragon when he laughed. "I guess there's that too, then," he said. "I never wanted kids or a wife, but...I can appreciate why people do. It's comfortable."

That wasn't the most passionate declaration in the world. Hill appreciated that. Out of the corner of his eye, he saw something pale flap in his direction. He looked over, and to his surprise saw Hen duck out from behind a tree, gesture emphatically at him, and then nip back out of sight again.

He hesitated. She poked her head out and looked at him expectantly. The chicken beak was missing—reminded, Hill felt for it in his pocket, ready to offer it up--replaced by a wooden mask of interlocked fingers. She gestured urgently for him to come over to her.

Hill took an uncertain step in her direction, and then another. A glance back over his shoulder showed that Davy hadn't even noticed he was gone yet. Emboldened by that, Hill covered the rest of the ground to where Hen was hidden.

"Hen," he said. "You're OK?"

She came in for a hug. Hill froze, his body at odd angles and his back hunched to compensate.

"Oh," he said. "That's what we're doing. Didn't realize."

She squeezed him tight, rubbed his back with both hands, and then leaned back. "I'm OK," she said. "You need to come with me."

Hill stepped back. She tried to cling to him, but he'd had a lifetime of extricating himself from over-affectionate people. He squirmed free.

"I can't," he said. "There's not much time left. I have to—"

"That's why I'm here," Hen said. "I found your father."

Hill froze. Figuratively, of course, but it didn't feel that way. The chill of the Beyond sank right down into his bones and made him feel stiff and slow. He opened his mouth to say something, and where his words had been there was just a hollow.

"You have to come with me." She tugged on his arm.

A second try and Hill found a few words. "Is he..."

What? OK? Albie Rosen was *dead*; that was the definition of not OK.

"He's here," Hen said. "But he can't be seen. You can't be seen. There's things we couldn't tell you before. Come on."

She grabbed his sleeve and dragged him with her. Hill dug his heels in for a minute, but the promise of being *right*—that people really had kept secrets from him—was hard to resist. He checked back on Davy, who was still making awkward conversation with Fraser, and then gave up and fell into step behind Hen.

Maybe Davy could talk Fraser into his redemption, Hill could find his dad, and things could all be set to rights by Christmas morning.

Everyone—his steps slowed without him meaning to, his feet dragging through the dull, dead grass of the Beyond—back where they belonged. That was it, wasn't it? The closest thing to a happy ending they could get.

"Come on," Hen urged him. "Hurry up. He can't wait to see you."

Hill did as he was told. They cut around the back of the house and headed toward the stables. They had never had horses. A donkey one year—he didn't remember why, or how—but no horses. They still kept the stables, because apparently, it improved the value of the property if they ever sold. As they got closer, Hill saw vague flickering lights at the small square windows.

"You said you didn't remember Dad," he said slowly as he watched the lights.

Hen clicked the fingers of her muzzle together as she looked around at him. Her eyes glittered in the moonlight.

"I lied," she said, smooth as icing. "I had to, because we couldn't tell anyone what was really going on."

She nodded in agreement with her own statement. It made Hill want to buy into it, even more than just his basic desire for this to be real.

"Tell me something about him," he asked.

"He's your dad," Hen said. She gave a little laugh at the silliness of the question.

Hill dug his heels into the grass. Her hand tightened on his arm, sharp nails pinching his skin.

"What color are his eyes?" he asked.

"Blue," she said immediately.

Hill thought she was wrong, but the confidence in her voice made him hesitate. His dad's eyes had been hazel. That was right. He was sure of that, but he didn't know if he actually remembered it or not.

There was one thing he definitely remembered, though. No matter how much he tried to forget.

The grass underfoot turned to the cobbles of the stable yard. Hill pulled his arm out of Hen's grip.

"Where were you that day?" he asked. "When he killed himself, where were you?"

She spun on her heel to glare at him.

"Do you want to see him or not?" she snapped. "It wasn't easy to make this happen, you know. It's only because you're special, and it still wasn't easy. Look what they did to me!"

Hen snatched the mask off her face. The skin had been peeled off before, to leave bare bone for the mask to catch on, but now it was scraped down to the bone. Tool marks scored over the white surface of her jaw and cheekbone.

"Where were you?" Hill insisted.

She heaved an aggravated sigh. "At work!" she said. "I had a job, didn't I?"

That sounded like a real question, not a rhetorical one. And she'd been dead a good year when Albie killed himself. She might have been at work, but it had been here. Not in the living world.

"Why?" he asked.

Hen stared at him, then turned and bolted for the stables. "He's here!" she yelled as she grabbed the doors and threw them open. "You can get him. I'm sorry I helped him before!"

The Hound shoved her out of the way. There was no malice in it, just impatience. It still bounced Hen off the wall. She slid down to sit on the ground, her arms folded over her head, as the rest of the Hunt followed the lead out.

Five of them, although one of them was dragged out on all fours, the bridle twisted around his head and gripped in another Hound's gauntleted hand.

"I'm sorry," Hen said into her knees.

She might have meant it for Hill or the Hounds. It was hard to tell.

"Me too," Hill said.

He turned on his heel and ran. Back the way he'd come at first, but when he got to where he'd left them, Davy was gone. Fraser was still there, his cigar smoked down to a stump, but he stared through Hill with those cold, heavy eyes.

Hill muttered a curse under his breath, changed direction, and ran back toward the house. He didn't have a plan. It might be OK. Davy always made that work.

He crashed through the kitchen doors shoulder-first and rolled over the floor. The staff, the living ones, stepped through or on him without noticing as they fed in and out of the party. It was only the dead, with serving trays of steaming roast things and pitchers of milky cocktails, that stepped over or around him.

Hill pushed himself back to his feet, hands slipping on the floor, and shoved his way through both toward the doors. He wasn't quick enough.

Someone behind him grabbed a handful of hair and yanked him back.

The dead servers cringed back against the wall, eyes wide and beaks agape with panic. The bright pink insides of their mouths seemed to pulse as they stared at the Hounds.

Dangled from one of the Hound's pawlike fists, Hill managed to stretch up onto his tiptoes to take his weight. He swiveled around to stare at the Hound, both hands raised to claw at the big gauntleted hand.

"Why?" he asked. "I've only got three hours left. Why can't you leave me be?"

To his surprise, the Hound actually looked sympathetic. Not enough to let him go, but his eyes looked soft, and the long jut of his muzzle was relaxed.

"Because it isn't right," the Hound chewed the words out. "The dead and the living don't mix. It opens doors."

Hill kicked at him. It didn't do much good. "Once it's Christmas Day, I'll be living again. I'll not have anything to do with the dead until I'm dead. I swear."

For the first time, the Hound curled its lip. Over the words, not the kick.

"You lie."

"No," Hill said. "I'm not. I won't."

"There's always someone," the Hound said. "There's never not *someone* you'd lie for."

It backhanded him. Hill's vision ran black at the impact; then he hit a table and crashed to the ground. He took a stack of plates and serving trays with him that landed with a clatter around him. Hill tried to get up. He thought he was doing a good job until he realized the Hound had dragged him by the collar.

"After a while," the Hound said as it handed him off to two other Hounds. They grabbed his arms and kept him on his feet, "You won't even mind."

They dragged him, ankles uncooperative, out of the kitchen.

Hill couldn't focus on despair or anything else through the rattle in his skull. He dangled from their grip as they marched through the party. The dead quailed back as they passed, hands up to cover beaks and maws and mouth parts in polite shock.

Just as Hill was about to give up, he saw his mom stride across the room, dodging around the living who got in her way. For a second,

Hill felt like a kid at school again, not sure if he was happy to see his mom ride to the rescue or humiliated.

Both, maybe.

"What are you *doing*?" Trudy demanded of a server. "I told you, the champagne is for the toast! Take it back."

Hill clung to the feeling with both hands. It might only be the memory of despair—and a kid's sharp, here today and gone tomorrow despair at that—but it was all he had. It wasn't enough. The world cracked around him—shattered white lines spreading out across the world—but before it could break completely, one of the Hounds grabbed him by the hair. A yank pulled his head back, throat pulled tight and exposed, and then a bridle was shoved in his mouth.

Nothing happened at first; then his skin turned to acid and his bones to liquid fat. He could feel skin and flesh peel away from his bones, absorbed by the mask as it grew new bone spurs to hook onto his skull. The teeth bit down into his tongue and...

It was like food. But inside the little boba pops of life he'd stolen from cookies or coffee or the taste of a tentacle on his tongue, this was death. Someone's death. The death of every tooth that gashed his tongue.

The painful, airless squeeze of his chest as he struggled for just one more breath of air that tasted of bleach and shit and other people's vomit.

Blood spread in a slow, glossy pool under it. He could see his face in it, the reflection blurred and dark, and the mess the bullet had made of his skull.

Water, bitter and chlorinated in his nose, as she sank under. Again. This time, she just let it happen and sank

...down

....down

The deaths drugged Hill and dragged him down into the cold, heavy grave with them. The Hound let him go with a shove and he slumped to the ground. That was what a dead man did, after all.

Chapter Eighteen

Dec 24, 9.10pm

DAVY HAD EXPECTED TO be angry when he came face to face with Fraser again.

Sure, he'd always expected to die young and, if he was honest, which wasn't like him, he'd probably deserved it. Not for whatever reason Fraser had for the murder, but in general. He'd not been a good man in life.

Or death, but there wasn't really any consequence for that. It seemed to be an advantage.

His little brother *had* still murdered him, though. That was the sort of thing that stirred up all sorts of things from the silt. Or that's what he'd thought anyhow.

Instead, maybe because he didn't remember the murder, Davy just watched Fraser avoid a good time like it was a job and felt...

OK, he couldn't put his finger on it exactly. It was one of the ones he wasn't good with, but it wasn't angry or vengeful.

Easy, maybe?

Close enough.

Davy still had a job to do, though. Sentiment and business—or afterlife mystical contracts—didn't mix.

"Do you ever wonder if my Dad would have done a better job?" Davy asked.

Fraser drew on the end of his cigar. He held the smoke in his lungs as he flicked the ash onto the wet grass.

"No," he said, the word escaping on gray wisps that filtered up into the leaves of the tree. "What would be the point?"

"I've been thinking about him," Davy poked at what was hopefully a sore spot. "About why he'd do what he did."

Fraser glanced over at him, his face unreadable. "Is that why you were at the graveyard on the Solstice?"

Davy ducked his head, scrubbing one hand through his hair as he glanced around for Hill. There was still no sign of him. Davy's tentacles picked fretfully at the grass and foliage as his unease soaked down into them.

With no one to consult on a Hill-approved response, Davy had to try and improvise.

"I guess?" he said. "I suppose I thought about it, but what if I didn't like his answer? What if I had to do something about it?"

Fraser gave him a confused look. "Like, what?" he asked. "Therapy, so you don't't--?"

He trailed off as he pointed the cigar at his forehead and mimed pulling the trigger. It wasn't like Davy was that socially astute, but even he was pretty sure that was a bit inappropriate.

"No," he was. He reached up and hooked his finger into the collar of his shirt to tug it loose as he thought. "I mean, what if he was pushed to it? If there was someone who made him do it?"

Fraser dropped the cigar to the ground and stood on it. He twisted his foot from the ankle to grind it out. "You should have asked me if that's what you were worried about," he said. "After the funeral, I had my people go through his life with a fine-tooth comb. There were no irregularities, no unexplained absences or travel, no new people in his life, no unexplained money in or out. None of the pressure points I'd have used."

"Then maybe he did something that drove him to it," Davy said. He hesitated—worried he was going to be too obvious—but there wasn't much time left. If Fraser was going to learn some sort of lesson from this, he needed to get on with it. "Or someone helped him along. When I was a kid...after you'd married mom...sometimes I wondered if you'd done it."

Fraser stared at him for a moment. The corner of his mouth twitched, and then he started to laugh, a snorted, rusty cackle of amusement.

"So I could have had dead Albie Rosen to contend with?" he said and tipped his head back to look skyward. "What's wrong with that? Too easy?"

They both waited a beat. Just in case. If there would ever be an answer to that question, it was this time of year. Not this time, though. Fraser wiped under his eyes with his thumbs and composed himself.

"I have never had any truck with...feeling bad about things you've done," Fraser said. "What's the point? I knew what I was going to do, and I did it anyhow. Who am I trying to fool crying about it in the aftermath?"

"I've noticed," Davy said. That was a safe answer to run with. Hill wouldn't have reached out to the dead to get his stepfather to change his ways if he'd believed Fraser's conscience worked.

"But you were meant to be a younger brother, like me," Fraser said. "And it's my fault we aren't anymore. That...that's always felt like guilt? I think"

Davy hesitated, caught off guard by the confession. Had the haunting actually worked?

He fumbled for a noncommittal answer that would encourage Fraser to keep talking.

"I don't understand what—"

"It was a long time ago," Fraser said dismissively. "One of our rivals tried to wipe us out during a business trip. Your mother was there and pregnant at the time; she lost the baby. Your brother. It nearly destroyed Albie. For a while he wanted to leave the company and go straight. But...what they didn't know was that I'd incited the attack so I'd have an excuse to wipe out our rival. We all knew it was necessary, but Albie and Mark wanted to try and find a peaceful solution first. So, I took matters into my own hands. And the thing is, I didn't feel bad about it then. It worked, and pregnancies are lost all the time."

Davy bit the inside of his cheek. The pain helped him keep his temper. Habit made him run his tongue over the inside of his mouth to feel the old scarred lumps his teeth had left over the years. The smooth skin he felt instead reminded him of the odds. He swallowed the thirty-plus years '*I fucking knew it*' and '*you could have killed us all*' and went with,

"Why tell me this now?"

Fraser pushed himself up off the tree and brushed his hands together.

"Because when you were born, I realized what I'd cost you," he said. "What I'd cost myself. Your brother is the only person who's stuck with you. No matter what's wrong with you or the things you do. Friends can cut ties, spouses can divorce you, but your brother will always share your blood and bone. They've no way out of it, except to die. I felt bad you'd never have that, for what I'd taken away from you. I didn't care for that. Guilt's an awful feeling. So I wouldn't take anything else from you. I didn't kill Albie, so if you'd dug him up...he'd have no bone to pick with me."

Davy wasn't sure how he felt about that. It definitely felt like something he could argue—if that was an option—was some sort of lesson learned. On the other hand, *his* murder apparently hadn't triggered any sort of epiphany.

"The original miscarriage and near-death experience might have still been a sore point," he pointed out. "Even if he didn't blame you for his death."

Fraser shrugged. "Even if he did, it's the Invoker who sets the rules of engagement," he said. "And you aren't like me. You'd want answers, not revenge. Which I would have given you if you'd just asked."

"Liar," Davy said. That slipped past his attempt to pretend to be Hill, who'd have tried their best to soften the blunt statement with mitigating excuses. Fraser caught the slip and gave Hill a mildly surprised look.

"I suppose that's true," Fraser admitted after a pause to consider the accusation. "There's been plenty of times I could have told you and never did. I suppose...I never had much faith in the confessional, but it seems prudent not to die with too much on your conscience."

"Does that mean that you've...had a visitor?" Davy prodded carefully.

Fraser's mouth twitched into a sketch of a smile. "A powerful man turned pensive about his past on Christmas Eve?" he said. "What other reason is there?"

Davy reached up and pulled a leaf off the tree. He shredded it absently with his nails.

"You mentioned your brother," he said. So maybe his murder hadn't been what had given Fraser his encounter with a moral, but if his was the first name that sprang to mind, then it had still weighed on him. "Is that who..."

Fraser twitched his chin in a nod. "I know where all the other bodies are buried," he said. "Mark's the only one whose corpse is still in play."

Mark? Who the fuck was—

Oh.

Davy stitched the pieces together, finally. It was him. That was the name he'd forgotten. Mark. He waited for it to become part of him again, to rewrite the gaps where it had been. It just lay on the bottom of his brain like a wet fish. He didn't feel like a 'Mark'. Mark Jones?

Fraser hadn't noticed his distraction.

"I'm at peace with the pound of flesh I owe my brother," he said. "And I'm willing to take one more stain on my soul to make sure Tannenbaum doesn't get to think he won."

What?

"What's the deli guy got to do with—" Davy blurted out.

Fraser blinked at him as if he'd forgotten he was there. He hesitated for a moment, the habit of being guarded tightening his eyes. Then he glanced at his watch to see the seconds tick by and shrugged.

"Tannenbaum's the one who killed my brother," he said. "And he's the only one who knew where he was buried. I always knew...I *knew* if I kept the pressure up on him, if I kept shitting on his life, he'd break eventually. I just thought the stupid ginger bastard would tell me whose pocket he'd been in. I didn't expect him to flout the Church and summon the dead."

Davy stared at him.

Why lie about that? Now. That didn't make any sense, it was...

No. It made sense. That actually made everything fall into place, as long as Davy moved *one* building block in his half-assed recreation of his death.

His little brother hadn't killed him.

And he'd actually been upset enough about it to spend thirty years ruining a man's life.

Davy didn't know what to do with that, to be honest. His sinuses felt weird and he felt the urge to grab Fraser in a headlock, or something, like when he used to torment him when they were kids. He thought that *maybe* he wanted to hug him—his tentacles splitting the difference as they tried to futilely grab the living man in an affectionate tangle--but there was nothing in their relationship that he could use to imagine that.

Fraser hadn't murdered him.

It mattered more than he'd thought.

...but, did it actually solve Davy's problem or just give him more? There was still the Christmas Eve deadline to get Fraser to learn some sort of lesson, and being sad enough over your brother's death to torture a man for thirty years probably wasn't going to cut it.

"Fraser—" Davy said.

"Hold on," Fraser interrupted him as he fished his phone out of his pocket. He held his hand up to Davy in a 'just a minute' gesture as he answered it. The glow of it lit the side of his face.

"Reynolds," he said. "Tell me you've pulled it off."

The muscles in his cheeks tightened in reaction to whatever Reynolds said. He muffled the phone briefly against his shoulder as he turned to look at Davy.

"I have to deal with this," he said. "But whatever happens tonight, it shouldn't splash back on you and Trudy. I kept you both clean."

He turned and walked away before Davy could untangle the knot of 'being Hill' and 'confession' and 'he'd forgotten about Reynolds hadn't he?'. Left under the tree, Davy watched his brother walk away and then turned and kicked a lumpy root.

"Fuck," he spat out. Then grimaced as he stumbled backward. *That* was a lot more satisfying to do in combat boots instead of sneakers.

Right. Plans changed. That happened all the time. Davy scrubbed his hands through his hair and took a deep breath of night-sweet air. He just needed to find Hill. That would be a start.

"What are you *doing*?" Trudy demanded of a server. She shooed them back towards the kitchen. "I told you, the champagne is for the toast! Take it back."

The server rolled his eyes but did as he was told. Before Davy could duck past, Trudy turned and caught sight of him. She started to smile and then turned it into a mock-frown as she looked him up and down.

"What happened to the costume?" she asked as she put a hand on her hip. "After all I had to do to get everyone to fall in line."

Davy's tentacles lashed restlessly around him as they pinched and slapped at things that Davy couldn't see. He left them to it—whoever it was probably deserved it—as he reached back to pull his costume on. The folds fell around him with a rustle, and he held his arms out to display it.

"A ghost," Trudy said. "I suppose it counts. What do you think of mine?"

She did a spin on the toe of her pink stiletto, arms held out so he could see the pink tweed suit she had on.

"Barbie?" he guessed.

That got him a sigh. "Cher," Trudy corrected him. "From *Legally Blonde.* Although at this point, I should just go with the flow and give them Barbie."

She took his arm, fighting briefly with the folds of the sheet, and guided him toward the buffet.

"Are you having fun?" she asked as she loaded up a plate with crudities and pastry puffs. "I know these events aren't your thing and you're only here to please your therapist, but if you give it a chance—"

"I am," Davy said. It was a bit of a lie, but he thought Hill would appreciate it. "And I appreciate the whole fancy dress thing. I know it wasn't easy and you didn't have to do it..."

His voice trailed off.

You didn't have to do this...

It was the last thing he remembered saying before the updates between body and spirit had fallen into the death-gap. He'd thought it had been a plea, but when he played it back now it was...

Thankful.

Careful, even. The way, maybe, he'd have talked to a woman who'd recently suffered a loss and had still answered the door to him?

A green door. He could still feel the gloss of it under his fingers, had it been the same color as the one in Hill's picture of his Dad?

"I wanted to do it," Trudy said. "I'd do anything for you, sweetheart. I'd have done anything for your Dad, too, but he wouldn't let me in. He wouldn't tell me what was wrong. So if you need something, anything, you ask?"

She pushed the plate of finger foods at him. Davy looked at it and then slid it back onto the table.

"Why did he kill himself?" he asked.

Trudy stared at him. Her face went blank. It was a familiar expression, the holding pattern of someone who needed to run through a filofax of reactions and pick the right one. She went with a wrinkled nose and a shrug of pink shoulders.

"I don't...I don't know," she said. "He did a lot of things he wasn't proud of, I think, at work. Maybe that just got on top of him? It was never anything to do with you, though. We both loved you so much. You were the reason he tried so hard."

From behind the veil of the ghost's sheet, Davy felt cold and a bit tired. He had met her. The memory was blurred by the chunks of Albie that had apparently been scooped out of his memory, but he could see her. Younger. Snappier. Somehow even blonder.

"I know about the house in Player Street," he said. "I know about the body in the basement. I just don't know which of you killed me and which of you dug my grave."

A flood of emotions washed over Trudy's face. Some of them didn't sit easily together. The brief glimpse of relief surprised Davy, although that was quickly unseated by fear. She grabbed his hands. Her fingers traced over Hill's knobbly knuckles and the faint spray of freckles as if to confirm it was his.

"My son," she asked. "Is it...is he gone?"

Her voice, other than a brief catch, was surprisingly composed. It was her fingers that shook. Davy took her hands in his and held them still. He was surprised at how gently he did it. Maybe even without Hill *in* it, the body remembered something of the man.

"He's not here. At midnight, when this is over, I'll go back through the Veil and Hill will get his bones back," Davy said. With any luck it wouldn't be a lie. "What happened to me, Trudy?"

She chewed her lower lip, worrying off the coat of Pepto-Bismol pink color.

"Do you need to know?" she asked. "For this to...end well?"

Davy studied her face. She'd had work done, from the woman he remembered, but it was subtle. In the circles she moved with Fraser, there was a fine line between not trying and trying too hard. He had the feeling that she'd been clinging to that line by her fingertips for a long time.

"No," he said. "Hill might, but that's up to you."

She looked down at their linked hands and, very deliberately, pulled hers away from him. She straightened the collar on her jacket.

"So, I don't have to say anything?" she said.

"You don't," Davy said. "I'm just curious if Albie killed himself from guilt or shame."

That made her flinch. The surprise on her face was sharply obvious as she looked at him. She tilted her chin and smiled thinly.

"And to think, I never thought you were smart enough to be cruel, Mark," she said.

The 'Mark' still didn't feel right.

"No, just lazy," Davy said. At least, that had been what every teacher who'd tried to motivate him as a kid had said. "Did you—"

He broke off as, over Trudy's shoulder, he saw Reynolds in a Prince Charming outfit shoving a middle-aged man in shabby overalls through the crowd. Davy didn't recognize him. The pieces only fell into place as the man looked around, and he saw the freckles swimming on drink-ruddy skin and the dregs of ginger at his temple.

Fraser *had* always hated to leave a job unfinished.

"...killed you," Trudy's confession pulled his attention back to her. For a second he weighed the satisfaction of knowing against the embarrassment of having to ask her to repeat that. He supposed he already knew more than he had to start with, so... Luckily, she touched her stomach as she went on. "I wanted Albie to get us away from you, but he wouldn't listen. He just kept talking about loyalty and how he'd known the risks the same as you when he'd signed up. But that wasn't true. You were violent people; he wasn't. We weren't. We shouldn't have been part of that world."

"So you killed me?" Davy asked. He kept one eye on Reynolds as the man headed toward the back of the house.

"I didn't really think it through," Trudy admitted, with a half-hearted laugh she choked on. "Sorry...I...I was sorry. It was just that you came to my house for something, and I was so angry. Then you were dead. I don't really remember the bit in the middle. Just hating you, then you were dead. It was like it just happened, on its own. Except for the blood all over me. When Albie came home, he said we couldn't let Fraser know what had happened. That we had to get rid of the body...you."

"So he dug the grave."

She nodded. "He cried the whole time," she said. "He never even liked you that much, but it broke him doing that. That night, I knew we'd not survive what I'd done, but I didn't realize he wouldn't. Now you know, what are you going to do?"

Davy sighed, blowing the sheet away from his face. He leaned over the dropped a kiss on Trudy's forehead.

"I'm going to go and stop my brother from making the worst mistake of his life. Or, at least, what would be the last one," he said. "Then I'll go back to being dead and leave you to pick up the pieces."

She laughed shakily at that. "Son-of-a-bitch," she said as she sniffed back tears and wiped her nose on her hand. "You fight dirty."

Davy shrugged his acknowledgement of that. He turned to leave her there as he pushed through the crowd of vampires, cats, and serial killers after Reynolds. Before he got far, Trudy grabbed hold of his sleeve from behind and fell in next to him.

"What are you--?"

"I don't love Fraser," she said. "He'd not have appreciated that, but we have a good life. I don't want to lose it. And I don't want to lose Hill the way I lost his Dad. He can't think that anything that happens here tonight was his fault. I'm not sitting this one out. You can't make me."

Davy begged to differ. He *could* have made her, but...

"Fine," he said. "Let's make it a family affair, sis."

She looked disturbed by that. Davy snorted to himself as he paused to scan the crowd for Reynold's. It was a good thing Trudy didn't know what he'd been doing to her kid recently. She'd really hate him calling her 'mom'.

There. He caught sight of Reynolds on the stairs, struggling briefly with Greg, who'd realized it was now or never. The huge swags of cloth and bauble garlands that decorated the bannister helped disguise the brief tussle that ended with Greg pale and sweaty as he was shoved up the last few steps.

Davy nudged his new sidekick and pointed in that direction. As they reached the bottom of the stairs a sudden crack of sound cut through the chatter of the party. People glanced around and headed for the doors, peering up at the sky for the smear of colored lights from fireworks.

Of course that's what they thought it was. When you hear hooves, think horses not zebras. At a party, think fireworks not gunshots.

Unless you had the context to know the gunshot was more likely.

Trudy had been around Fraser long enough to recognise the noise too. She bolted up the stairs, all long legs and heels, before Davy could stop her. As he followed her the the Beyond smeared suddenly into view. Glitchy and staticky as it faded in and out.

He saw a Hound.

The cowed and muzzled dead as they shied back and muttered.

Hill. Davy looked around quickly. Hill had to be close for Davy to peek through the Veil again, but...

It was gone again.

Davy's tentacles slapped out at whatever he'd just lost sight of. He could feel the agitation feedback down them as tension in his arms and across his spine.

"What?" Trudy asked as she looked back him. She was tense, caught between him and her anxiety about what had happened upstairs. "What is it?"

Davy clenched his jaw and breathed out through his nose.

"Nothing we can do anything about," he muttered. "Come on, let's deal with what we can."

Hill had raised the dead all on his own; Davy just had to hope that he could survive them as well.

Chapter Nineteen

Dec 24, 10.40pm

IT WAS TO HARD to think while dying.

...blisters popped on the backs of her hands as she fumbled at the window. She was crying, but the heat of the flames dried them on her lashes before they could cool her cheeks. Smoke stung her nose and eyes. Every breath made her lungs crackle like bacon...

The Hound yanked Hill's lead, and that—at least—was something to do that wasn't...

...the world had narrowed down to the beep of the machines and the strange, forced pressure of air in his lungs. Even the soft murmur of his

wife's voice as she filled him in about people he didn't know, whose lives he'd forgotten, had fallen silent. Maybe she'd left. He was mostly dead already. He could feel it spread through him like rot despite the machines and the drugs' attempts to ward it off.

He stumbled along behind the big, dog-headed man, vaguely aware that the rest of the pack hung around their heels to watch the woods suspiciously. The thing was...

...earth underfoot instead of stone. It crumbled and he fell. For a second it felt like flight, then he bounced off the first spur and felt his ribs give.

Hill had spent his life working out how to function through things that *felt* like he was dying. He hadn't been, but it had felt just as real and overwhelming as the...

...warmth. Softness. Milk. A sound that wasn't a heartbeat, but felt the same. It had hurt a little, but now it didn't and...

That one made Hill stagger. It was the first *kind* death, the first that hadn't been shackled about with fear and resistance. It felt like he could have sunk into it and given up.

He wasn't sure, as he went down to his knees on the wet mulch, that he should have fought it. Davy wasn't here. Fraser's money or his mom's connections couldn't help him. What happened to polters to take them from a danger to useful?

"Up," the Hound on the other end of the bridle snarled. He twisted it hard and the bit sank sharp, broken molars into Hill's already ragged tongue.

...she screamed

Hill got his hand under him...

The gun tasted sour and oily on his tongue. The muzzle scraped the roof of his mouth as he tightened his...

...and pushed himself up. He swayed uneasily on his feet as he tried to focus.

He couldn't pull together enough of him to...

...the wheels of the truck tore up the bike first. She thought that would save her. The driver would stop before it ran over her. It would stop. It didn't.

...do anything, but he could listen.

"Where are they?" one of the Hounds asked. It seemed strange to recognize anything human in that snarled, chewed-on voice, but he sounded afraid. "Are you sure they'll be here?"

"The birds said this is the closest corpse near harvest," the lead Hound said. "You want to ask them more?"

Apparently not.

Hill pressed his tongue down against the bottom of his jaw and tried to lift his head. The bone bridle felt like it was strung with weights, dragging him down and making his back ache, but he managed to catch a quick glimpse of their surroundings.

That didn't help much. Trees and the night sky. They weren't far from the house. He could still hear the party, but too far for him to stagger in this state. His feet caught in torn-up earth, and the lead Hound had to grab his shoulder to keep him upright.

A second later Hill saw the corpse they'd been talking about. A teenager sprawled across the path, head and body twisted in opposite directions. His slack, discolored face didn't look surprised, but Davy had died that way a few times now. He had been. The dirt bike he'd taken his spill from hung nearby, strung up on the fallen tree trunk he'd not *quite* been able to take.

...his heart had stopped. His chest felt like it was going to explode and...

"He's ready for harvest," the lead Hound said. He dragged Hill forward and kicked his feet out from under him. A paw on the back of Hill's neck pushed his head down into...

Into the dead man.

He tried to scream, but nothing but garbled howls came out through the bridle. The Hound shoved harder. Hill grabbed at him, clawed at the corners of his mask as *this particular horror* cut through the rest like a knife.

"Stop it." The Hound slapped his hands away and forced them down to match the dead man's sprawled limbs. It wasn't exact, but the Hound made him fit. "This is how we all die. You just fucked it up."

There was someone else in the body. Hill didn't know how there was room for them both, but somehow it worked. Somehow it worked. He was scared, but they were screaming because...because they weren't dead.

Not yet.

"It's done," the Hound. He glanced at someone who must have been already there, waiting on them, and cocked a curious ear. "Will you do the honors?"

There was a grunt and then a cold hand under his chin tipped his head around—still *in* the dead body—so he stared up at Seb. He felt a brief stab of excitement, but the expression of flat irritation in Seb's eyes quashed it.

"I told you," Seb said. "Call me before the men with nooses and sticks get you. You should have listened."

He slapped the side of Hill's face and pushed himself back up out of the crouch. There was a chain strung around his neck. Hill watched as the dog-muzzled man pulled a whistle from under his shirt. It shouldn't have been possible for dog lips and tongue to blow a whistle, but he managed it.

It was silent.

It ripped Hill apart like tissue paper, leaving him desperate as he tried to wad what was *him* back together. That wasn't his mother. It was his Dad, he thought.

Seb nudged the dead man with the toe of his boot. "You'll feel better once it's over," he said. "They all do. Once the Harvest is finished, you won't mind much at all."

He was going to say something else. Then he glanced into the trees, flinched, and quickly retreated. The rest of the Hounds went with him, ears flat and fur slick to their body.

Hill tried to roll his eyes to see what was coming. He couldn't make them out, just the crunch of their feet on the leaves and the long, hooded shadows the moonlight cast.

"The tally's off," someone said. The voice *hurt.* It sounded like a broken bone felt; it tasted like marrow. Hill tried to spit it out, as if it had gone in his mouth instead of his ears, but it didn't help. "We came for one."

"Call it a bonus," Seb said. His voice was tense, drawn out thin and nasal with fear. "You've been doing good work."

He laughed at that, like it was a joke. No one else did.

Then the men got to work. On the dead boy first. They shucked him out of the body with dry-bone fingers and hooks, then strung him up. He hung by his wrists as they used loops of rough, hemp ropes that scraped his skin dry and raw, a slough of wet ectoplasm dropped into a reed basket they kicked under him.

Hill, left in the corpse, screamed against the bridle as he tried to work out how to claw or chew or just squirm out of the cold meat. One of the men glanced his way, the moonlight catching on a scrawny jaw and dirty cheek under the stained burlap. Then they stepped away and looked again.

He wiped his brown, bony fingers on his leather apron and limped over to the body. Whatever passed for joints popped and crackled as he knelt down. A dry, rough finger that felt like jerky touched Hill's jaw, and then the man pushed his hood back.

"You shouldn't be here," Albie said. His eyes were hazel. Hill had remembered that right. "I didn't want you to see me until this was gone."

Hill didn't know what that meant. He tried to grab for Albie's hands, to beg for help. Nothing came out. Albie pulled one of the hooked knives from his belt and tested the point on his finger.

"I never planned to let them hurt you," he promised, his voice cracked and broken like ribs. "But you have to get home....Home by midnight, you understand."

Hill wasn't sure, but he nodded desperately anyhow.

Albie's dry mouth folded into a smile that cracked his lips. He reached down and grabbed Hill by the hair. A yank pulled him halfway out of the dead man, his feet still—somehow—caught in the bony arch of his ribs. Another yank made him scream and dropped him, wet and sobbing, on the ground.

The rest of the hooded men, there for the harvest, turned with the rustle of heavy burlap. One of them dropped something they'd winkled from the dead man with a wet slop of noise.

"What are you doing?"

"You can't do that?"

"It's forbidden. How do they know you?"

"It's forbidden?"

Their voices, smashed against each other, felt like an abbatoir. On the sidelines, the Hounds yelped and covered their eyes, muzzles screwed up in distress. Seb grabbed one by the ruff and shoved him out of the way as he stepped forward.

"What's going on?" he yelled. "What are you doing?"

Albie looked down at Hill. His face softened and it was just Dad again, under the dirt and the filthy clothes.

"Let it go," he said. "Let me go. Now. RUN!"

He snapped the instruction as he lunged forward to block the first of the hooded men who tried to swarm them. A short, brutal swing of that hooked blade caught under the man's dirty coat and pared out a white, half-bone arm. The sleeve flapped, suddenly empty, as the arm dropped to the ground and melted like dew into the dirt.

Hill tore at the muzzle and managed to rip it off. He spat the bit out, bloodied and clotted with tongue. Then he scrambled to his feet and hesitated.

It was his dad. His *dad.* The reason that he'd done all of this, the big gap in his life. He couldn't just leave him here to fight whatever the hooded men were.

"I said, run," Albie roared at him. One of the other men threw a noose around him, the rough rope sparking against burlap. He managed to get his fingers between the knot and his neck as he reached over his shoulder and dug the hook of his blade into one of the other hooded men as they swarmed him. "It's nearly midnight! Go *home.* Go!"

Hill made a desperate, *hurt* sound in his throat, threw the bridle into the darkness, and the dirt bike hung up on the old tree exploded. Chunks of metal and burning gobs of rubber rained down as the Hooded Men yelped in surprise and shied away. It was all Hill could do.

He took one last look at his Dad and ran. As he vaulted over the old, dead wood trees, he heard Seb roar behind him as he tried to rally the cowed Hounds to pursuit.

How close to midnight was it? Hill didn't know. He glanced up through the tree branches at the sky. Even if he'd known how to tell the time by the moon, it was obscured by clouds.

He wasn't even sure, he realized as he blocked the swipe of a low-hanging branch with his forearm, that he was going the right way.

Panic threatened briefly as he stopped to try and orient himself and heard the low sound of the Hounds coughed howls behind him. What would they do to him if they found him this time? He had the creeping feeling there would be no second chances.

Somewhere, in the dark, there was the brittle sound of a tree cracking and he felt the polter-white glaze of nothing eat the sides of his mind. He cursed under his breath and thumped the heel of his hand against his forehead. Not now. It wouldn't help, and he didn't know if he'd have time to make it back from where it dragged him down to.

Or what would happen if what the polter made him into got back into his skin.

No, Hill took an unnecessary breath and let it out. All he had to do was find Davy. He could do that. It had worked before.

He closed his eyes and tried to *feel* what way to go. It might just have been wishful thinking, but...that way.

Hill opened his eyes and forced himself into a jog, pushing through bushes and undergrowth.

Home was that way.

He slowed to a stop as he approached the lake house. The party—the one on this side, at least—was over. The muzzled dead that remained milled around in small, nervous groups as they were herded around by grim-faced Hounds and stork-headed dead.

From the way even the Hounds fell back when the Storks passed, it seemed that they were in charge.

Hill caught an odd, suspicious look from someone he thought was a server—their muzzle just paper and print. He turned away and caught a glimpse of himself in a window, his face scarred where the bridle had scored the skin and his lips rimmed with ash. Even if no one recognized him, he realized as he reached back to grab his hood, he didn't look like he belonged.

As he yanked the hood up over his head, he felt something bump against his side in his pocket. He reached in to see what it was and felt the bony angles and sharp, jabbed point of Hen's stolen beak. The memory of the bridle's weight made him hesitate, but when he glanced back he saw the server murmuring to someone else. There was a finger pointed in his direction, and then they turned to look for...the Hounds, probably.

It looked like he didn't have much choice. He pulled the chicken skull out of his pocket. It was deceptively light in his hand as he gripped it, the beak jabbed down into his palm. There was no time to think it through. He lifted the mask and pressed it against his face.

Nothing happened at first; then he had to bite back a scream as he felt the familiar pain dig in. He could feel skin and flesh peel away from his bones, absorbed by the mask as it grew new bone spurs to hook onto his skull.

Someone grabbed his shoulder.

"Who—" the Hound swallowed the demand as he jerked Hill around long enough to catch sight of his face. His lip twitched and a sneeze flared his black nose. "Sorry, Sir. Fucking help think there's a reward. They said...the polter was here."

"Well, you better hope he's not," Hill clipped out. He could feel the click the beak made around the words, but it still felt like his mouth and tongue that made them. It was an effort not to look confused by that. Instead, he tried to pretend he was Fraser, the same irritated 'I'm surrounded by idiots *and* I pay them' weariness that he had when someone was on his last nerve. "Last I heard, your people had custody. I'd hope they could finish this without any more fuck ups. Or did another of you get bridled?"

The Hound put his ears flat. Those mostly dog eyes looked woeful as he hunched thick shoulders up.

"Hope not, sir," he muttered. "I'll let you get back to work."

He shuffled backward and then loped away. Hill watched him go and then felt his face surreptitiously. He found an unexpectedly warm, dense beak and the heavy, rough-textured sag of the chicken's wattles.

Hopefully it would buy him enough time to find Davy before...

Reminded, he looked around, but, right now, he couldn't remember where any of the clocks were. He turned and made eye contact with the server who'd tried to turn him in.

"You," he said as he crooked his finger. The man shuffled reluctantly over. Hill didn't bother with pleasantries. "What time is it?"

That got him a confused glance over his paper mask, and then the server shrugged. "It's nearly midnight," he said. "Ten minutes and the doors will close again until next year. If we aren't back in Dudley town limits by then, we lose our visas. We might get stuck out here with the hooded men and the horrors."

Hill stared at him. The horrors. Death really made you want to live, he thought with an odd, distant panic.

Ten minutes.

"Well, Happy Christmas," he parroted in a tight voice that didn't hide his panic as well as he'd hoped. He took a step back and clicked his beak nervously. "You can go. Tell them I said so. I have more important things to do than herd contractors."

The server didn't wait around to make sure that Hill meant that. He just looked relieved and took off at a jog, arguing and pointing back at Hill when a Hound tried to stop him. Hill left them to sort it out as he ducked inside the house.

He could still feel the faint tug of 'home' when he concentrated on it. It was hard to tell if it had really gotten fainter as the Veil got ready to close, or if that was his imagination. Hill tried not to think too hard about that as he followed the tug of it toward Davy and his body.

As he hit the steps up to the second floor, though, he felt the resistance of the air thicken. Every step felt like there were lead weights on his feet. He had to drag himself up, one painful step at a time, like a fish swimming against the current.

Somewhere downstairs, he heard a door slam open.

"Rosen!" Seb's rough voice echoed through the dead reflection of Hill's childhood home, rattling the dusty baubles from Christmases long gone that hung from the stairs. "Come out, come out, wherever you are. I know you're here, but there's no time left to win. So just give up."

Hill really hoped the dog-faced man wasn't right about that.

Chapter Twenty

Dec 24, 11.40pm

"I'll admit," Davy said as he wadded up his costume and pressed it against the bloody wound in Fraser's thigh. He hoped Hill hadn't planned to try to return the outfit tomorrow. There was no way he could pull off 'I didn't wear it' now. "Things have gotten out of hand."

Fraser lifted his head off the wall he was pressed against and gave Davy a sour look.

"You," he said. "You died, and I forgot all this. The chaos. The lack of planning."

Despite the pressure he had on the wound, Davy could feel the slow leak of blood well up under his fingers. He pressed down harder, but that was a stopgap measure. At *best* that was what it was. His tentacles tried to help, bunched up in knots of muscle and flesh that slipped off and through the wound.

"I'm sure you'd have done a much better haunting yourself," he said.

"Me too," Fraser said.

Reynolds turned on his heel and glared at them. He had one hand clenched in his hair, chunks of his curls stuck up between his fingers as he dragged on it. There was a spray of blood across the front of his floppy-sleeved white shirt and dark, sweaty stains under the arm.

"Shut up!" he ordered as he waved his gun in the air. The silencer made it look clumsy, the weight awkward in his hand. "You have to shut the fuck up. I need to...I need to think. I need to...think."

Trudy cowered politely in the far corner of the room. Her blonde hair was tangled in fresh knots, and she held Tannenbaum's head on her lap. His overalls were ripped open from where she'd already done CPR, bruises livid on his chest as they spread and darkened under the skin. It probably wasn't the time to pay attention to things like that, but Davy couldn't help but notice that his ex really hadn't kept himself up.

Of course, a gym membership had probably been low on his list of priorities. What with Fraser kicking his life over every few years.

"He needs an ambulance," Trudy said, in a calm voice that assumed Reynolds would *of course* see reason. It was an effective approach. "He's having a heart attack."

Reynolds turned away from Fraser and Davy to glare at her.

"I kidnapped the bastard," he said. "On your husband's orders. His surviving isn't going to do any of us any good. Is it?"

It turned out that though Davy might have addled him a bit, the man still wasn't stupid.

"You...You're Hill," he said as he looked at Davy.

"If you want," Davy said. "I can be whoever you want me to be."

Fraser made a disgusted sound in the back of his throat and then wheezed in pain as Davy dug his thumb down harder into his thigh. It was medically necessary, but also satisfying..

"Bastard," Fraser muttered through clenched teeth.

"Shut up," Davy told him.

"He told me," Reynolds muttered to himself as he started to pace again. "He *told* me he had a visitor. That someone had called up the dead, and that was the source of everything that's gone wrong. He told me."

Reynolds rapped his fingers hard against his forehead to hammer that thought home.

"I was wrong," Fraser said.

"He was right," Davy said.

They spoke at the same time, with identical levels of confidence.

"It was Hill," Fraser argued. "He set this all up. The ungrateful little bastard thinks I did something to his coward of a dad."

There was a soft, pained gasp from Trudy. She might have *known* it was a lie, but she couldn't stop the hurt 'don't' that escaped her.

"I gave him a job at the company because he couldn't hold one down anywhere else," Fraser sneered, ignoring her. "He used that access to find out how to attack us from within. It had to be an inside job. How else could he have known where the bodies were buried? And look at you. For fuck's sake, Reynolds, you're one of my top contractors and you're sweating like a whore in church over *Hill?* You ever even sucked a cock?"

Trudy closed her eyes and primmed her lips together in a thin, waxy pink line. She rolled her eyes up behind her lids as if she were looking at the heavens. Davy imagined the 'Jesus' that she probably captioned the gesture with.

"That's bullshit," Davy said. "I knew where the bodies were buried because I buried them, thirty years ago, before someone buried me. You really think Hill could have pulled this off, could have turned you?"

The flattery was a bit obvious, but Reynolds wasn't at his best. He visibly reacted to the appeal of that idea as he stared at Davy.

"Some of the old guard used to talk about you," he said. "They called you Davy. Davy Jones, because you knew—"

Davy nodded his encouragement of that line of thought. "We can work together. You and me. It's been a while, after all, since I was in the game on this side."

The muzzle of the gun swung indecisively back and forth between Davy's head and Fraser's. After a second's thought

Reynolds pulled his lips tight against his teeth and shook his head.

"He's your brother," he said. "You expect me to believe you'd turn on him? Huh?!"

Davy traded a brief, confused glance with Fraser. The idea that they *wouldn't* turn on each other had never come up before. It had always been taken as a given, if anything.

"Have you met him?" they both asked at the same time.

"Then why are you trying to save his life?" Reynolds asked.

"Because he can't sign the company back over to me if he's dead," Davy said. "What do you think, that I want to go back? Do you know what it's like on the other side, Reynolds?"

The hook swung in the air. Davy had baited it, now to see if Reynolds would bite. There weren't many people in their line of work who wouldn't. After you'd sent four or five people ahead of you, most people started to wonder. A few near-death experiences of their own, and it kept you up at night.

"What is it like?" Reynolds asked with a sort of queasy fascination.

"Boring, mostly," Davy said, falling back on the truth when he couldn't come up with a lie that sounded better. "And the cost-of-death is sky high around here."

Reynolds looked irritated. "Are you mocking me?" he asked. "I *love* you. I did this for you. It was your idea to kill him."

"Yeah," Davy said. "Are you ever going to?"

Reynolds flushed. Two spots of red rode high on his cheekbones as he took a step forward and lifted the gun jerkily to point at Fraser's head. His finger, nails bitten down to the bloody quick, tightened.

"Look at my desk," Fraser blurted out. "The first envelope. Look at it. He's lying to you. My brother isn't dead. He's probably behind this, but not as a spirit."

Reynolds licked his lips. "You're trying to fool me," he said.

"No."

"He is. Don't listen to him."

Reynolds hesitated a second and then stepped forward to shuffle, one-handed, through the paperwork on the desk. He picked up a heavy, manila envelope and shook out a handful of documents.

"See?" Fraser said. "He's alive. My brother faked his own death. This was all Hill."

The gun sagged slightly as Reynold let it drop while he fumbled through the IDs. Fraser dug his own hand down on the makeshift dressing as Davy pushed himself quietly to his feet.

"How do I even know this is real?" Reynolds muttered in protest as he opened the passport to look at it. "This could be anyone."

Davy grabbed a chair by the back, stepped forward, and swung it in one smooth movement. The arc ended as the chair shattered against Reynolds's back. Two legs snapped, splinters dug into Reynolds's shoulders, and the leather seat flapped forlornly from studs as Davy dropped it.

When people heard someone was good in a fight, they always expected something out of the Karate Kid. In Davy's experience, that wasn't necessary. A crane kick might look impressive, but it didn't accomplish anything that the application of something heavy to the back of the head would do just as effectively.

Of course, he *could* do both.

Reynolds staggered and Davy swept the man's feet out from under him. As he went down, Davy grabbed his gun hand. He dug his fingers in, crushing Reynolds's hand as they wrestled for control of the weapon.

"This was what you wanted," Reynolds snarled into Davy's face. "This is what you asked me to do so that you'd love me."

Davy shrugged. "Plans change," he said as he shoved his tentacles up Reynolds's nose and into his brain. The static discharge of lust and twisted memory poured back and forth between them. Davy gritted his teeth against it. "And I lie. If you love me, you have to accept that about me."

Rage twisted Reynolds's face and, a little too late, Davy wondered if repeated exposure might have helped the man work up some sort of resistance. The answer was probably yes, since instead of staggering off to puke, Reynolds snapped his head forward. He drove the top of his skull into Davy's face, the almost airy *pop* of a broken nose spilling hot, wet pain into Davy's head.

Davy recoiled, blood dripping down his chest, and realized it didn't hurt as much as he expected. The pain was there, but it felt like being scorched through a layer of silicone. Distanced, insulated. Realization made him glance at the clock on the wall. It was an aesthetic but unnecessary bit of interior design in a digital era, but it provided a suitably sombre notice that there were under five minutes to midnight.

"I don't have time for this," he said as he wiped his nose on the back of his hand. "And you're not good enough for this."

Reynolds swung the gun up. "I'll see you soon," he said. The muzzle jammed under his jaw, dug in so deep the stubbled skin looked ready to split. His finger tightened on the trigger. Davy lunged forward to try and pull the gun away. He wasn't sure *why*; this solved his immediate problem. But he did it anyhow.

He was too late.

The gun went off. Whatever flesh made Reynolds into Reynolds sprayed over Fraser's desk and what was left toppled over backwards onto the floor. The gun dropped out of his hand.

Davy took a step forward, running on very old instincts, and kicked the gun out of the way. It skittered under the desk and came to rest somewhere out of sight with a thump.

"It's nearly midnight," Fraser said. "What happens then?"

"I don't know," Davy said. He stared down at Reynolds as he wrestled with an unfamiliar feeling that twisted sour and green in his gut. It could either be guilt or the creeping suspicion that a dead Reynolds would be no more easily scraped off than a living one. He could work it out later. Davy spun around and hurried back over to Fraser's side. "But before midnight, you need to learn some sort of lesson about treating people better."

Fraser closed his eyes in a slow, exhausted blink. When he opened them, he looked disgusted.

"Can't you just kill me?" he asked with a weak sneer.

"Trust me, that's the idea I started with," Davy said. "But you raised a bleeding heart."

Fraser looked sullen. "Anything I've done, I'm willing to answer for," he said. "But I won't ask forgiveness for doing what needed—"

Trudy's voice cut through Fraser's attempt to talk himself into damnation.

"I killed Mark," she spat out. "I hid his body. That was me, and you've spent the last thirty years treating me well for it. Instead, you blamed this man? Tormented him because of what you said yourself, because you made a mistake. Admit it."

Fraser looked stunned. "You did what—"

"ADMIT IT!" Trudy yelled, her voice cracking. "For *fuck's* sake, our son needs you to just this once accept you fucked up."

If anything, Fraser looked more shocked by the cursing than the confession. He opened his mouth a couple of times and then gave in with a mumbled admission.

"Maybe I should have...looked for more evidence," he said.

Davy waited for a sense that the geas had lifted from him or for the Veil to split and a forgiving light from heaven bathe them both. None of them happened. He shrugged and slapped Fraser on the shoulder.

"Yeah," he said. "Good enough. Buy him another deli or something."

Fraser curled his lip in something that didn't *quite* manage to be an expression as he rolled his eyes to the side to look around the room. "I may be dead before that goes through," he said. "Or in jail."

"As long as you mean to do it until midnight," Davy said. He squeezed Fraser's shoulder quickly before he pushed himself to his feet. "When you do die, look me up. I'll put a good word in for you with people."

Fraser snorted.

"People don't like you."

He had a point. Davy shrugged. "Look me up anyhow."

Fraser smiled. His teeth were bloody. "Those IDs you had made?" he said. "I think you pissed Gallagher off. She made you bald. Trust me, you were lucky you died with hair. It didn't look good."

The moment was interrupted by Trudy's strained, desperate voice. "You have a minute left," she said. "Whatever you have to do to get my son back, do it now."

She also had a point.

Davy took one last look at his brother, gave Reynolds's leg a kick, and then headed out into the hall. Now that he wasn't otherwise occupied, he could feel the tug of something insistent in the pit of his chest. It was anchored just under his backbone and dragged him down the hall and toward the stairs. Just before he stepped down onto the first step, Hill appeared below him. Davy hesitated for a second as the sharp-beaked muzzle made him doubt himself, but he knew Hill's eyes. His hands.

Long legs carried Hill up three more steps, and then he staggered to a stop just before he reached the top, arms windmilling for balance until Davy lassoed him with a tentacle.

"What happened?" he asked. His eyes flicked past Davy, and then he looked back over his shoulder as he clicked that borrowed beak together nervously. "Did you kill Fraser?"

"He's not dead," Davy said, "He just looks like shit."

Hill reached up to touch Davy's bloody face. For a second Davy thought he could actually feel the cold brush of spectral fingers.

"Are you OK?"

"Reynolds," Davy said with a shrug. "You were right about swizzle-sticking his brain. It wasn't good for him. But he's dead now, so that'll be my problem moving on."

Somewhere, a bell started to toll. It didn't sound like the sort of bell Trudy would have in her *House and Garden* spread house. Davy swore under his breath as he wrapped his tentacles around Hill, caressing his face and memorizing the nape of his neck.

Hill looked up. "Already?" he said. "I'm not ready. Davy, I think I lo—"

A tentacle wrapped under his beak and shushed him.

"Save it," Davy said. "For someone who can do it back. Who can kiss you and give you a life. When that's over, then you come find me...and I'll make you fucking forget him."

Davy unhooked the muzzle with his tentacles and slipped it off. He wanted to see Hill's face one last time He caressed the side of Hill's face with a tentacle and traced the line of his mouth.

"Fraser didn't kill me," Davy said. "He didn't kill your dad either."

Hill shook his head as he refused to accept that. "No. No, that makes no sense," he said. "If Fraser didn't kill you, how did you end up buried in the basement of a house my dad owned?"

It wasn't a hard question to answer. All it took was a second's thought. Davy had hoped that Hill would just accept his word, but he should have known better. He saw the pieces fall together as Hill's face sank.

"No," he said, his voice cracked. "He wouldn't."

"I guess he regretted it," Davy said. "And he already paid the price, more than once."

Hill kept shaking his head. "No," he said. The certainty was already gone, though. "My dad?"

"Fraser never knew," Davy dodged that question with a different truth. "He thought Greg—the deli guy—had killed me for another player."

The bell tolled again. That was four.

"The Hounds are here," Hill said. He pressed a kiss to one of Davy's tentacles. Part of Davy had always, no matter how useful they could be, hated the pale, visible manifestations of his sin. Not right now. "Will you be OK?"

The bell struck five.

"Fraser learned a lesson," Davy said. "He's going to make things right."

At least, one thing. That was probably enough.

"Once everyone is back where they belong, there's nothing in it for the Hounds to hassle me," Davy said. "You're the one who shook things up."

The bell struck six, and Davy felt the pressure suddenly intensify. He sucked in a startled breath as he was squeezed out of Hill like toothpaste out of a tube. The empty body dropped onto the stairs like a puppet with its strings cut. Someone in the party that was, Davy realized, still happening downstairs, screamed in shock. Then the living world faded as the Beyond reasserted itself on his senses.

Hill was still there. He stood in front of Davy, his silver green eyes wide with surprise.

"Hey," Davy said. He reached up and cupped the side of Hill's face with his hand. "I guess we get a minute."

"It's not enough," Hill said.

"No."

Over Hill's shoulder, Davy saw one of the dogs, snub-faced, brindle muzzle scored with scars and jabbed with thorns, step onto the stairs.

Seb? He thought that was it. They'd done business before. He knew Davy, anyhow. His battered muzzle stretched into a dog's wet, pink smile.

"Be smart, Davy," Seb said as he started up the stairs. Two Hounds followed him, although they looked worse off than he did. "The dead stay dead. It might be useful if that wasn't true, but it is. We can't have him going back to the world with all this locked in that pretty head of his. Imagine what he could ask of us to do our bidding, what he could tell the living."

It was hard to tell if that was a threat or a suggestion.

Davy twitched as the clock struck nine. He wrapped a tentacle around the back of Hill's neck and pulled him into a kiss that was cold and electric and tasted of bones. They kissed with the frustration of two days of only being able to touch through proxy, and the slow, cold knowledge that it would be sixty years before they kissed again.

Finally, Davy pulled back. He stroked Hill's mouth with his thumb.

"Don't miss me," he said.

"Don't tell me what to do," Hill answered.

Davy grabbed him by the arms and waist, tentacles hooked around the waistband of his jeans, and tossed him up onto the landing. Close enough to his body. While Hill spluttered a startled protest, Davy, now back in the clothes he'd died in, brushed himself down and grinned at Seb and the Hounds as they stalked toward him.

"I don't suppose we can discuss this?" he said.

Seb glanced around at the Hounds that flanked him, then back to Davy.

"Maybe some other time," he said. "Right now, get out of my way."

Davy grabbed a champagne bottle someone had left on the stairs, tentacle wrapped twice around the narrow neck, and swung it around to smash against the side of the Hound's head. He might not win this fight, but he'd make them remember it.

The bottle smashed, green bits of glass scattered on the carpet, and then the Hounds were on him. They tore and battered each other. The Hound's teeth ripped Davy's hand down to the bone, and he ripped its ear off with a twist of a tentacle. They slid and slipped on stairs slick with ectoplasm as Davy grabbed at muzzles and dug into eyeballs, and they shredded and ripped at him.

Eleven.

"Davy," Hill blurted from behind him. "I can't just..."

But it was too late for him to do anything stupid. The bell struck midnight, the Veil snapped closed, and Davy turned around just in time to see Hill's body stir on the steps as its owner slid back home.

He was safe.

Davy grinned in relief and then swore as Seb grabbed him by the hair.

"You," the Company dog said through bloody, broken teeth as he pulled Davy's head back at an uncomfortable angle. "Owe me a polter.'

Davy spat at him.

That was dumb, but it was Christmas. He deserved a treat.

Epilogue

21 Jun, 11.30pm

THE 447 PULLED IN at the bus stop. The doors whooshed open as Hill grabbed the back of the chair in front of him to pull himself up out of the seat. He juggled his shopping bag over one arm and his stick tucked under the other, pinned to his ribs with his elbow.

He could see the driver's irritated expression mellow into something like pity as he limped down the aisle toward her. She should have seen him six months ago. Death took a lot of PT to get over. His body had only started to feel like his again, instead of a heavy, borrowed glove.

"Are you sure you want off here?" the driver asked. "It's not the best part of town. Especially at night. Especially..."

She changed her mind about whatever the last "especially" was. Hill could, he supposed, have made her uncomfortable by pushing her to put it into words. He had things to do, though.

"I'm sure," he said. "Thanks."

He scrambled off awkwardly, his leg managing to be both stiff and weak, depending on how he put his weight on it. Once he was on the sidewalk, he pulled his stick from under his arm and let it take some of the weight. It helped.

Some.

On balance, though, he couldn't complain. There had been a span of time where the doctors had thought he'd never get back his mobility. A shorter period when amputation for both him and Fraser had been on the table. Now, six months on, they said that, eventually, he should be able to do anything he could before. Just slower and with more pain.

So he fumbled with his stick, juggled his bag from arm to arm, and limped on his way to make a deal with the devil.

Lowercase d.

He was fairly sure.

Hill stopped in front of 145 Player Street and looked up at the house.

It hadn't changed since he was here last. Not much, anyhow. There were some more cobwebs in the windows, a few more weeds on the path. The neighbors had taken down all their Christmas decorations, but put up new curtains. They always had to flex.

They'd also offered to buy the property.

Hill had turned them down. He still—or that was the plan—had a use for the basement.

He tucked the stick back under his arm so he could fish his keys out as he struggled up the few steps. The dead didn't break a sweat. That was one advantage he could list if it came up. Hill fumbled with the key, neglected for a year, until the rust gave and he was able to force it open.

Hill paused in the hall for a second to hang his coat up and deposit his stick in the umbrella basket. It rattled pointedly around until it came to rest against the wall. He ignored it. Just because he could use the stick indoors didn't mean he was going to.

He went into the kitchen. There was no pot on the stove, no jackrabbit in the fridge. His research had been a lot less extensive—due to the time crunch—but this ritual was a lot simpler.

Mostly, Hill reminded himself, because it was a spell.

The Church frowned on people using the Invocation of the Spirits these days, but it wasn't forbidden like what Hill was about to do.

This was necromancy. He could technically still be put to death for it, although no one had been for over a century. The Church was especially unlikely to make an example of a tragic, rich young man who'd only barely survived an attack by an obsessed stalker. One who had, to boot, allowed the Church to keep Reynolds under the care of exorcists instead of pursuing a legal complaint.

Still, you never knew. Hill paused at the top of the stairs and let that reminder sink in. He could still change his mind.

No.

He took a deep breath, braced his hand against the cold, rough brick, and limped down the steps. The remnants of the Invocation still lay where he'd left them at Christmas. At this point they had mostly withered past the gross stage, but he still felt oddly embarrassed at the mess. He used the side of his foot to shift the scabbed-over pot to the middle and clumsily lowered himself down onto the tarp.

All the spell took were three simple items. In this case, a dried pig's ear, a cup of coffee that Hill uncapped and poured in, and a blank business card that quickly stained from the coffee. Hill took a box of matches out of his pocket, struck one, and dropped it in. The edges of the card caught, smoldering sullenly.

"You said to call you if I changed my mind," Hill said. "I've changed it."

He pulled a dog whistle from under his sweater and blew it as hard as he could. All he could hear was a faint droning whine, but dogs up and down the street suddenly started to bark. That was it, though. Hill clenched his hand around the whistle. Had he done it wrong? Was it the wrong time of year? The sites he'd found on the dark web said the Veil was thinner during the equinox, but not as thin as during the Solstice. Maybe...

The coffee bubbled, and a foul pork and paper stew smell seeped out of it. The greasy trickle of smoke thickened until Hill had to fight the urge to recoil. He covered his mouth with his arm and squinted into the smoke. Finally, it started to clear.

"The offer was for when you were the Invoker," Seb said. He squatted opposite Hill on the tarp, as naked as Davy had been. Bits of coffee and leather caught in his snaggle teeth as he chewed on the pig's ear. "You invoked and went home. Our business was done."

His body was marked like a brindle dog, in stripes, with black and pink toenails on his feet.

Hill kept his eyes up.

"If that was true, you wouldn't be here," he said.

Seb finished the ear, burped, and picked up the pot. He took a sip of rancid meat and burned coffee.

"Maybe we could make a new deal," Seb said.

"Maybe," Hill said. "What are you offering?"

Seb grinned, his mouth spread ear to ear and his tongue dangled out. "Like I told you, death's not so bad," he said. "If you know the right people, and the right people know your worth. I can always use a polter in my kennels."

Hill smiled back at him. "Oh, see, I'm not the only one making the deal," he said. "My stepdad recently had a transformative Solstice experience and wants to get himself ready for the afterlife. He's not really interested in starting from scratch when he gets there, and he's got a lot more influence on this side than I ever would."

They stared at each other for a second. Seb picked a bit of meat out of his teeth.

"Usually they just do good works," he said.

"He bought a deli," Hill said. "Now he's working for himself."

"I might be able to work with that," Seb said slowly. "In fact, that could actually work out well indeed. But what's in it for you? Most people who escape death, don't come courting it again."

Hill took a shallow breath. Months on...sometimes it still felt strange.

"I want to live," he said. "*And* I want Davy."

The ache in his voice was so raw, so obvious, that Hill could feel Fraser's disappointment in him from halfway across Dudley.

Seb looked surprised, and maybe interested.

A pale tentacle, scored with old, pink welts of scar tissue, reached out to grab a bottle of whiskey. It lifted it and poured a glug of memory into a smeared shot glass held in scarred hands. Dark blonde hair curled damply against the back of his neck and a black t-shirt pulled tight over broad shoulders.

"I don't like doing this any more than you like me doing it," Davy said conversationally as he took a drink of the whiskey. The dead man he held upside down, dangled from one ankle, made a sound that didn't sound entirely like agreement. It didn't seem to bother Davy. "So why do you keep making me do it, Carlisle? Pay your debts, and I won't have to—"

Hill smoothed his hair back from his face with one hand. He felt the—or *didn't* feel—the dead scar tissue on his palm.

"Davy," he said.

Carlisle, whoever he was, hit the ground with a thud as Davy let go of him. The glass of whiskey followed suit as Davy bolted up out of his seat. He turned around and stared at Hill. The flash of dismay that crossed his handsome face made Hill's stomach twist with anxiety. Before he could panic himself into something stupid, Davy crossed the distance between them with three long, quick strides.

Tentacles whipped around Hill's waist, shoulders, and thighs as Davy pulled him into a deep, frantic kiss. It was a good thing neither of them needed to breathe, they wouldn't have been able to.

"How are you—" Davy finally pulled back enough to ask. He cupped Hill's face in his hand, grazing his thumb over the curve of his lower lip. "Hill, what did you do?"

Hill leaned forward and rested his forehead against Davy's. He tangled the fingers of both hands in unruly, cropped blonde hair that was just as dense and soft as he'd imagined.

"Not that," he said. Promised. "I wouldn't do that to you, or mom. I made a . I don't know what it will cost me, in the end, but it's worth it."

Davy started to stay something. Then he stopped. Tentacles tightened around Hill to pull him closer, warm and forward and familiar. He closed his black eyes and breathed in as if he could inhale Hill.

"I missed you," he said.

It shouldn't have been *enough*. Hill had seen enough declarations of love and devotion on TV to know what he *should* expect, what he should want from this. Except Davy was Davy and Hill was Hill.

Somehow, it was more than enough.

It was everything.

From behind Davy's back someone cleared their throat. "I can leave," Carlisle offered from where he still dangled. "Come back later?"

About the Author

TA MOORE is a Northern Irish writer of romantic suspense, urban fantasy, and contemporary romance novels. A childhood in a rural, seaside town fostered in her a suspicious nature, a love of mystery, and a streak of black humor a mile wide.

Coffee, Doc Marten boots, and good friends are the essential things in life. Spiders, mayo, and heels are to be avoided.

TA Moore can be found at the following locations:

Blog: www.tamoorewrites.com

Facebook: www.facebook.com/TA.Moores/

Facebook Group: TA Moore's Trouble in a Teacup https://www.facebook.com/groups/troubleinateacup

Twitter: @tamoorewrites

If you've enjoyed this book, please consider leaving a review for TA Moore on Amazon and other book retailer sites. Actually, it would be great to leave them for any book you've enjoyed. Authors truly appreciate it.

To catch up on all Rogue Firebird Press authors, please visit www.roguefirebirdpress.com

Author Catalog

Published by Rogue Firebird Press

NIGHT SHIFT

Shift Work

Split Shift

Shiftless

DIRTY DEEDS

Dirty Work

Dirty Job

YULE LADS

True North

North Star

BABYLON BOY

Hex Work

Hex Sells

DIGGING UP BONES

Bone To Pick

Skin And Bone

WOLF WINTER

Dog Days

Stone The Crows

Wolf At The Door

LOST AND FOUND

Prodigal

ISLAND CONFIDENTIAL

Wanted - Bad Boyfriend

Island Love

BLOOD AND BONE

Dead Man Stalking

THE PRODIGIUM

Cash In Hand

STANDALONE BOOKS

Liar, Liar

Every Other Weekend

Swipe

Take The Edge Off

Footwork

Sting in the Tail (Carnival of Mysteries)

Other Publications

Labyrinth of Stone

Red Milk (Requiem for the Departed)

The White Heifer of Fearchair (The Phantom Queen Awakes)

A Different Kind of Monster (Blood Fruit)

Words of Wisdom (Barefoot Nuns of Barcelona & other short stories)—Finalist in the Orange Northern Woman Short Story Prize

Island Life (Ulster Tatler) —Winner of the Orange Northern Woman Short Story Prize

Elf Shot (Bad, Dad, & Dangerous)

Despite what his co-workers say Belling, Montana paramedic Dylan Hollie does not hate Christmas.

It's just that as an ex-foster kid he learned early on that Christmas just didn't have much relevance to his life. He's seen no evidence since then that he's wrong.

That said, if Santa ever delivered a six-foot plus wall of hot muscle under his tree he'd be willing to reconsider. He's even sourced an available one locally in the taciturn Somerset North and his impossibly blue eyes.

So really, at this point the ball is in Santa's court.

There's just one problem. Well, just one to start with anyhow. The battered, dying man someone dumped from a height onto Dylan's car outside the Just-as-High, Somerset's bar. He gave Dylan an old, well-worn watch and begged him to keep it safe.

Now Christmas is relevant to Dylan's life in the worst way. The Winter Court has loosed their Wolves on the world and Dylan is on the run with Somerset North. A man who seems to know a lot more about what is going on than a Montana bar owner with exceptional shoulders should.

It turns out that Santa is missing, presumed dead. And the key to the hotly disputed succession crisis is a foster kid who never celebrated the season.

Cloister Witte is a man with a dark past and a cute dog. He's happy to talk about the dog all day, but after growing up in the shadow of a missing brother, a deadbeat dad, and a criminal stepfather, he'd rather leave the past back in Montana. These days he's a K-9 officer in the San Diego County Sheriff's Department and pays a tithe to his ghosts by doing what no one was able to do for his brother—find the missing and bring them home. He's good at solving difficult mysteries. The dog is even better. This time the missing person is a ten-year-old boy who walked into the woods in the middle of the night and didn't come back.

With the antagonistic help of distractingly handsome FBI agent Javi Merlo, it quickly becomes clear that Drew Hartley didn't run away. He was taken, and the evidence implies he's not the kidnapper's first victim. As the search intensifies, old grudges and tragedies are pulled into the light of day. But with each clue they uncover, it looks less and less likely that Drew will be found alive.

You'd think the werewolves would be the worst thing about the Night Shift; you'd be wrong.

All Officer Kit Marlow wanted was a cup of coffee and some downtime before his next night shift. Instead, he got a naked man in the elevator and an unaccounted-for dead girl in the morgue. He's going to need to deal with both before he can head for his bed.

Or anyone else's. Although not much chance of that.

Reluctantly partnered with the acerbic security consultant Cade Deacon—last seen naked in the elevator—Marlow delves into the dead girl's life. Between them, they uncover a new crime scene with the whiff of old corruption. A corruption that, five years ago, nearly took Marlow's life and ended his career.

Finding out who killed the dead girl on the slab might only be the start of this investigation. Oh, and it's the second night of the full moon. So 80% of the city, including Cade, will turn into werewolves in the middle of the case.

So, there's that.

A Wolf Winter Novel

The world ends not with a bang, but with a downpour. Tornadoes spin through the heart of London, New York cooks in a heat wave that melts tarmac, and Russia freezes under an ever-thickening layer of permafrost. People rally at first—organizing aid drops and evacuating populations—but the weather is only getting worse.

In Durham, mild-mannered academic Danny Fennick has battened down to sit out the storm. He grew up in the Scottish Highlands, so he's seen harsh winters before. Besides, he has an advantage. He's a werewolf. Or, to be precise, a weredog. Less impressive, but still useful.

Except the other werewolves don't believe this is any ordinary winter, and they're coming down over the Wall to mark their new territory. Including Danny's ex, Jack—the Crown Prince Pup of the Numitor's pack—and the prince's brother, who wants to kill him.

A wolf winter isn't white. It's red as blood.

Divorce lawyer Clayton Reynolds is a happy cynic who believes in hard work and one-night stands. He also believes that being an excellent lawyer means he never has to go home to the miserable trailer park where he grew up and that volunteering at a women's shelter will buy off the conscience that occasionally plagues him. So when Nadine Graham comes in with a broken arm and a son she desperately wants to protect, Clayton can't turn down their plea for help.

Taking the case means appealing to investigator "Just Call Me Kelly" for help. That wouldn't be so bad if Kelly weren't a hopeless romantic... and the hottest man Clayton's ever met. Kelly has always had a crush on the unobtainable Clayton Reynolds. He agrees to help, even though he has enough on his plate with the motherless baby his widowed brother left him to care for.

As Nadine's case turns dangerous and the two seemingly opposite men are forced to work together, they discover they have a great deal in common—but solving the case and saving Nadine's life might cost Kelly everything.

https://mybook.to/eelISaB

Bode Harlan has never claimed to be a good guy, but he's trying to keep his nose clean and his head down these days.

After a year in prison for assault--and to be fair, he did it--he isn't looking to go back. Admittedly, his pretty face being the star attraction in an illegal underground fighting ring seems to run counter ato that goal, but he's gotta pay the bills and there ain't much else he's good at.

And it keeps his parole officer off his back...since she runs the place.

Then his mom skips town and her boyfriend kicks Bode's 14 year old brother out on the street. Bode grew up in and out of foster care, he doesn't want that for Danny. It's not like he can take the kid in, though. He's an ex-con who gets beat up twice a month for money. That's how he ends up on his good-natured ex-boyfriend's doorstep.

Sonny is a soft touch. At least he always was for Bode.

All he wants is somewhere to crash for a couple of nights, nothing more. Sonny's got his life together now--a home, a boyfriend, even a dog--and it would take a real asshole to want to blow that up.

...of course, Bode's never said he wasn't an asshole.

www.ingramcontent.com/pod-product-compliance
Lightning Source LLC
La Vergne TN
LVHW030909080826
845145LV00010B/2821

* 9 7 8 1 9 5 4 1 5 9 8 1 5 *